Last Chance
SEDUCTION
A MONTGOMERY INK LEGACY NOVEL

CARRIE ANN RYAN
NEW YORK TIMES BESTSELLING AUTHOR

Last Chance Seduction

Montgomery Ink Legacy

Carrie Ann Ryan

Last Chance Seduction
By: Carrie Ann Ryan
© 2025 Carrie Ann Ryan

Cover Art by Sweet N Spicy Designs

This book is a work of fiction. Names, characters, places, and incidents either are products of the author's imagination or are used fictitiously. Any resemblance to actual events, locales or persons, living or dead, is entirely coincidental.

No part of this book can be reproduced in any form or by electronic or mechanical means including information storage and retrieval systems, without the express written permission of the author. The only exception is by a reviewer who may quote short excerpts in a review.

All content warnings are listed on the book page for this book on my website.

NO AI TRAINING: Without in any way limiting the author's [and publisher's] exclusive rights under copyright, any use of this publication to "train" generative artificial intelligence (AI) technologies to generate text is expressly prohibited. The author reserves all rights to license uses of this work for generative AI training and development of machine learning language models.

Praise for Carrie Ann Ryan

"Count on Carrie Ann Ryan for emotional, sexy, character driven stories that capture your heart!" – Carly Phillips, NY Times bestselling author

"Carrie Ann Ryan's romances are my newest addiction! The emotion in her books captures me from the very beginning. The hope and healing hold me close until the end. These love stories will simply sweep you away." ~ NYT Bestselling Author Deveny Perry

"Carrie Ann Ryan writes the perfect balance of sweet and heat ensuring every story feeds the soul." - Audrey Carlan, #1 New York Times Bestselling Author

"Carrie Ann Ryan never fails to draw readers in with passion, raw sensuality, and characters that pop off the page. Any book by Carrie Ann is an absolute treat." – New York Times Bestselling Author J. Kenner

"Carrie Ann Ryan knows how to pull your heartstrings and make your pulse pound! Her wonderful Redwood Pack series will draw you in and keep you reading long into the night. I can't wait to see what comes next with the new generation, the Talons. Keep them coming, Carrie Ann!" –Lara Adrian, New York Times bestselling author of CRAVE THE NIGHT

"With snarky humor, sizzling love scenes, and brilliant, imaginative worldbuilding, The Dante's Circle series reads as if Carrie Ann Ryan peeked at my personal wish list!" – NYT Bestselling Author, Larissa Ione

"Carrie Ann Ryan writes sexy shifters in a world full of passionate happily-ever-afters." – *New York Times* Bestselling Author Vivian Arend

"Carrie Ann's books are sexy with characters you can't help but love from page one. They are heat and heart blended to perfection." *New York Times* Bestselling Author Jayne Rylon

Carrie Ann Ryan's books are wickedly funny and deliciously hot, with plenty of twists to keep you guessing. They'll keep you up all night!" USA Today Bestselling Author Cari Quinn

"Once again, Carrie Ann Ryan knocks the Dante's Circle series out of the park. The queen of hot, sexy, enthralling paranormal romance, Carrie Ann is an author not to miss!" *New York Times* bestselling Author Marie Harte

Dedication

To Maxie.
Thank you for nearly twenty years of being at my side.
You were with me before I wrote my first word. Thank you for countless early mornings, late nights, and cross country trips.
I know you're dancing along the rainbow bridge, closing doors in others' faces if they dare to get in your space.
Say hi to Dan and Miley for me.
I miss you already.

Prologue

Lexington

2 Years Ago

"I can't believe I'm getting married tomorrow."

I leaned back in my seat, one leg propped on the chair beside me, my arm draped over the back of it, and raised my brow at Justin. The man had said that a few times over the past couple of hours and while it should bother me, it didn't. I had been through enough family weddings to know that nerves were *always* an issue. Even if they pretended they weren't.

Of course, this wasn't a Montgomery wedding. Meaning there was a distinct lack of cheese and dairy jokes at this rehearsal dinner. However, I wasn't about to complain to Nina, the wedding planner who had been running from one side of the room to the other all night. I didn't know how the woman did that in stilettos that seemed to be so tiny they could break at any moment. That's why I stood clear of heels.

There had been that one time at the family barbecue when we had needed some way to pass the time during a random obstacle course. My mom had laughed at all of us, though we had broken two of her shoes. Dad ended up getting her the fancy red soled ones as an apology, considering it was his idea.

"Why are you smiling like that?" Justin asked, pulling me out of my thoughts.

I sipped my whiskey and shrugged. "I was just thinking about a family story. Nothing important."

"I don't know how you can even think with so many family members around you all the time. I'm an only kid, and sometimes even my parents are too much."

My lips quirked. Not everybody understood our family. My father had five brothers, and my mother had six. My mother also had four male cousins on one side, and a few others on the other side, while my dad had sixteen cousins, plus the countless people who had married in or just became family versus friends.

That meant my family was slightly boisterous. In

fact, compared to the rest of my cousins, my brother and I had the most members. It was a little ridiculous.

"You do realize I only have one sibling, right? Silas and I were rather quiet."

Justin snorted before downing the rest of his scotch. He tapped the bar with two fingers, and the bartender poured another shot.

I was a little worried how much he was drinking the night before his wedding, but I knew Justin could hold his liquor. Plus he was staying at my house, so I would make sure he had enough water and caffeine to get through the evening.

Justin scoffed. "You say that, but you hang out with your cousins more than any other person I know. It's nice, but it's a lot."

"True. It can be a lot. But you're not marrying me. So you don't need to know everybody's name."

Justin narrowed his gaze at me. "Does Gia hate your family?"

I winced. "No. But she's an only child like you and didn't really understand family dinners."

In fact, Gia nearly ran in the other direction when the loud and boisterous Montgomerys and Wilders had shown up. It wasn't as if my family circled her and tried to induct her into a cult. They just wanted to get to know her.

I drained the rest of my glass, not really in the mood to talk about that memory.

"She'll get used to my family." I hoped. "But this is your wedding. Let's not talk about my girlfriend." Who wasn't even coming to the wedding since she had another event. I'd have thought she'd want to come to this one because there wouldn't be any of my family here, but I'd been wrong. And that was probably not a healthy way to think considering I loved my family and liked spending time with them.

"Yes. Because I'm getting married tomorrow. To Mercy." He gave me that faraway look, and I just smiled at the man.

"You are. And we just finished your lovely rehearsal dinner. Let's get back to my place so that we can sleep this off, and make sure you have your vows written."

Justin's eyes widened. "Shit. Was I supposed to write those?"

I froze, blinking at my friend. "What?"

"Kidding. You know Mercy, like she'd ever let me not have my vows perfectly done."

I studied his face, wondering where that tone came from, but smiled as Mercy, the bride herself, walked forward.

Her long dark blonde hair was piled up in a weird bun thing, and she'd painted her lips bright red. She had on a dark gray dress that matched the bridesmaids in some form of theme, and I lifted my water glass in a toast.

"Hello there, Bride."

She rolled her eyes at me. "Oh, Lexington. Are you getting my betrothed in trouble?" She wrapped her arm around Justin's shoulder, and he leaned against her. The two looked so comfortable with each other, completely in love. And I was only a little jealous. Not of either one of them, but the fact that they'd found someone. Much like many of my cousins had. Maybe Gia would be the one. It could happen.

Maybe.

"I thought you were heading out?" Justin asked as he set down his empty glass.

"I am. I just wanted to say goodbye." She looked over at me and winked. "Cover your eyes, Lexington. There's about to be PDA."

I laughed, and then jokingly covered my eyes.

There was a wet sound, and a little bit of moaning, and I groaned. "Are you two serious right now?"

Mercy threw her head back and laughed. "Okay, take this man home. Get him sobered up. We have a wedding to attend."

"You got it. Where's your ride?" I asked, looking around the emptying rehearsal hall.

Another woman with dark brown hair and pink colored lips came walking forward and stood at my side. Emily grinned before wiping her forehead with her arm. She'd been tired all day but I knew she worked long hours. "Don't worry. I got her. I mean, my twin sister is getting married tomorrow. We have to do our ritual."

"Do I want to know what this ritual is?" Justin asked with a snort.

"Is it a sexy ritual?" I teased, wiggling my brows.

Emily gagged, while Mercy just beamed. "You know it. I might be getting married tomorrow, but we do have to throw some herbs into a cauldron and dance around naked."

"Well, why can't we come to that?" I asked as I stood up to hug both of them goodbye. "I got this one, you guys take care of yourselves. We have to be here at eleven tomorrow, right?"

The twins laughed, but Nina came running up, panic etched on her features. "That's when the wedding begins. I thought we went over the schedule today."

I held up both hands, feeling bad that the frazzled wedding planner had overheard me joking. "I'm just teasing them. We had everything written down. You're doing great, Nina."

"Thank you, now everybody go get some sleep. We do not want dark circles tomorrow." She squeezed everybody's hands tightly, before running back to do something else.

"She scares me," I whispered.

"One of our friends used her before. I kind of wish we would have used Claire, your friend, since Nina stresses lots, but my mother loved her. So this is where we are."

"I will mention that to Claire," I teased.

"Good, because one day I will get married, and I will need someone who doesn't stress me out," Emily whispered.

We laughed, parted ways, and I dragged the groom back to my place. The night went off without a hitch, with Justin passed out in my guestroom, and me alone in bed while I went through what seemed like a thousand emails on my phone for the business, and the constant group chats for the family.

I muted them often because there were so many. With dozens of cousins, let alone friends and other family, subgroup chats and big group chats were always there. And yet, nobody cared if we went on mute. Yes, we were always in each other's business, but it was because we loved each other. We were *needy*, as my other girlfriend Carly had once said. I shook my head, pushing her out of my mind before I plugged in my phone and went to sleep.

The alarm came far too early the next morning, but I rolled out of bed with a pep in my step. Justin and I had coffee, ate breakfast, and then headed out to meet the groomsmen. Today was going to be a big day, and Justin looked nervous as hell.

"Are you doing okay?" I asked as we got ready in the groom's suite.

Justin's hands shook as he tried to tie his tie but he nodded. "Is it wrong that I just want to get this over with?"

"No, because that means you get to the wedding night," one of other groomsmen said with a sneer, and I glared at the other man.

Before I could say anything though, Nina was there to tie Justin's tie for him, and then she patted his chest. "You've got this."

"I do. Thanks, Nina." Justin smiled at her, before the wedding planner turned to all of us and held up both hands.

"You look amazing, let's get this done." Then she clapped her hands twice and led us out.

The place was all done up in golds and grays, which I wouldn't have thought would look nice together, but somehow it was classy and soft at the same time. I stood up next to Justin, rings in my pocket, and went through exactly what I was supposed to do thanks to the rehearsals. My job was easy. I got to see one of my good friends get married to one of my childhood friends. I couldn't ask for better.

Bridesmaids made their way down the aisle, with Emily last as the maid of honor. She winked at me, and I did the same to her, trying not to smirk.

And then Mercy was there, no veil because she would never hide her face, and she grinned over at Justin. She walked herself down the aisle, because of course she did, and I knew she was holding herself back from running.

Justin's hands were shaking as he reached out for Mercy.

"Are you ready?" she asked, all smiles.

Justin nodded in answer, and then the two of them were standing at the altar.

"Friends and family, we are here to celebrate the love and promise of two wonderful individuals," the man began.

"Wait," Justin called out.

I froze as Mercy blinked up at the man she loved, and Emily went pale, the color draining from her face.

"Is something wrong?" Mercy asked, her voice soft, tentative.

"I can't do this."

There were gasps and murmurs in the pews, and I

tugged at Justin's shoulder. "Is this really the time?" I bit out.

"Now or never." Justin shook his head, pushed off my grip, and looked at Mercy. "I'm sorry. I'll explain later." And then he looked toward the back of the long room and tugged at his tie.

"Nina. I can't do this anymore."

And then the wedding planner burst into tears as the groom ran from his bride down the aisle. As the two left, the silence was so thick you could cut it with a knife. And I felt as though I was having an out of body experience.

"Mercy," I whispered as I looked over at her.

But she just shook her head at me. "Did you know?"

"No!" I practically shouted. "Shit. Let's get you out of here."

"Mercy?" a soft voice said from behind her, and we both looked to see Emily staggering toward us. Alarmed, I nearly cursed again at the gray pallor of her skin.

I was moving toward her without even thinking, arms outstretched. Because there was blood seeping from her nose, and when she coughed, blood sprayed over the white of Mercy's dress.

"Emily!" Mercy cried out.

And as I caught Emily in my arms, taking her to the ground, the bride knelt beside me. We shouted for an ambulance, and people started screaming, pulling out their phones to call for someone or to record because that's what people did.

But it was all I could do to hold the mirrored copy of the bride in my arms as tears slid down Mercy's cheeks.

All thoughts of a runaway groom and broken promises gone.

And I knew the nightmare was only just beginning.

Chapter One

Mercy

It would truly make a better day for all involved if Mr. Darcy would stop glaring at me. That attitude of his was nothing new, but for once, it would be nice if he'd blink at some point.

I stared down at my all-black cat, and knew if I blinked first, it would be all over. I would have to get up from my desk, walk to the back door, and let my lovely cat out on the catio. Not that catio was an actual word, but I went with it anyway. Because my beautiful, darling, adorable son, Mr. Darcy, needed to be outside, but I wasn't about to let him roam through the neighborhood to either get hit by a car, eaten by an animal, or adopted by another family. Hence the catio was where he was usually allowed to be. My beautiful porch was now screened in and an oasis for me considering the mosquitoes during certain times of the year.

"Mr. Darcy, I have to get back to work. I can't be outside with you. And the last time I left you alone on the catio for too long, you learned how to unlock the door."

Mr. Darcy finally blinked, but didn't stop staring at me as he lifted one paw and licked it. Then he proceeded to bathe, leaning back so he could lift his back leg and show me exactly how annoyed he was with me.

"Really? That's how you're going to play it? We both know I'm not that flexible, and seriously, gross."

I shuddered as he continued to clean himself and went back to my paperwork.

I needed to get in the booth soon, as I had a deadline coming up. And other than speaking with my cat, I hadn't used my voice for most of the day. Vocal rest was important in my line of work. I opened my notebook and highlighted a few starred items that would be needed later.

"This shouldn't take long," I muttered to myself, keeping my voice calm.

I only had to record a short story today, and with the amount of effort I had put into the prep work, I should be able to have it down as long as my mouth didn't get tongue-tied on a few words that I usually messed up. And they were never difficult words. My mind just decided to be a little silly when it came to reading a book out loud.

I grinned, thinking how I'd had the same issues when I had been a drama student back in college—a theater kid at heart. I always tangled myself up over the easiest things, focusing on making sure I was perfect on the most difficult words and themes.

I was sure there was probably some psychological explanation to that, something I didn't want to get into too deeply. After all, I read books for a living, as well as a few other voice acting skills. I didn't need to dive deeper than that.

Mr. Darcy immediately jumped on my desk, startling me.

"Are you serious right now?" I asked the cat as he delicately pawed his way over my desk, knocking my pen to the ground and proceeding to lay on his side half over my notebook, his other paw dangerously close to my hot tea.

"Oh don't you dare," I warned, narrowing my gaze at him.

I wasn't quite sure when I had become the woman who merely spoke to cats for a living. But here I was, alone in a home that I had bought with my own money, as well as the bank's, and spoke to cats more than I spoke to people.

Yes, one of my good friends came over occasionally, but she was also a voice actor, and both of us in the same house doing the same work wasn't physically possible. Not when I needed to get in my booth and start working.

"Okay Mr. Darcy, I'm going to have to set you on the ground. You know I hate doing that, as you deserve everything in the world, but come on."

He leaned forward, moving his paw to press something on my keyboard.

The computer made a sound, and I looked up at the screen, hoping he didn't email my client something or somehow send money to his own special bank account off in the Cayman Islands.

I snorted, wondering exactly when I had lost my mind, thinking that my cat had somehow siphoned money off from me.

"You need to get more sleep." I glared through the side window, knowing the source of my irritation wasn't exactly my cat, or my new working schedule.

No, it was *them*.

And as if they knew I was talking about them, the sounds of hammering echoed through my home.

My beautiful, peaceful, quiet home.

Or rather, *formerly* quiet.

Workers spoke and shouted to one another, laughing with one another, as they continued to do their jobs. I didn't want to hate them for doing their jobs, after all, they seemed to know what they were doing and were efficient about it. But why on earth was my new neighbor deciding to expand his beautiful home already?

Of course, it wasn't as if I had *met* the new neighbor. No, the elderly couple who had lived in that home for most of their lives, had moved out to be closer to their children, and the new person had found their way in. I hadn't lived here long, but long enough for me to feel as though I'd finally found my home. But I hadn't met this new person.

And whoever this person or family was, decided to make my life a living hell.

Because even though the booth that I had spent far too much money on was soundproof, it didn't block as many sounds as one would like.

Namely the sounds of a jackhammer breaking through whatever stone happened to be in the ground back there. Part of me had wanted to research that stone, to figure out what could possibly be making that terrible racket, but I had work to do.

Work I now had to do in the evenings and nights,

because I couldn't very well narrate a book with construction going on.

This was not what I signed up for when I had bought this home. And whoever had moved in next door was going to rue the day they had ever decided to build onto their home and restore it without asking any of the neighbors.

Jason and Nancy on the other side of me were also perturbed because they had two-year-old twin girls who still needed their nap time, and of course the construction went on. However, apparently, they had spoken with the neighbor when I had been out of town and had known ahead of time that the construction was happening.

I grumbled to myself, because it seemed whoever this new neighbor was, had spoken to nearly everybody on our cul-de-sac, giving them a baked good, as well as a thank-you-for-welcoming-me-to-the-neighborhood present, to explain there would be construction.

I attended a conference and had missed out on meeting the new guy. And I wasn't grumpy at all that I didn't get a baked good or welcome gift. No, instead I got the sound of hammers hammering themselves on my brain and making my job twice as hard.

Mr. Darcy rolled onto his stomach, then stood up

before stretching to his heart's content, yawning as he did so.

"Ooh, good stretch," I said and rolled my eyes.

Why did I say that every time my cat stretched? And I knew I wasn't the only one who did it. It was like a reflex at this point.

My phone chirped beside me, and I smiled down at the readout, grateful for the distraction. Because there was no way I was going to get actual voice work done until they were done hammering whatever the hell they were hammering today.

"Hello Posy," I answered.

"I was going to ask how you were doing, but I can hear the hammering from here," my closest friend said with a laugh.

I paused at that thought, wondering *if* Posy was my closest friend. Maybe she was my closest friend locally, I had a huge group of friends online, because I hadn't lived in Colorado for the past couple of years. I put my hand over my heart, rubbing at the sharp pain there, thinking of why I had moved away. But no, I wasn't going to think too hard about that. I was better now. Breathing, finding my happiness.

And I was building a local community. With my neighbors who weren't annoying the hell out of me, and with people like Posy, who made me smile.

"It's never ending."

"Have you met your neighbor then? I mean, has he even explained what he's doing? The houses aren't that old. What could he be adding?"

"I have no idea. He hasn't said a darn thing to me. Which is very annoying. So I have no clue what he's doing over there. But it's not like I have a choice in the matter. He didn't have to tell anyone or ask."

"I'd say you can come over here and work, but I'm on as many deadlines as you. I shouldn't be upset that we have work, but it is a little overwhelming."

"I am grateful for the jobs, but you're right. I'm just having to become an owl now."

"I'm sure there's a 'whoo' joke in there, but I'm tired after finishing that fantasy novel."

"How many words did you have to ask the author to pronounce for you?"

"I'm not even going to count at this point."

We both laughed, and I shook my head, petting Mr. Darcy as he found his way onto my lap.

"Anyway, I just wanted to check in on you. Because I have to go back into the booth."

I leaned into my chair, comfortable for the first time in a long while. "Thank you, I'll get back into the booth once the hammering ends."

As soon as I spoke the words into existence, the

sound of a saw whirling echoed through my home, and I groaned. "And apparently saws."

"You know, if you go over there, maybe you could ask the contractor or owner what's going on. I know that they have a job to do, but you never know, you could find a window during the day to work."

"We all know that construction crews never work on time."

"Maybe this one does. I know that the one Cullen works for is usually decently on time."

"So how are things with you and Cullen?" I asked, teasing.

"We're having dinner tomorrow."

"And is dinner all you're having or are you just calling yourself dinner at this point?" I asked dryly.

"What do you mean?" Posy asked, truly not understanding the innuendo. I swore the two were already dating, though I knew Posy and Cullen didn't believe so so I didn't even bother answering the question. Posy was more of a hermit than I was and rarely left the house. If she did, it was sometimes with me, but more often than not, it was with Cullen. But if the two wanted to remain friends, and be each other's safety, I wasn't going to complain or say anything about it.

"I should at least get some work done, even if it's not voice work. And rest."

"Okay then. Maybe we can do coffee at Lattes on the Rock in a couple of days?"

"That sounds perfect."

We hung up, and I once again ran my hand over my chest. Because Lattes on the Rocks happened to be in the same building as Montgomery Ink Legacy. And from what I could tell, Montgomery Security, and the gallery owned by the Montgomerys. One huge family, so many opportunities to see the people I hadn't kept in contact with in the past two years.

It wasn't that I was hiding from my former close friend, it was that seeing him reminded me of the day that changed everything.

When being left at the altar wasn't even the worst thing that could happen in those few moments.

I shook off that melancholy note and pulled away from the desk.

Mr. Darcy immediately jumped off my lap and proceeded to prance over to the back door. He looked over my shoulder as if ready to roll his eyes, exasperated with me.

"Fine. You win. I'll garden and pull out whatever weeds have decided to annoy me today."

Even though it was winter in Colorado, with Christmas and New Year's and every other holiday squeezed into a three-week period coming up, there were still a few plants I needed to deal with. Ones that hadn't gone dormant. They would soon, but if I didn't take care of the plant bed now, it would be terrible by the time spring came around. I pulled on my jacket, slid my feet into my old worn gardening shoes, and opened the back door. Darcy jumped onto the catio, sniffing around for any new scents, before jumping onto the outdoor couch I had out there, and proceeded to make biscuits as if it was his only thing in the world.

"You go there, Mr. Darcy. I'm proud of you."

I opened the back door and quickly shut it behind me before Mr. Darcy could escape and went to the side garden. It was closest to the back gate that opened to the field beyond the cul-de-sac. I kept a lock on it usually but had unlocked it the day before to bring a few things in the back way. I scowled, reminding myself to lock it again. Most of the homes around us had the same walks, that way we didn't have to go all the way around the cul-de-sac in order to reach the walking paths that were through the treed area. I lifted my face up to the sky, knowing that the clouds would probably go away soon. It was a little misty, and I was grateful for it. Colorado was so dry, that no amount of lotion could help my skin some days. But the mist was desperately needed. It wasn't biting cold, just chilly enough that I had my fall coat on in December, rather than my winter coat. I knew that when my friends down south came to visit they would probably be in a full parka at this point, but you got used to the altitude and cold eventually.

I had been in New York for the past two years, so getting used to zero humidity, higher altitude, and less oxygen had taken me a couple of months. But now I'd been home for a little while, and in that time, I had already gotten a new neighbor.

One who proceeded to annoy the heck out of me with all of that sound. I put on my noise-canceling headphones, turned on an audiobook, one actually read by a friend, and proceeded to whack away at the weeds.

I was not a good gardener, but I read books, and I did my best. Sometimes my best wasn't going to be enough, but I could try.

Emily was always better at gardening. She knew the Latin and English names for nearly every plant we came in contact with. And if she didn't know, she would by the end of the day.

I wiped a tear away from my face with the back of my hand, knowing that this was a part of grief.

There might be five stages, but you didn't go in any order. You followed your way through the path, and it circled back numerous times. And, because of the human condition you could go through multiple stages simultaneously.

It was a wonderful experiment, this life of mine. But Emily wouldn't want me to linger in any stage for too long. So I was doing this for her.

Whatever this was.

Mr. Darcy came towards me, face pressed to the screen, and I smiled up at him, before going back to my audiobook and gardening. I rolled my shoulders back, about twenty minutes into my foray into this new non-talent of mine, when I turned off my audiobook and decided to just let the headache have its due course, considering all I could hear was the damn hammering.

I looked up, and Mr. Darcy wasn't in front of me anymore, instead he was closer to the corner of the catio, back arched, hissing.

I froze, wondering what he could see, and swallowed hard as something began to slither towards me.

Emily would know exactly what kind of snake this was, but I knew the pattern on that body, and it should not be awake in December. No, they should be hibernating, far away.

But as it slithered towards me, moving a little drowsily, I didn't think, I did the one thing that I swore I would never do. I screamed.

I staggered back, as Mr. Darcy hissed, slashing at the screen.

"No, no, get away." I didn't know if I was talking to

Mr. Darcy or the snake, but the shaking in my voice didn't invoke much confidence.

I didn't have a weapon, and it was just a snake moving towards me, but it could strike at any moment. And I didn't know if it could strike my cat somehow through the holes of the screen.

My earbud fell out, and I reached for my tiny shovel, knowing it wasn't going to be enough. Because I finally remembered what Emily had taught me. The rings on the length of the snake made sense now.

Not just a snake.

But a venomous snake.

"Are you okay?" a deep voice asked as footsteps on grass and gravel sounded towards me from my backyard. I didn't turn to look who it was, but instead, tried to stand up, and tried not to make it too sudden. The snake came forward again, jerking slightly, and another shout escaped my lips.

"Holy crap, we've got this," a deep voice ordered as a man in jeans and a layered flannel came forward, shovel in hand, and did what I couldn't do.

I shuddered, shame sliding over me, realizing I had just screamed, not only probably hurting my voice, but doing something that I didn't want to do. Because I didn't need help. I could do everything on my own. Why did I react like I had? It was weak. So damn weak.

"Miss? Are you okay?"

I looked up at that voice, that familiar voice, and froze.

Lexington Wilder-Montgomery blinked down at me, those dark blue eyes vivid against his pale skin. His beard was thicker than I had seen it before, covering that strong jawline, but I knew those eyes, that face.

My former fiancé's best friend, and the man who had held Emily as she had nearly died the first time.

"Mercy?" Lexington gasped, as he leaned forward and picked me up by my elbows as if he had done it a thousand times.

When it had only been a few.

"Are you okay? I didn't know you were here. Holy hell."

And then he crushed me to his chest, and I stood there, frozen, hating that I had needed help.

And hating that it had come in the shape of this man.

One of the only people I had never wanted to see again. And not for his actions, but for my own.

Chapter Two

Lexington

It only took a moment for the woman in my arms to freeze at my hold before she pulled back, eyes wide for a bare instant, before her face blanked.

"Mercy. It is you."

I was usually far better with words than this. Only I wasn't sure what I was supposed to say in this moment. It had been over two years since I had seen her. Two years since everything had been beyond reality and unable to actually see reason.

She looked much the same, though I knew her reality was anything but. With her dark blonde hair pulled back from her face, dirt on her chin, and pale underneath those red cheeks from either embarrassment, or fright, she was the same Mercy she had been before. But that wasn't true. There was no way she could still be that same Mercy.

"Lexington."

I held back a wince. I'd used to be Lex to her. I loved both of my names, but I'd never just been the mouthful of Lexington when it came to the woman I'd grown up with and had once called my good friend.

"Is this your house?"

She nodded before wiping her hands on her hips. "Yes. I didn't realize you were working on the house next door. The Montgomerys really are everywhere, aren't they?"

I opened my mouth to say something, but she turned to the person beside me.

"Thank you for dealing with that. I hate having to kill any living creature, but it was venomous, and I don't really want it to go into another yard and harm a child or small animal. So thank you. Now if you don't mind, I need to go inside. I'm late for work." She gave me a look then. "Work that's a little difficult with all the noise going on."

I winced. "I didn't realize you lived next door. When I went to visit all the neighbors to tell them we were adding onto the home, you weren't here. I'm sorry if we're too loud for you."

"You own this place?" she asked and shook her head.

"Of course you do. Of course Justin's best friend lives next door to me. Because why wouldn't you?"

I couldn't help the scowl that covered my face at the mention of my former friend's name. "I haven't spoken to Justin since the day after and..." I let my voice trail off. "Well, the day after I saw you last."

Because after Mercy and Emily had gone to the hospital, I hadn't seen them again. They'd packed up and headed to a hospital with better care and on the top edge of research for Emily's particular cancer.

I hadn't even been able to check in on them because they had been so focused on keeping Emily alive, that I couldn't even express my sorrow, or anger at Justin, to Mercy. The two women that I had hung out with as a child and grown up with had cut me out of their lives with a precision scalpel just like they had with Justin. And I had resented it.

Then again, my world had upended on its own a few times since then, so it wasn't as if I didn't understand finding a way into this new world. Only mine paled in comparison.

"I see."

She didn't elaborate and I had no idea what to say. But I didn't want her to leave. Damn it. I used to be better at this. *We* used to be better at this. "I do own it. I wanted a house that the Montgomerys didn't build, and

I could make it my own. I guess I moved in right after you did."

Out of the corner of my eye I saw the rest of my crew that had run to Mercy's backyard at the sound of her scream head back to the project site. And for that I was grateful. I didn't need anyone else to see me fumbling like this.

"Well, I guess I'll leave you to it. But if you could let me know exactly when you guys are working, especially with the loud noises, that would be great. My sound booth only works so well."

I winced once again. "I can text you every day what we're doing, and if you're behind on deadline or something, let me know, we can work something out."

"I didn't realize that you were able to control contractors like that? Isn't timing important?"

"I'm the boss, and it's my house. And I do remember how you work, Mercy."

"I'm not the same person, Lex. And work changes over time. So do people."

"You're right about that." I slid my hands into my pockets, rocking back on my heels. Mercy and I had been friends once. I wanted to believe the resentment in her voice was because of Justin, but maybe I had done something wrong as well.

"I didn't know, you know."

She winced, and I knew that was the exact wrong thing to say. "I need to get back to work." A loud meow echoed from behind her, and she sighed. "And Mr. Darcy needs his food."

I looked past her at the familiar black cat. "Hey there, Mr. Darcy. Long time no see."

Mercy just nodded at me, before she turned on her heel, and walked carefully back to the closed-in patio. Then she picked up the meowing cat and walked into her house, closing and locking the door behind her.

I stood in her backyard, hands in my pockets, wondering what the hell I was supposed to do now.

"Hey, Montgomery, are you going to come back here and help out?"

I shook myself out of whatever the hell my brain was doing in that moment, and walked through her backyard, and through the back gate. I closed it behind me, noting that she hadn't locked it from the other side.

I took my phone out of my pocket, ready to text her and tell her to lock it, and realized that she would probably do it herself, and I wasn't even sure if she had the same number. Because she hadn't answered a single call since I'd watched her and Emily get into that ambulance, red sprayed over all of that beautiful white lace Mercy had worn.

Sighing, I walked the slow path to my backyard, and through the open back gate.

"Everything okay?" Cullen asked, and I nodded at the large, bearded man. He was one of our main plumbers for Montgomery Construction, and we were grateful to have him. He had more experience than pretty much anyone on our crew considering he was a full decade older than most of us. But he didn't mind calling the rest of us boss. He was just good at what he did, and he didn't complain much.

"Sorry, you need me?"

"Mercy okay? I heard there was a snake. What kind?"

"Something venomous. You know Mercy?" I asked, wondering why that tickle of irritation rolled up my spine. It wasn't as if I had been on site recently to meet the rest of the neighbors other than that first time. I was the lead for the entire company, and our architect. We had multiple projects going at once, and my house wasn't on the top of the list. I wasn't even living here full-time because I was working on multiple bids, so I still had my apartment.

It was easier for me to go back into the office if I only had to drive less than a mile. But my lease was up soon, and I would be living full-time in my home, complete with construction noise. No wonder Mercy looked perturbed. And it wasn't just for the snake.

Not only did she get a blast from the past from seeing my face, but she also had to deal with construction noise. And that had to be killer for a voice actor.

"I'm friends with one of her friends. I don't know her too well, but yeah, funny coincidence."

"Oh," I said before another worker called me over.

"Anyway, everything okay?"

"All good here. We're all set with the bathroom addition, now we just need to work on a few other things before I get to head to another project and then come back here to do the big part."

"I swear, you move around from project to project more than Dash does."

"Did someone say my name," my cousin said as he strutted over, a grin on his face.

Dash was my age but sometimes acted like he was a decade younger than me. Mostly because it made him stand out amongst the rest of us. He liked being the easy, happy-go-lucky guy, and while that was usually my thing to do, recently, I wasn't in the mood to keep up with that appearance.

"I'm headed out back to the office, I know Jamie and Brooklyn need to have a meeting. Are you going to head that way soon?"

"No I have to work here, sign a few things, and then I have that house up in Aurora."

I nodded as we pulled out our phones and went through our schedule.

We weren't the first, nor were we the second, construction and contracting company within the Montgomery family. My cousins' grandparents had actually begun the first construction company. Montgomery Inc. They had made a name for themselves, and then the next generation, my aunts and uncles had come along and expanded the business to the point that people sought them out even in other states. In fact, a family in England had a Montgomery Inc. home thanks to a friend of a friend, so now it was an internationally known company. My aunts and uncles, as well as my grandparents had started another company, Montgomery Builders. Apparently, there had been beef between the two sets of grandparents, and though the companies had never been one, they had been trying to outdo each other. Or at least, they had been on the Builders' side.

My mother had done some of the art for the family, but it was my father who was a Montgomery Builder. Dash did what my father, Beckett Montgomery did, while I took my Aunt Annabelle's place as architect and lead. While we could have continued on in the Montgomery Builders name, I had wanted to start fresh. Because it wasn't as if my parents had retired yet. They were still young enough that they had plenty of time. In twenty years, if we all decided to combine companies, we could, but for now, we were a subset, our own group that instead of building from the ground up, did more of restoration and updating. We liked to keep a little bit of the historical parts but use what we had.

Hence my home.

In other words, the original Denver branch, Montgomery Inc., was still working full-time, and had expanded beyond just the Montgomerys. They had even pulled in one of the other cousins' branch the Gallaghers, and somehow, they were this mega company that worked well. We worked alongside them on some projects, but we have our own LLC. And the Montgomery Builders, based in Fort Collins, worked with building new environmentally focused buildings and projects.

Montgomery Construction worked between the four major cities. Therefore we were a little overstretched at this point.

However, there was a bid coming up that I knew my cousin Brooklyn desperately wanted, and I was on the same path as her.

I said goodbye to the crew and did my best not to

look over at Mercy's two-story home with the black shutters and white framing. It was a fantastic house that had been upgraded in the past few years. In fact, many of the homes had been, but my home hadn't. So I was going to play catch-up, and make it my own, while letting it blend. That was my job as architect.

I drove the forty minutes to my office, grateful that I hadn't dealt with too much traffic, and pulled into the parking lot. I knew I lived probably a little too far from the office, but I loved my new house and didn't want to change the office location as of yet. If my family began to move like the cousins were warning, then we'd figure it out. I let out a breath, knowing we had far too many things on our plate to worry about an office some of us were rarely at. Jamie, another cousin, and our admin who kept us on the straight and narrow, parked right next to me.

She got out of the car, her pink-tipped white-blonde hair flowing in the wind. "I picked up a bunch of coffee from Latte on the Rocks after I had lunch with Riley. Sound good?"

"Did you bring me a sandwich?" I asked in answer.

"Of course I did. I brought everybody sandwiches. But I got the best one."

"Thank you," I said dryly. I rolled my eyes, and took

the coffee tray from her, as we made our way into the small office that we called home.

Dash was rarely here. He and most of the crew were out on projects more often than not. I tended to need the office more seeing as I was the architect, but I did spend as many hours onsite as possible. Brooklyn was the same, considering she was the lead landscape artist and architect. And Jamie was the one who glued us all together. Because without her, I was pretty sure we would all be at the wrong project site half of the time.

"There you are," Brooklyn said as she came down the hall, her hair pulled back from her face, dirt on the cuff of her pants, and with actual dirt handprints on the front of her jeans.

"I'm so glad that you showered for this occasion," I said dryly.

"I would flip you off, but there are cameras in here, and well you know one of the parents would see."

"As if our parents don't curse more than us," I said dryly.

"This is true," she said with a laugh.

"Ooh, coffee and sandwiches? Why does that sound disgusting and amazing at the same time?"

"We don't ask these things," Jamie answered, and we headed into one of the main meeting rooms. Other people were working around the building, but most everybody was out on the project sites. We weren't as big as the two original companies, and this is where we liked it. We would grow eventually, because I knew we wouldn't only hire Montgomerys as our main crew.

"So, how's the house coming along?" Brooklyn asked before she took a huge bite of her sandwich.

In answer, I took a bite of my own, groaning at the spiciness.

"First, I'm so glad that the Montgomerys married into the sandwich-making people."

"You do realize that we're allowed to go to places that the Montgomerys don't actually own or are a part of, right?" Jamie asked dryly.

"True, but I love Raven and Greer. Because now that they've added more sandwiches and soups to the menu, I don't need to go anywhere else."

"True, we just need someone to open a restaurant. Maybe Italian. Do we know anyone that we could marry into our Montgomery mafia?" Brooklyn asked, blinking those light blue eyes of hers.

She had more freckles than any other Montgomery I knew, and didn't bother covering them up most days seeing as she was out in the field with only sunscreen as her makeup. And considering her twin older brothers, Nate and James were constantly around, ensuring that

Brooklyn never had a date, I understood why Brooklyn made jokes about marrying into the family.

"Montgomery Mafia? That's a good one."

Brooklyn rolled her eyes. "It's what Lance called us."

"Lance?" I asked, leaning forward. "Do I have to kick his ass?"

"No. My brothers already decided to do that. Lance was only four dates, and then he met the Montgomerys. Not even all of us, just two of them. And it was an issue."

"Do your brothers know?"

"Do they know that I kicked him to the curb? Or that he ran away because he was afraid of the Montgomerys? I don't really know which, and we're just going to pretend that I did it on my own. Duke is at least able to stand up to us," she added, speaking of her current boyfriend.

"If a guy can't handle our family, then he's not worth handling," Jamie said with a shrug.

"Is there someone I need to worry about with you?"

"You know, this is the problem with working with family. Because if this was an actual place of employment, I'd have to talk with HR. But I think I'm HR," she said with a blink.

"Maybe we should write that into our bylaws. That

Montgomery boys can't ruin the Montgomery girls' dates."

"Here here," Brooklyn said as she toasted her coffee cup in the air.

"Oh am I outnumbered? I'm not usually outnumbered," I mumbled.

"It's because the rest of them are out on the project site, and you're stuck with us. So, how are the bids going?" Brooklyn asked, all business.

I sighed. "So far we're three for four," I answered, explaining each of the projects that had already signed us on. Jamie took notes, and I knew she would have everything set up for our major meeting next week.

"What's the fourth?"

"The Arnaults account."

"Oh, I so want that estate. Can you just imagine the crowns if I could get my hands on them. Do you think we actually have a chance?"

I looked down at my sandwich, suddenly no longer hungry.

"Wait, Arnault as in Gia Arnault?" Jamie asked, and I looked up at my two cousins who gave each other a look. I did not want to see the pity on their faces.

"Yes, as in my ex-girlfriend Gia. As in the one who left me for another man and seems happy."

"Well at least you didn't break her heart or

anything." Brooklyn winced. "I just meant that if it's her father that has to make the decision, he's not going to hate you, is he?"

"I don't think so, but the meeting's coming up, and I'm going to have to grovel most likely."

"Because she cheated on you?" Jamie asked.

"There's a huge holiday retreat coming up, and I'm going."

"You got the invite?" Brooklyn asked, and Jamie beamed.

"I have skills," she said with a laugh.

"Skills I'm grateful for, and I don't want to know what kind of favors you had to pull."

"HR!" Jamie called out.

"So yes, I'm going to go to this event, I'm going to work on the bid, and I'm going to hopefully not have to deal with Gia at all. It's not like she's ever been to that estate. Her dad never let her be part of the business."

"Oh, that's good. I mean, not good, but weird. I don't know, do you need help?" Brooklyn asked, and I saw the sincerity on her face.

"I can handle it. We want this estate. It would not only do great things for the company, we'd make a huge profit on it, and it's a building we really want to work with. It's good all around. Except for the pesky ex-girlfriend problem."

"Speaking of ex-girlfriends that aren't your ex-girlfriend," Jamie added in, and I narrowed my gaze.

"Who texted you?"

"Dash of course."

"Wait? What did I miss?" Brooklyn asked.

"I figured out who my new neighbor is in the two-story next door." At Brooklyn's curious look, I sighed. "Mercy Caddel."

My cousin's eyes widened. "Oh no. I mean, it's great. I haven't seen Mercy in well... Damn it. How is she? I mean, I guess you can't really ask how she is. It's been, what, a year since Emily passed? Poor Mercy."

I ran my hand over my chest, wondering why once again I felt as helpless as I always did when it came to her. "I didn't even have a chance to say my condolences or truly mention how much I hate Justin. Not that I wanted to bring up Justin."

"Yes, he's such an asshole."

"And he lives nowhere near here, so I don't have to see him again. And Mercy is never going to have to see him."

"Well her being next door's going to be good for you guys. I know it sucked when you lost touch after everything happened. She was always running around with you Fort Collins Montgomerys," Brooklyn, the Denver Montgomery kid, said with a laugh.

"I didn't really get to know her, and I wasn't at the wedding, so let me know if you want me to stop by, and I don't know, mend fences?"

"Jamie, I love you, but there's no need to mend fences. I was childhood friends with Mercy, then I wasn't. Now we're neighbors, and it's all going to just work out in the end. We're adults. I just hate the fact that we couldn't go to the funeral."

"Mercy doesn't have any other family, does she?" Brooklyn asked.

As someone with more family than I could deal with, it seemed unheard of to me that she wouldn't have anyone else in her life. And I didn't feel pity, because Mercy would hate that, but I did feel for her.

"Well, I'm just going to do what the Montgomerys do best and wheedle my way in so she knows she doesn't have to be alone if she doesn't want to. Though, she probably hates me right now."

"Because of Justin?" Jamie asked.

"No, because of the construction."

Both girls winced, and I snorted.

"Yes, that. One more strike against me."

"That ass was cute you know, at least from what I remember," Brooklyn provoked.

I shook my head and pulled back from the table. "And with that annoying look, I'm going back to work.

And don't even think about calling Mercy and doing whatever witch work you do."

"Oh, interesting," Brooklyn teased. "Now I have ideas."

I ran away as quickly as I could, once again afraid of the Montgomery women.

If my mother, a Wilder and a Montgomery had taught me anything, it was that you didn't have to be fearful of a Montgomery woman, you just had to understand that you would never win an argument.

And you also had to be a little crafty when it came to making sure they kept out of your life. I was going to go back to my desk, get to work, and focus on the bid that was going to change our business.

And not on the neighbor that I had done my best not to think of for the past two years. And knew just like I had failed for the past two years, I would fail in this once again.

Chapter Three

Mercy

"What do you mean you don't know where the invoice went?"

I lowered my voice, relaxing my tongue as I spoke. "The invoice isn't here. You must have forgotten to send it."

I leaned back, raising my voice slightly. "No, it was right on the email."

"Why did you lose it? We're going to be late because of you."

I lowered my voice once more. "You don't need to blame this on me. I know that you're just trying to find a reason to be angry with me because of what happened, but you don't have to make something up."

The banter went back and forth, and I paused my

narrating every once in a while, marking moments where I knew I would have to go back, or let my mouth rest. The current forced proximity, workplace rom com on my stand made me smile. Considering I hadn't slept much in the past few days getting work done in the few hours that I had available at this moment, it was good to smile.

I reached for my water bottle and winced as the sound of a saw echoed through my tiny booth.

Of course.

Why wouldn't there be a grating noise out of nowhere when I needed silence for my job. Sound that hadn't been there when I'd bought my home. Racket that no one had asked for. Commotion that threatened my sanity as it was louder than anything that had occurred in the neighborhood so far.

I had never had this issue in the past, not even with high wind, or massive trucks moving in and out of the cul-de-sac thanks to a neighbor moving. Even in my old place, when I had had a weaker booth and thinner walls, it hadn't been this loud.

And yet Lexington Montgomery was going to drive me insane. Of course, he had done that when we had been children as well. Always a little too enthusiastic even though he'd dragged me along with him, so I never felt alone. Not that a twin could ever feel alone.

My heart raced and I swallowed the bile that crept up my throat at the thought of Emily.

Lexington.

I needed to think of Lexington. Like how he'd try to run everybody's lives even if you weren't prepared for it. He liked to organize everyone to the nth degree and had worked alongside his cousins and Emily to ensure that all our lives and playgroups could go off without a hitch.

There was no time for spontaneity or anything off the beaten path.

I frowned at that, realizing that I was probably being a little too harsh when it came to reflecting back on our childhood. Because Lexington had *enjoyed* a little randomness. It was Emily that had been a little more type A, even more than me. But I did have the creative streak. Like when I was younger, I had wanted to join the circus and then become an acrobat. After I had given up that dream, I had decided I wanted to be an actress—racing from Broadway to the Oscars. It hadn't mattered which, I wanted to perform.

And then I'd realized that I did better with voices and projecting, than I ever did using the rest of my body to act. The voice acting was really where I had leaned into it. I could do impressions and other aspects of that role, but being a comedian had never appealed to me. So my current job was truly a perfect fit.

Except for the fact that I couldn't focus with whatever the hell they were doing next door.

Of course, if I would have just asked Lexington that morning, maybe I would be a little more in the know.

My phone buzzed and I looked down at the unknown number. I wouldn't have normally answered, but I was waiting on a call from a friend's producer.

"Hello?"

Silence.

"Hello? Are you there?"

A click and the call discounted. How strange. Frowning, I picked up my phone and looked at the text that Lex had sent that morning.

> **LEX:**
> I really hope this is your current number and I'm not just texting a random stranger. But here's the schedule for this week, and my goal is for us to stay on this path. But if something happens, I'll let you know. I'm sorry that we're at the point of the project where it's a lot of noise outside of the house versus in it. But if all goes according to plan, we'll be done soon, and you'll be able to work without having to hear hammering all day.

> **LEX:**
> By the way, I picked up your latest book, and I'm totally listening to it while on the job site. Your voice has gotten better, which I didn't think was possible considering how good you were when we were younger. And congratulations on that award. Not that I was stalking. Okay, I might be stalking.

I had refused to smile at that, knowing it wouldn't do anybody any good if I let myself laugh over whatever ridiculous thing he was saying next.

After all, I was back in Colorado to find my feet again. Not to jump back into old connections and relationships that would just remind me of everything I lost.

But I clicked the link and looked at the calendar he'd sent over.

Everything was laid out, color coordinated, and signed by not only Lex, but by Jamie. I frowned, trying to remember if I knew that particular Montgomery. Probably, as I had a feeling I had met nearly all of Lexington's cousins over the years, but it shouldn't matter. This was my work, something I needed to focus on, and I shouldn't have to put aside everything for a man once again.

I scowled at that, wondering where that came from. Just because Lex knew Justin didn't mean he was exactly like Justin. In fact, the two had always been nearly opposites. With Lex being a little more easygoing, and yet at the same time, focused on making sure that others around him were taken care of. Sometimes to the detriment of himself. It was probably why we had gotten along when we'd been younger. Because we were birds of a feather and all that.

And that was why Emily had such a crush on him for so long.

I pressed my lips together, hating that once again I was thinking about that time in our lives.

It was always funny to me that Emily's major crush years ago had been on Lexington of all people. Nothing came from it, and I was pretty sure that Lexington knew of Emily's crush for all those years. But by the time I'd met Justin, and I'd thought I was in love, ready to marry him and spend the rest of my life with him, Emily moved on, and I'd thought Lexington was on the path to getting married as well. In the time since I'd been gone though, I'd only heard rumblings that he had been in that serious relationship with Carly, and then another woman named Gia, with both of those relationships fizzling out quite spectacularly.

I had never gone out of my way to find out more information about him because when I thought about Lex I thought about Justin. However, we had so many similar overlaps in our connections over the years, that I couldn't help but hear some of it.

Though it still surprised me that I hadn't known he was my neighbor, and that he hadn't known either.

The idea that I had even gone out of my way to *not* buy a house built by the Montgomerys, just told me that maybe cutting myself off from my past while moving back to my home state, didn't make any sense in the long run. With a sigh, I saved all of my work, grabbed my notebook, and figured I would do a few other things around the house and get back to my narrating later. My throat was a little sore, considering I had been up far too late the night before, so maybe I should actually pay attention to the schedule Lex had gone out of his way to send me and not grumble.

Except as I went upstairs, the sound of construction echoed throughout my living room, and I couldn't help but glare through the wall.

Mr. Darcy wound his way through my legs, tail up, apparently annoyed with the noise as well, and went to the back door.

"I'll let you out on the catio, but I am not going out there. Way too much noise."

Mr. Darcy just blinked at me, and I sighed, realizing I was now having a full on conversation with this cat.

I cracked open the back sliding door, let him out on

the catio, and then closed the screen door so that way any bugs that might've made their way through the chilled Colorado afternoon wouldn't be able to enter my home, but I would still be able to hear Mr. Darcy if he was in trouble.

I made my way to my kitchen and scowled as I realized that my refrigerator was far emptier than I thought. Apparently, grocery shopping was next in my future instead of working. Which was probably a better idea anyway.

I looked out the window above the sink and caught a glimpse of Lexington on his roof.

I blinked, wondering exactly how safe it could be for him up there. Wasn't he an architect? I hadn't realized that he was the one who would put on a tool belt and do such a dangerous task. But with those tight Wranglers of his, the well-worn boots, and ball cap turned backwards, he apparently knew what he was doing.

Tight jeans? Why the hell was I noticing Lexington Montgomery's tight jeans?

I shook my head and went to get ready to head out to the grocery store. I slid on comfortable leggings that didn't have holes in them, cute knee boots, and an overlarge sweater. It sort of worked as a tunic, and I called that a win. I quickly made up a weekly grocery list, forced Mr. Darcy back into the house much to his discontent, and headed out to my car. I had parked in the driveway the day before as I had moved around a few boxes in the garage and wasn't sure what I was going to do with those books that I couldn't quite lift.

"Mercy!"

I froze in the act of opening my door and steeled myself for that oh-so-familiar voice.

"Lexington."

"You should just call me Lex you know. My name is a bit of a mouthful."

I raised a brow. "I do call you Lex." When I cursed him in my mind. Though I knew leaning into calling him Lexington was childish. What was wrong with me?

"Sure you do. Did you get my text? It is you, right? Not some random person."

"I got them. Thanks for the schedule. Though it does seem to be all noise all the time."

"We'll be done in an hour with this, and then there won't be anything loud for the next two weeks. Promise. We're hitting the holiday season, and I'm giving my team time off."

I blinked at him. "Oh?"

He winked and I swallowed hard. "I do like to be a nice boss every once in a while. Where are you off to?"

"Well since I couldn't get most of my work done today, I'm off to grocery shop. Is that okay with you?"

Why was I acting like this? Lexington had been my friend. We had been friendly. Nice to each other. I didn't know what it was that got my fur up when it came to him these days. But maybe it was because once again he had seen me at one of my lowest points.

There had been a reason I hadn't invited anybody to Emily's funeral. Because she hadn't had one. She hadn't wanted one. And I had acquiesced to her request. So nobody had been with me to say goodbye. It had just been me and her ashes, and a sense of loss that would never be repaired.

"Merce? What's up? What's wrong?" he asked as he reached out and slid his fingertips over my cheek.

I flinched and took a step back so my body pressed against my SUV.

"I'm fine. Just lost in thought."

"Okay. I'm sorry. But for real though, you should be able to get all the work done you need to soon, okay? We're almost done with the outdoor projects. Promise."

"It's your house, Lexington. Don't worry about it. I know you already talked to everybody else about timing. I just wasn't here for that."

"I can still feel bad about it."

"And I can still apologize for being grumpy."

"You never need to apologize for that, Merce," he said, his lips quirking into a smile.

I was aware that some of his team members, as well as probably a few Montgomerys, were stealing curious looks over at us, but I ignored them. It would be best for everybody if I continued to do that.

"Anyway, I just wanted to let you know we'll be out of your hair soon."

"Thanks. It'll be nice actually, since I have a bunch of deadlines I want to get ahead of during the holidays."

He frowned. "You're going to be working the whole season?"

"Of course. It's a great time for me to get some work done because there's not that many people out and about. You know?"

He looked like he wanted to say something, but one of his crew called him over, and I waved him off.

"Get back to work, I'm going grocery shopping."

"Okay. Yeah. Well, it's good to see you, Merce."

I nodded in answer, and he made his way back towards the house.

With a sigh, and wondering why everything just felt off, I got in my car and headed to the grocery store.

I wasn't planning on celebrating the holidays this year. It was just me after all. What was the point of putting up a tree, setting lights, or buying myself gifts? I had friends all around the world, and I could visit any one of them. Many had even offered, but I didn't want to invade their time with their families. I just wanted to be by myself and try to figure out how to enjoy the time that I had on this earth. Which might not sound too productive or healthy, but for me, it was a step in a different direction. I wasn't drowning myself in sorrow, wasn't hiding from my own feelings. I was moving on in this new life of mine. Alone.

But I was good at being alone.

I put one earbud in my ear, had my phone out with my grocery list, and set about to get through this part of the day quickly.

I hummed along to my favorite contemporary artist, focusing on trying to breathe through the day, rather than on what I didn't have anymore. Holiday music blasted through the speakers overhead, while the aisles were filled with different seasonal purchases and offerings, and I added a box of specialty chocolates to my basket, I ignored the other red and green items surrounding me.

Images of our family holidays blasted through my mind, that bittersweet feeling taking hold once more.

My mother and Emily had always been the ones who pushed us to go all out for the holidays, while my father and I had smiled along, but enjoyed it, nonetheless.

When Mom had died when we'd had been juniors

in high school, Emily had gone full tilt to make sure that we still celebrated the way that Mom had always loved. And I had joined in, knowing that my sister had needed me.

Then Dad had died just three years later, leaving us alone in a world where we still did everything for each other to bring that joy.

Now it was just me—and Mr. Darcy. Celebrating didn't really seem high up on my list of priorities.

With a smile, at least a forced one, I was nearly done with my grocery shopping when the hairs on the back of my neck stood on end. Frowning I turned around and saw a familiar man walking the opposite way down the aisle. Now that I thought about it, he had been down nearly every single aisle I had been throughout this entire shopping day, but that wasn't too crazy. After all, it was grocery shopping, and it wasn't as if people didn't have similar lists.

Still though, it felt a bit odd.

Or maybe I was just seeing too much considering I had just read a thriller book the night before.

Nonetheless, I finished my shopping quickly and kept an eye out for him on my way out. But I didn't see him again.

"You're losing your mind, Mercy," I whispered to myself.

I drove home, pushing the odd experience out of my mind, because it was just me seeing things after all, and pulled into my driveway soon after. The construction crew seemed to be done for the day, and only Lex's truck and another SUV I didn't recognize sat in the driveway. I quickly pulled my groceries out of my SUV and brought everything inside. Mr. Darcy meowed angrily at me because I wasn't going to let him outside yet, considering the temperature was beginning to drop quite quickly, and I immediately put everything away. The doorbell rang soon after I was finished, and I frowned, wondering who that could be.

When I checked the app on my phone, I blinked, seeing a familiar face.

I went to the door, opened it, and smiled at the woman who had done her best to bring joy into my childhood. "Mrs. Montgomery. Oh. Hi."

Eliza Wilder-Montgomery smiled brightly at me and opened her arms. "Mercy. Lexington said you were back." I immediately hugged her, and she enveloped me in her arms, that familiar mother's touch nearly bringing tears to my eyes.

"It's so good to see you," I whispered, my voice breaking.

"Same here, baby girl. Well, let me get a look at you." She pulled back and studied my face. I didn't know what she saw there, and I wasn't sure I wanted to know. "It's good to have you home, darling."

Tears pricked at my eyelids, and I blinked them away, wondering at the odd reaction.

I had grown up with the Montgomerys and run wild with them. Then I had run away to the best hospital in the world for my sister and then continued to run to save myself.

And in the end, I had left everybody behind.

And I was only just now realizing that.

"I didn't realize that you guys live so close." Of course, I shouldn't have been surprised. The Montgomerys had always been a tight family. They might not live on top of one another, but there always seemed to be one nearby. Case in point: my neighbor.

"Oh, I'm just here to annoy my son. But he said you moved next door, and I had to say hello." She squeezed my hand and I relaxed.

"Well I'm glad that you're here."

Her smile brightened her face, and though I knew she wasn't Lex's biological mom, she looked so much like him then, I couldn't help but smile back. "Me too. And I'm inviting you to the Montgomery Christmas party at my house in Fort Collins. It's coming up soon, and I'm not taking no for an answer."

I blinked, suddenly unsure. "Oh. I don't know."

"I told you I'm not taking no for an answer. You used to come to them when you were younger, and now you're doing it again. Lex can drive you if you want, because we don't know about the roads, however, I just want you to know that you are required to come. I'm sorry, it's a mother's prerogative."

I blinked, wondering if there was a way out of this invitation, but from the determined look on her face, I didn't think there would be.

"Oh...Mrs. Montgomery."

She waved me off. "Call me Eliza. There are way too many Montgomerys out there. You know that."

"I don't think I can call you Eliza," I teased. "My mother would shake her head at me from above."

Her eyes warmed at the mention of my mother, and she sighed. "You're home now. And that means the Montgomerys are here to make you one of our own. We tend to do that. Believe me, I wasn't born a Montgomery."

"Mom, are you annoying Mercy?" Lex called out.

"You are not too old for me to wash your mouth out with soap. Don't be mean to your mother."

"I'm just saying, Mercy has to get to work. It's finally quiet over here."

"Mrs. Montgomery. Eliza," I corrected at her look. "You don't need to invite me."

She winked. "I just did. And Lexington will take you. You don't need to bring anything, just yourself. I want to stuff you full of cheese, and joy. Even for a few hours, okay? Let me do that."

Tears once again threatened, but I swallowed hard through the tightening of my throat. "Okay. But only because I feel like if I don't, you'll drag me anyway."

"You always were very brilliant, my dear."

"Were you always this threatening when we were younger?" I asked, laughing.

"Yes, but I was a lot more subtle about it. Now I don't have to be subtle because you're all adults." She leaned forward and kissed my cheek. "Welcome home. Don't worry, the Montgomerys will take care of you. You really don't have another choice."

And as she said the words, I had a feeling I only knew half of exactly what that meant.

Chapter Four

Lexington

ME:

You must have typed incorrectly. What do you mean I'm driving Mercy to the family party?

MOM:

That's exactly what it sounds like. I invited your neighbor to the Montgomery Christmas party because all are welcome, and I've missed seeing her. Now drive her so that way she doesn't have to deal with parking. It's only nice.

I crossed my eyes and had to wonder exactly what my mother was getting at. Because *I* should have been the one to invite Mercy to the party. Frankly, the only reason I hadn't was that every time she saw me these days, she got grumpy over the noise. And I didn't blame her one bit for that. However, inviting her to the family party felt odd for some reason. She had been to a few back in the day of course. This wouldn't be the first time she had hung out with the family, but it would be the first time since everything had changed.

And I wasn't quite sure what I felt about that.

> **MOM:**
> I am not trying to set you up with her. I do realize that some mothers constantly want their children to fall in love, make a family, and be happy, but I just want you to be happy. I promise never to set you up on a date. In fact, I think I've made this promise before.

> **ME:**
> I don't know if I believe you.

My phone rang in that instance, and I laughed, seeing my mom's face on the screen.

"Hello dear Mom."

A familiar deep growl of a voice came on the line. "It's your father. Don't call your mother a liar. Because I'm going to have to beat you, and I never beat you as a kid, so maybe it's time that I did."

"Oh, thanks. Threatening your favorite child."

"I can hear you, you know," my younger brother, Silas called out from the other side of the line.

I laughed full out. I loved this damn family. "Silas, what are you doing there?"

Silas chuckled. "Because I am the good son, and I'm prepping the house. You just have to bring a girl with you. I wonder if you actually know what to do when it comes to girls."

Dad snorted over the speaker phone. "Boys, don't make me reach through the phone and strangle this one, and don't forget, you're closer to me."

"You know, that's the holiday spirit, my boys. Threatening each other and doing it out of love." Mom laughed, but I knew she was most likely glaring at my father and brother.

Considering my mom had six brothers of her own, as well as four male cousins that all had grown up together, she could handle any one of us with her pinky. And pretty much had when we were growing up.

"Okay, I'll bring her. And I do trust you not to try to set me up on a date, Mom. I'm okay not dating," I lied.

Because I was the perpetual last man standing. Not exactly with my family and friends, but close to. My best friend in the world was engaged to my cousin, and my other closest friends, who happened to be my cousins, were each married to the loves of their lives. Many of my cousins who were at my age within the generation were married and having children and moving on. Yes, some weren't, but many were in serious relationships.

And I had been in two serious relationships in my life. And both of them I had ended up being the perfect man to date before you found your forever.

I was going to put that on a business card.

Want to meet the love of your life? Date me, and you'll find him. Then you can dump me along the way, leaving me all alone, and move on.

It was hard not to feel bitter at that, considering both women that I thought I had loved had not only cheated on me, but had immediately found themselves engaged to the person that they thought they could be with forever.

No, no, I wasn't ready to date. Wasn't ready to be set up.

Because once I did, Mercy would just find the love of her life. And she had already thought she found that once with my former friend. It was way too complicated.

"I will see you in a couple of hours then, and you do not have to bring anything. Seriously, you don't need to bring wine or cheese or anything else. The rest of the Montgomerys have brought so much food, we will have too much for even us."

"How many people are you expecting?" I asked, a little worried. My parents had a big house, especially since it had only been the four of us growing up. But my family was in construction, and liked building homes, it caused a vast quantity of Montgomerys in our lives. And they had gotten lucky with the land that they had been able to purchase, because they could just add on buildings over time. You couldn't find that type of land these days for any reasonable cost.

"I think about a hundred. Fewer than last year."

I shuddered at the sheer number. "You know, we have a problem."

"Yes, we do, but it's not like I invited all of your cousins from Texas. Just imagine if the Wilders and the Montgomerys showed."

"Don't put that out in the air, we'd start a war or something. They'd see so many people congregating in one area, they'd be afraid."

"As they should," Silas put in, and then my brother let out a grunt, and I knew he and my father were most likely wrestling.

I rolled my eyes, even though I heard the humor in my mom's voice as she said goodbye, and I went to get ready. I had already packed the wine and cupcakes that I had purchased from a local bakery earlier.

It wasn't from Latte on the Rocks, but I knew that my family who owned that cafe would be there as well. This was from another local bakery, a small mom-and-pop shop that was just starting. And me buying fifty cupcakes had really made their day.

So of course I was bringing desserts, and wine because I liked wine. It wasn't Wilder wine like my mother's family made, but it was decent enough. Colorado people knew what they were doing.

At least I thought so.

So I'd be going against my mother in one aspect, meaning I couldn't when it came to bringing Mercy.

I rubbed my temple and pulled out my phone again.

ME:
> What time should I be over to pick you up?

MERCY:
> I can just walk to your car next door. And I can be ready in twenty minutes. Did you want to get there early?

ME:
> No, that's perfect. And I'm sorry my mom most likely cornered you into this.

MERCY:
> I like your mom. And I like Montgomery parties. And I guess she's right, I do need to get out of the house.

I frowned at that, wondering exactly who she had to

speak to these days. Who she hung out with now that she was back in town. Most of her friends had been Justin's friends, and the Montgomerys. And when she had moved away, she had cut all ties from us. I had tried not to take that personally, because I had understood it. Between needing to get away from everything that Justin had done, and taking care of her sister, reaching out to us after ignoring us for so long probably wasn't high on her list.

I did not blame her for it, but now that she was back, I was going to show her that she didn't need to be alone.

But not in an awkward way.

Because that made so much sense.

I finished getting ready, and made my way out to my SUV, and blinked when I saw Mercy was already there.

"Oh. You're fast."

She shrugged, and I smiled at the bags in her hands.

"I've been pacing all day, wondering exactly what I was supposed to bring or wear to this. I'm sort of out of habit when it comes to Montgomery parties. But my friend's going to be there, so I'm not going to feel too badly or out of place."

I set my things in the back seat and took the two bags from her. "You know, we're friends. At least we were."

"I guess so." She shook her head. "Sorry. I feel awkward all the time these days."

"Same here. But if you're not talking about the Montgomerys, which friends are you talking about?" I asked as I got into the driver's seat. She got into the passenger seat, and I started the car, wondering if I was going to be able to make it through this hour-long drive. It didn't usually take that long, but with slightly icy roads and traffic, it might take even longer. "So wait, who do you know going to this other than Montgomerys?"

"My friend, Posy. She's friends with Cullen, and I think a few of your cousins."

I nodded and turned on my turn signal so I could merge onto the highway.

"I know Posy. She's nice. I didn't know you knew her. Or did I?"

"We're in the same profession and live near each other, and we've become friends since I've moved back. She's wonderful. She keeps to herself more than I do, however."

"I've met her a couple of times, though I don't know her well. I thought she was dating Cullen, turns out I was wrong."

"I thought they were too, but they're just friends. It's

nice, you know, having friends. And that made me sound sad and depressed."

I shook my head and got into the middle lane as people going ninety passed me, and people going thirty stayed in the right lane. "I think the only time I leave the house these days is with family, mostly because we're all friends. I've been working overtime in order to get a few projects done and out of the way, including my own house."

"Why is that?" she asked and sounded honestly interested.

I kept my fingers against the steering wheel and nodded. "There's a contract for a large project coming up that I really want. We've all been working double time to get our proposal ready, it just comes with a complication."

"What kind of complication?"

"It's the Arnault estate."

When she didn't say anything, I realized that we had been out of each other's lives for a little while now.

"It's the largest estate on the north side of the city, beautiful views of the Rockies, and one of the most historic areas that we have. It's also owned by my ex's family."

I caught her wince even as I moved around a slow

SUV in front of me. "Do you think it's going to be a hindrance?"

"Honestly, I don't know. Gia didn't have anything to do with her father's line of work or that estate, but I also don't know what she might've told her father. I didn't realize it until later, but she was far more vindictive than I thought. She liked to push the happiness of our relationship at the time in others faces. And we didn't end on the best of terms and when we saw each other afterward, she liked to show off the happiness she had with the other guy as if she hadn't dug a hole in my chest." I hadn't meant to blurt all of that out, but apparently it had been at the surface. Considering the amount of time I'd put into the proposal itself and getting ready for the upcoming bid retreat, I guess it made sense.

"Didn't she cheat on you?"

"Yep," I said, popping the P.

The little growl escaping her mouth was hot as hell. "Well, I can hate her for you if you'd like."

"I truly appreciate that." My lips lifted into a smile.

"At least my ex had the decency to move across the country."

"Damn straight." I shook my head. "I'm still sorry that Justin did that to you."

"He doesn't matter anymore. Seriously, there are way worse things going on in the world, and in our own lives. And we are headed to a Montgomery holiday party. Meaning there's going to be wine, cheese, and probably a few stories to share. I'm glad your mom got me out of the house."

"Make sure you tell her that. And that I didn't have to drag you out here."

"I'll do that," she said with a laugh, and we settled into the drive, speaking of work and things we had missed.

And in that instant, it didn't feel as if any time had passed, but then again, so much had happened since.

The party was in full swing by the time we got there, as the Montgomerys liked to be early, rather than late.

My mom had only rolled her eyes when I handed over my cupcakes and wine but had been ecstatic when Mercy had shown up with a cheesecake.

"It's not homemade, it's from this little bakery."

I frowned. "From Savannah's?"

"Yes, do you know it?"

"It's where I got the cupcakes." I shook my head, my chest rumbling. "I usually go with a Montgomery place, but I knew they were all backed up with orders and I didn't want to use the family privilege to cut in line."

"Well, that's interesting," my mom said. I narrowed my gaze at her.

She just rolled her eyes and tugged Mercy away.

Taking her place, Dash came up to me, handing me a bottle of beer, and I moved into the party, finally relaxing after a long month of overtime and stress.

The Montgomerys tended to switch off where they had the main party every year. This year it was with the Fort Collins branch, next year it would be with the Boulder branch. We loved our holidays, and with snow on the mountains, the air crisp outside, but not so cold that you couldn't enjoy it, it was that perfect time of year. My family had gone all out with the decorations, and I knew my uncles and aunts had helped there. Everything was covered in green and red and sparkles and just looked welcoming. My cousins' kids were roaming about, at least those who could walk. The infants and toddlers were upstairs, already sleeping in the spare cribs that family had provided.

Nobody got rid of baby things in this family, because it could always be used for someone else. We Montgomerys liked to procreate.

I frowned at that, wondering when it would be my turn.

Forever the groomsman, never the groom.

Not that I would ever say that out loud.

Beer empty, I took a few drink orders from my family and headed into the kitchen to get something else. I bumped into someone as soon as I did and reached out and grabbed her elbow.

Mercy looked up at me then, eyes wide, and I swallowed hard, taking a quick step back once I found myself looking at her lips, and not into those beautiful eyes of hers.

Beautiful eyes? Well, it was time for me to go to water, and not that single beer.

"Having fun?" I asked before I cleared my throat since my voice was oddly scratchy.

"Yes. I'm honestly thankful to be out of the house. Thank you for driving me."

I wouldn't thank my mom later as I had a feeling she wasn't entirely truthful about the setting up thing. Then again...maybe I *should* thank her. "No problem. You just let me know when you want to get home, okay?"

"No, you let me know. You're the one driving and this is your family."

"Mercy, I'm not going to force you to do anything that you don't want to do," I said, and I realized my voice was low, and I was hovering way too close. I took another step back, and she frowned at me, before she blinked that look away so quickly that perhaps, I had seen something that wasn't there.

"Anyway, I need to get drinks for the others, have fun, okay? Let me know if you need anything."

"I'm a big girl. I can take care of myself. But thank you, Lex."

I grinned at that. "You called me Lex."

"I've called you Lex before." She met my gaze. "I'm trying. Or I'm going to blame the wine," she said, and that blush on her cheeks was so damn pretty, it reminded me of when we had been younger, and I had been the first one to see Mercy like that.

But then Justin had called dibs, and you didn't cross the bro code when it came to dibs.

And how shitty was that?

I pulled my gaze away from her, grabbed a glass of water, and the beers, and scurried away. Scurried, because I was a damn menace. A coward.

I had nearly kissed Mercy.

Why the hell would I have done that?

I shook myself, handed the beers over to my cousins, and chugged half my water.

"You okay? You look a little flush, bro," Dash said, and I cleared my throat.

"Nothing, I think I just need to go outside, get some air."

"Okay. You want some company?" he asked, and I heard the sincerity in his tone.

"I'm good. Thanks."

I drained my glass, set it on the table with the other

empties, and went towards the back door so I could take a deep breath.

I didn't know what was wrong with me, but there was no need for me to think of Mercy that way.

We were neighbors, friends. And she had enough on her plate rather than my mind going into a weird direction. Just because part of me wanted to settle down, didn't mean I had to fall for the first woman who looked at me.

And even thinking about going in that direction was ridiculous. Because our history with each other was so entwined, that doing anything to jeopardize what we had had before, let alone what we were making now, would be insane.

I went past the couch and bumped into someone again. With so many people in this house, it wasn't unheard of, but as I held onto Mercy's arm again, I had to wonder what exactly the hell was going on.

She looked up at me then and smiled wide. "Are you really just going to knock me on the floor one day?"

"You're just so little down there, I didn't see you," I tease.

She rolled her eyes. "Really? You're going with a short joke? You used to do that all the time."

"You're like a foot shorter than me, pipsqueak."

"You did not just call me pipsqueak."

"What? You didn't kick me last time I did."

"Because we were like fifteen. And I was a teenage girl. I'm a woman now. I could kick your ass."

Damn it, she was a woman.

And I could not blame those thoughts on the single beer I had.

"Look who's under the mistletoe!" one of my annoying cousins called out.

I froze, my entire body stiffening as Mercy blinked up at me, eyes wide.

"*Kiss! Kiss! Kiss!*"

"I am so sorry," I mumbled, though my heart couldn't help but race. My hands went clammy, and I licked my lips. Damn it. I shouldn't look or *feel* too eager.

Mercy just shook her head at me. "Can we run?"

"You would rather run and deal with the Montgomerys' wrath and leers versus just kiss me quickly and getting it over with?" I asked, wondering if I should be hurt.

"I hate that logic."

"Okay, so one, two, three?"

"You're going to count down for this?" she asked, as everybody continued to chant for us to kiss.

"You know what, fine." And with that, I leaned forward and pressed my lips to hers.

I meant to step back, to stop the kiss before it even started, but I didn't. Instead, I parted my lips and swiped my tongue along hers. She tasted of wine, cupcakes, and Mercy.

Fuck.

And when I pulled back, and stared at her, everybody cheered, and I realized the drive home was going to be hell.

Because I had just kissed Mercy.

My former friend's ex-fiancée.

And one of the first girls I had ever had a crush on.

Oh, and my new neighbor.

I guess hell had a new name. I guess hell had a new resident. And here I was, staking my claim.

Chapter Five

Lexington

Four Years Ago

"Is there a reason we're out here at a barbecue?" Justin asked, and I squinted at my friend, wondering exactly why he was asking this for the eighth time.

"Because we just celebrated our graduation, and now we're having a nice party before we split up and go about our days?"

"Well, it's not like you don't know what you're going to do for the rest of your life. You have an in when it comes to your family. You could have chosen any profession that you wanted within the Montgomerys, and look at you, you chose the one that had perfect space for you."

I scowled at the other man and tossed a bag of chips at him.

"Eat something, you get crabby when you're hungry."

"What? I'm not over exaggerating here. You have multiple construction companies in your family, and you guys are just what, going to open a subsidiary of one? Rather than forcing your parents out of their jobs? It makes sense. You don't have to go out there and figure out how to do interviews or make a resume. You have an in."

An odd sense of guilt swept through me, but I did my best to push that away.

"I didn't automatically get a job with my family. Yes, growing up when I had wanted to start working, I applied for any job I could get at sixteen within the Montgomery Construction companies. My parents had hired me because I had been the only person to apply for one of the jobs that required me to be knee-deep in mud and other things I'd rather not think about. Then I worked for another company while I was eighteen and in my first year of college, one that had nothing to do with the Montgomerys. I had wanted an outside take on what it meant to be an architect. Yes, my aunt Annabelle had taught me everything that she knew, but I had still taken the time to learn from others. If I had been given everything that I had ever wanted without having to work for it, why had I even bothered going to college?"

But Justin was right in some respect. My family never would've let me fail completely. If I had tried for other companies, and gotten the jobs, they would've cheered me on. If I would've found myself unemployed, they'd have made sure that I found a way to work with them. Just maybe not in the exact job that I wanted. Because we cared about each other, but we also wanted the best in the business.

I had wanted to be an architect and work with my family's construction company since I had been a little kid with a tiny tool belt and a little wrench. I had walked along the different sites with my little hard hat as I soaked in as much knowledge as I could.

And I was damn lucky and excited that Dash, Brooklyn, and even Jamie had wanted to join us. Jamie could've worked for any company out there, as she was a whiz with marketing, organization, and just keeping an office afloat. Plus she could make connections with anybody and make a bid worthwhile. We had wanted to start our own business because we hadn't wanted to stay in Fort Collins, and the company had grown enough that it was needed.

It was my job on the line, my money on the line, or

rather, my loans on the line, if we failed. Just like it was with every single person who had bought in.

Justin didn't understand that. And I tried not to be resentful for it.

"Sorry," Justin said after a moment, as if he read my mind.

"Yeah?" I ask, slightly grumbly.

"I'm in a shit mood, but that's no reason for me to take it out on you. I know you're damn talented. I'm just annoyed that I didn't get the job at Anderson's that I wanted."

"But you're at Clark's. That's an amazing law firm."

"I know, I know. And they'll give me great references and experience for my gap year."

"Look at you, able to take a gap year."

"Yes, because I'm privileged." He rolled his eyes as he said it, but the man wasn't wrong. I came from Montgomery money, which was blue-collar money. Hence the loans. Justin came from fancy money. He didn't have student loans, and honestly, I was surprised he hadn't gotten the job with the Anderson law firm. But maybe it just hadn't been a good fit. For all I knew, the interview hadn't gone well.

"Well, hello, who's that?" Justin said, pulling me from my thoughts. I looked over where he was staring, his heart in his eyes, and I grinned.

"Hey, Mercy! We're over here."

"I thought you were dating Gia?" Justin whispered.

"I'm not dating Gia. She's just a friend. So is Mercy."

Gia and I had been schoolmates, and I get the feeling she had a thing for me, but I couldn't help but keep my gaze on Mercy.

She was just so damn beautiful. She had put more highlights in her hair since I had last seen her, so now it shined bright blonde underneath the sunlight. Her twin, Emily, followed behind her, her hair a bright cherry red.

"Dibs," Justin called, and all thoughts of me finally getting the nerve to ask Mercy out after crushing on her since we had been years younger fled.

"What?"

"Dibs. You can take the redhead. I want the blonde." He winked and my stomach fell.

"Justin, they're both my friends."

"That means I have an in. Why don't you introduce me?"

Then Mercy smiled at Justin, that grin so bright that it nearly knocked me to my knees, and I did the only thing that a good friend would do.

"Mercy, Emily, this is Justin. Justin, these are the twins."

"I'm so glad that I have an identity outside of being a

twin," Mercy said with a laugh, and I took a step back and watched Justin up his game.

But that was fine, just fine.

It wasn't as if I had ever had a chance with Mercy. If something was ever going to happen, it would have before this.

My phone buzzed, and I watched Gia's photo flash on the screen.

Well then, maybe it was time for me to take a step in that direction and stop wanting what I couldn't have. And at the sound of Mercy's laugh, I answered the phone and realized it was time to grow up and give up that certain dream.

TWO YEARS AGO.

"I can't believe that he just walked out on her during the wedding," Gia said as we sat across from each other in the park, gray storm clouds on the way.

"He didn't answer my call when I tried to reach out to him to see what the hell he was doing, but I don't think I even want to talk to him at this point."

"He was always an egotistical jerk, you know."

"I don't know if *always* is a good word for that," I corrected.

"No, he was a jerk. Anyway, I'm thankful that you're here. Because I think it's time we talk."

I blinked at her, the temperature chilling as the wind began to pick up. "What is it that you wanted to talk about?" I asked, grateful that my voice was staying slightly steady.

"Lex, you know I've had a lot of fun with you. I mean, we've traveled, we've made great friends, and I really like you."

I swallowed hard and stuck my hands in my pockets. "But?"

"But I think you have to agree with me that this just isn't working."

"What's not working?" I asked, my heart racing. Oh, why did it feel like she had her hand around it right now, squeezing ever so slightly so the blood vessels began to pop one by one?

"I don't want to say it's not you, it's me. But honestly, the phrase is useful. I just don't think we click."

"Gia, we've been together for two years. We live together." Why the hell was I even trying? I saw that look in her eyes. I knew it. She was done. Already moved on. And just...just not *here*.

"I know, and I'll totally keep paying my rent on the

lease, but Lex, do you really see us with a future? You're a nice guy. You're a great boyfriend. But I want a *husband*."

My hand curled around the box in my pants pocket, the box I had hidden for months because I hadn't wanted to overshadow Justin and Mercy's wedding.

Because I was ready. I was ready for the next step.

And as acid coated my tongue, she continued to talk, but I just finally let go, knowing it was all for rote.

The first raindrop fell, hitting me in the face, and I didn't blink it away.

"I'll come pick up my stuff soon. But I hope we can be friends? I mean, you're a great guy, Lex. But I just don't see myself marrying you. And I want forever. I know I'll find it. But it won't be with you. You're just not it. I hope you understand that."

I watched her walk away, not a single word uttered. What more was there to say? I had never been more wrong in a situation, but then again, I had been. I'd been wrong about Justin, now it seems like I was wrong once again.

Rain began to fall in earnest, and I turned on my heel and made my way back to my car.

I thought Gia was the one for me. I thought she was my forever. It turns out I wasn't good enough.

And I wasn't going to be anyone's forever.

Thunder cracked, and I slid my face up to the sky, and let the rain slid down my face, doing what it did best—wash away the rest of the world. Or at least the problems I wanted to pretend I didn't have.

When my phone buzzed again, I looked down at the text.

> **MERCY:**
> I'm sorry to have to do this, but Emily and I need to head to New York. We got into the specialist that we needed. Can you handle the list we went through? I know it's too much but I just...I can't do it right now.

I finally got in my car and answered back. Because of course I would help.

The twins needed me. Just like my family did.

I was good at being there for them. It turns out I wasn't good at much else.

Today

"Are you really not going to let me work on your gardens?"

I looked up as Brooklyn got out of her truck and came towards me. I rolled my eyes at my cousin, shovel in hand. "I'm literally just digging right now. You are the one who gets to plan my front gardens. Don't worry. I'm not taking that from you. Although, that does seem like a bit of a downside for you, doesn't it?"

"Not really. I love working with gardens. Mom and Dad let me take over occasionally." She looked down at the hole I was currently working on and clucked her tongue. "What are you trying to bury here?"

"It's just an issue I need to deal with, I swear it's not for a body." I paused. "Okay I said that far too quickly. However, I will need your help soon. Again, not a body." She smirked. "I do plan on adding a couple of trees in the back. Mostly because we had dry rot with one of the originals, and then the previous owners had planted another tree so close to the foundation there was going to be issues."

"Poor tree."

"Both of them were already dying, well, which sucks."

"Tell me about it. Well, I'm here to make plans. Even if you hadn't let me in the first place, I was taking over."

"That sounds like the cousin I know and love," I teased. "But why are you really here?"

"No reason," Brooklyn sing-songed.

"Brooklyn."

"Fine, I just wanted to see if Mercy was home."

"And why would you need to see if Mercy's home?" I asked, slightly on edge. Because I knew exactly why Brooklyn was here.

And why Dash had shown up earlier, and even Livy had come by. Livy didn't even live in the state anymore, but she, her new husband, and daughter, as well as a couple of her new in-laws had come down to visit before Christmas. They were spending all of Christmas and New Year's up in Wyoming but had wanted to visit the family beforehand.

And every single person had wanted to know what was going on with me and Mercy.

Not that there was anything going on. It was just a kiss, a simple kiss that I had been waiting on since I was eight years old, even though I had completely forgotten that I had been waiting on it since I was eight years old. That's what happened when you lived in denial, sometimes the denial worked.

"You're welcome to go annoy her while she's working, but today's a relatively quiet day on my house, so she's probably in her studio. I'm not dealing with her wrath."

"Why would she be wrathful? I just want to say hi."

I raised a brow. "It was mistletoe. Stop it."

"Uh-huh. So you *are* thinking about that kiss. Because your kiss wasn't the only kiss that happened underneath the mistletoe. And people have questions."

"What other kiss was there?" What the hell had I missed? There hadn't been too many unpaired, non-family members there so there were only so many possibilities.

"Aww, it's so nice that you're focused on your own moment in time underneath the mistletoe."

"Let me guess, the only kiss you got last night was by a cousin on the cheek?"

"Rude. True. But rude."

"What about Rodney? I'm surprised you didn't bring him."

Brooklyn rolled her eyes.

"That's been over for a while now. I'm seeing someone else, though he didn't get to come to the party. He had other family obligations. As for Rodney? He didn't like that I disparaged kale."

I blinked, trying to catch up. "As in our friend's husband or the salad?"

"The salad."

A family friend of a friend happened to be married to a man named Cale, spelled with a C. He seemed like a nice enough guy, but I usually ended up just thinking about the vegetable.

"Anyway, I'm off to the office, because I have a few papers to sign, but let me know when you're ready to finish working on that bid. I know the retreat's coming up."

I crossed my eyes at that. "Don't remind me."

"I'll go with you if you want. I can schmooze just as good as you."

My lips twitched.

"Yes, you can. But it's the holidays. I'm not going to make you do that."

"The offer's still out there. Or hell, bring Mom. She's great at that."

"I don't know if bringing my mother to a retreat where everybody's trying to one-up one another is going to set the tone."

"It'll keep people guessing," she said with a laugh, before she got back into her truck, and headed off.

I shook my head, knowing that Brooklyn had taken time out of her day to come annoy me, and see what was going on between Mercy and me. Not that there was anything going on.

Another car pulled into my driveway, and I turned, with a glare at the ready for a family member, when a familiar brunette walked towards me.

She had her hair done in waves all the way down to her waist, with red and caramel low-lights artfully done in between some of the curls. The flowing dress she wore moved with each sure step, the wind in her hair and in her dress artfully done. Her makeup was done to the nines, and I knew her shoes and bags had to be worth more than my first car.

And I had liked that old junker.

"Gia," I said after a moment, looking at the woman who had broken my heart and hadn't even realized it.

She smiled at me, her eyes kind, but I had to wonder exactly what she was thinking.

"Oh, Lex. I'm so glad that you're here."

I set the shovel down and wiped my hands. I didn't offer to shake her hand or even hug her, considering she wouldn't appreciate the dirt.

"I didn't know you knew about this house," I said in lieu of a true greeting.

"Oh, you know me, I have spies everywhere." She rolled her eyes. "For real, though. I was working with Daddy on a few permits, and I realized that yours had come up. And well, I just wanted to see how you were after Carly's news."

I blinked, wondering exactly how Gia knew so much about my personal life, and work life for that matter. She might literally have those spies of hers.

"What do you mean Carly's news?" I asked, speaking of my other ex-girlfriend. She and I had started dating a few months after Gia had dumped me, and now Carly was married, and happy.

Again, I was the man you dated before you found your happily ever after.

I set my teeth at that thought and tried not to sigh.

"Well, I just got the news in the mail. About the baby shower."

My stomach fell, and I tried not to stagger back. "Carly's having a baby?"

Her eyes narrowed to slits before she smiled brightly. "Yes. Isn't it great? I just love the fact that you can be friends with your exes. Anyway, I wanted to see how you were doing. Because the retreat's coming up, and I know Daddy's working hard and trying to figure out which bid to take. And don't worry, I've made sure that he knows not to cut you off completely because we were dating. Heck, I'm married, very happy, and Daddy understands that. So don't worry, I'm putting in a good word for you for the Arnault Estate project."

She kept saying these things, as if they were supposed to make sense and not nearly push me over the edge.

Why the hell did I think that trying for the Arnault Estate would be easy? Or something I should do?

Except for the fact that every single person in my building wanted this, and I wanted to be the one who brought it. I didn't want my lack of personal life—or twisted one—to stand in the way.

And here I was, wondering what the hell I was doing.

"I'll need to tell Carly congratulations. I haven't checked my mail."

And I had a feeling the invite would be there. Because just like with Gia, I was cordial with my exes. And they felt the need to invite me to every important part of their lives.

Why did I suddenly resent that?

"Well, I just am so excited for her, and I wanted to see how you were doing. Oh, and who are you bringing to the retreat?"

I blinked. "Excuse me?"

"To the retreat. It's sort of a family thing you know, and Daddy's pretty conservative." She went on, "Which sounds terrible, but it's a family estate, and he's not just going to sign over to anybody. There are other companies there with similar proposals to yours that have more experience. I know there are a few other projects looking for contractors though, so you probably won't leave empty handed."

That didn't sound old school or ominous at all. I resisted the urge to fist my hands at my sides. "The Montgomerys is a family-owned and operated business with a long-standing family goal." Even saying the words made me want to throw up. Because I had a feeling this wasn't exactly what she meant.

She gave that sickly sweet smile that I'd missed for far too long. "I know. The Montgomerys do the best work in the state. You guys worked on my house."

"I remember," I said. Though it hadn't been my company. It had been the Denver branch, because of location. I would have worked on her home with her then boyfriend, because I was better than that, but I was glad that I hadn't had to. "The retreat though, what exactly do you mean?"

"I just want to make sure that you're not coming alone." She rolled her shoulders back. "Because there's a lot of other companies coming that are going to showcase how steadfast and steady they are. And while the Montgomerys themselves have a lot of depth, your section of the company is pretty young. I'm not saying this to be mean. I just want you to know that you're going to have to show that you guys have longevity."

I opened my mouth to say something, but Gia's gaze caught on something behind me, and I turned as Mercy walked towards me with a bright smile on her face.

"There you are." She ran towards me, wrapped her arm around my waist, and kissed me firmly on the cheek. Warmth spread through the ice that had slid through my system as Gia had spoken and I instinctively wrapped my arm around her waist. "Thanks for taking on a quiet day so that I could work. Now, why don't you introduce me." She turned to Gia and held out her hand. "Hi, I'm Mercy. Lex's girlfriend."

Chapter Six

Mercy

Was it really spying if you just happened to be in your living room at the front window drinking a cup of tea? It wasn't as if I had purposely tiptoed towards the glass, leaned forward, and pressed my ears so close I could possibly hear their words.

No, I had just opened the window earlier to let out smoke because I had forgotten I had put a pan on the stove and went to work. It had taken me longer than I'd wanted because of three more random calls that led to nowhere that were really starting to annoy me. Yes, I had only been working a room away, but boiled eggs that had been over-boiled with all of the water gone, made for a disgusting mess. I was just lucky I hadn't burned down my house.

So, that was why the window was open. And that was why I had been able to hear most of every conversation Lex had had over the past twenty minutes. Including one with Brooklyn.

It wasn't my fault that I had heard my name. Anybody would be curious. So I continued to sip my tea, because I was a voice actor. I needed to soothe my throat and practice voice rest so I could continue working on my heavy deadline. I was the one who put myself into this deadline over the holidays, but that was fine. I was making it work, and here I was, sipping the rest of my tea as I listened to Gia drone on and on about her perfect life.

I cringed. No, that was uncalled for. Gia had always been nice to me. At least the few times we had hung out together as a group. But she hadn't really understood why Lex had female friends and frankly, I didn't blame her. After all, my fiancé had ended up cheating on me with the wedding planner. So maybe having female friends when you couldn't trust the person you're with really didn't make sense.

But Lex was trustworthy. That much I knew after knowing him for so many years of my life. Gia had been cautious about his female friendships, and I had always understood. I had never wanted to be the person who could hurt someone's relationship.

But it seems in the time I had been gone, Gia had not only broken up with Lex and moved on, but Lex's other girlfriend was already married and having a baby with someone else.

I was terrible at relationships. Yes, I hadn't had one or frankly, hadn't had sex since Justin, and that was something I didn't want to think about. But it seemed that Lexington was as bad off when it came to romance as me. And that sounded like a terrible time.

When Gia continued on about family matters and what her father was looking for in terms of a contractor, the hair on the back of my neck stood on end.

None of the Montgomerys in that particular branch were married from what I remembered. Meaning none of the Montgomerys who wanted that job had family. Cousins, siblings, and loving parents counted as family in my book. Considering I had nobody left, it sure as hell counted. But I didn't think that was the family Gia was talking about. Somehow, I found myself outside of my house, walking down my path, doing the most insane thing I could possibly do.

I slid my hand around Lex's waist, gripping his belt loop with all of my strength. Then without thinking, I went to my toes and kissed his cheek like I had a right to do that. I ignored the odd warmth in my belly at the touch. This had to be an out of body experience, after all. I said a few words that might have made sense, then did the most ridiculous thing possible.

"Hi, I'm Mercy. Lex's girlfriend."

Hello, stupidity, my name is Mercy.

Gia knew who the fuck I was. Why the hell was I acting as if we had never met before? Of course, we each had different hair color then, and she had new jewelry. Like the biggest diamond I'd ever seen in my life.

But that wasn't even the crazy part.

Girlfriend. Lex. Me.

Well, at least Lexington had already dug a hole for me to dive into and never be seen from again. If he could just cover me up with that excess dirt, that would be great. Maybe he could plant some flowers over me, and I could bring beauty to the world.

Because there was no way I was getting out of this embarrassing situation with my pride.

All was lost.

"Mercy? What? Oh. Oh it's Gia." The smile on Gia's face brightened so much that I practically needed sunglasses. She had always been a beautiful woman, but right then, she was absolutely gorgeous. And from the calculating look in her eyes, she was also cunning.

And for some reason a slight tinge of jealousy trickled up my spine, but I ignored that. Because there was no reason for me to be jealous. She was beautiful but we'd seen beneath the surface.

"I recognize you. You look amazing. I didn't realize you and Lex were together." She turned to Lex, that Cheshire Cat smile on her face. "Oh, what a small world. And to think, you two were just friends when we were dating. It's so interesting how things turn out."

"Um," Lex said by my side. "Um."

Well, he had dug the hole physically, and I was just going to continue to dig it figuratively.

He cleared his throat. "Right. I'm so sorry. It has been a while, hasn't it? It's nice to see you, Gia. And congratulations on the wedding and everything."

That sounded like a goodbye if I'd ever heard one. And I wanted to eat my own foot.

"I guess we have a lot to catch up on. Will you be at the retreat? I mean, girlfriends are totally allowed. They may be traditional in some sense, but you're totally allowed to live together or share a hotel room when you're not married." Gia laughed, rolling her eyes. "I think it's more they want to ensure that you're steady and a true family business. Anyway, it's so good to hear about this. We're going to have to get drinks sometime so you can tell me exactly how this came about. You know what's funny? Back when Lex and I were dating, I was totally jealous of you."

Lex's hand around my waist squeezed so tightly I was afraid he was going to leave a bruise.

"Oh really? I'm sorry about that. I was with Justin then. And well, Lex and I didn't see each other that way. We were just friends."

He cleared his throat and I knew he had to be wondering what the hell I was up to. But with the way Gia was finally backing off...maybe it would be okay. Or maybe we were both losing our damn minds. "Yeah. Just friends. And well, sorry, this being out as a couple thing is new, and hearing the word girlfriend sort of surprised me."

"I totally get that feeling. Anyway, we'll have to do drinks so you can tell me all about it. Or, how about we all get together at the retreat? I know you'll be working at the JW for bids and everything, but we will have to take some time to just get things caught up. This makes me so happy to hear. I mean, to be honest, Lex, I was worried that Carly's news would be hard on you during the holidays, so I wanted to make sure that you were okay. But this just makes me so happy. I will see both of you at the retreat." She leaned forward, kissed my cheek, then Lex's, before she ran off to her car, as if she hadn't contradicted herself eight times, and made me feel as if I had lost my damn mind.

"Oh," I said, my arm still around his waist as Gia

drove off. "I don't know exactly what happened, but I'm pretty sure my tea was drugged."

"You had tea? There was tea?" Lex pulled away from me and then began to pace. When he nearly fell into the hole he had just dug, I reached out for him and caught his arm.

"Don't fall. I'm sorry."

"Well maybe me falling and cracking my skull open would make more sense than what just happened." He whirled on me, his eyes wide. "Why the hell did you just tell Gia you're my girlfriend? You can't even stand me. Not that that matters. What the hell?"

"I don't know. She just bothers me. She's always bothered me." I put my hands over my face and tried not to growl.

"I'm going to need you to explain that very slowly because I have a headache now. And I think that headache is named Mercy," he snapped.

My lips twitched, but I did my best not to laugh.

Because he was panicking way more than me and to be honest that was probably the correct thing to do. Yet, I was going to have to deal with what the hell I had just done.

"The thing is, I was boiling eggs and then they got burnt and so I had the window open."

"You are saying words, and I understand that they

are full sentences, or at least mostly full sentences, but not anywhere near the explanation I need from you."

"I had the windows open, and I was drinking my tea to soothe my throat."

"Again, not helping."

"I'm getting there. First, I heard Brooklyn come over and give you trouble or at least razz you like a cousin does. And I know you guys were worried about the bid and the whole estate thing, and I didn't mean to listen, but I was just there. And Mr. Darcy was there."

"You mean the cat and not the fictional character from *Pride and Prejudice*?"

"You aren't helping here."

"How am I supposed to be helping right now? Keep going." He froze for a moment, the blush on his cheeks deepening. "You heard everything she said?"

"Yes. Like teasing the fact that we kissed." I paused. "Underneath the mistletoe. But I'm continuing on. Then Gia came, and frankly, she sounded like she wanted you to be upset that Carly was pregnant. Or upset at the fact that both of them are married. I'm not quite sure, but I didn't like it. And then I didn't like the fact that it felt as if she were dangling the job that you really want for your family in front of you. And one thing led to another, and I kind of wanted to just kick her."

"So you kicked her with an imaginary wedding?" he asked, his voice going high-pitched.

I looked around, afraid somebody would hear what had just happened.

"Come on in with me. I don't want to be overheard."

"Who the hell is overhearing this? Unless another neighbor has their window open!" He was practically shouting at this point, so I pulled him by his arm, past the hole in the ground, and into my house.

His nose scrunched up as soon as we walked in, but he knelt down, petting Mr. Darcy's stomach as if the cat hadn't just bit my hand earlier for daring to do the same thing.

Traitor.

"From the look on your face you do smell the eggs."

"What the hell did you do?"

"I told you. I forgot they were on the stove. And well, that's why I had the window open."

"It's not helping."

"I realize that. And me standing at the window for that long to try to get the smell out of my nose clearly wasn't enough either."

"Mercy. What the hell did you do?"

"I don't know. Your family has just been so nice to me over the years, and your mom enveloped me into her fold for that party, and I don't know what I just did. I love your family. I love what they do for the community. And I didn't want you to lose out on something good for your company because you're not married. And frankly, I didn't like the fact that Gia seemed to be rubbing her marriage as well as Carly's in your face. I'm a little testy when it comes to marriage," I put in, and Lex blinked at me before standing up.

"I'm just as touchy with marriage as you are. Considering the last wedding I was best man in turned out the way it did."

"I don't even think about Justin most days. Because him walking away from me wasn't the worst thing that happened to me that day."

My heart ached, my fingers going numb just remembering it. So when Lex reached for my hand, squeezing gently, I froze, wondering why that felt like a lifeline when I was the one who had just altered his axis.

"I don't know what I'm supposed to do now. Because Gia's probably already told her father about the whole relationship thing, and I can't show up without a girlfriend. Let alone any member of my family could find out about this, and either spill the beans, or be very worried that I didn't tell them."

"I know, I know. I didn't like the look on Gia's face. There. It makes no sense. I could have done anything else, but no, I had to pull out the fake relationship card."

"I didn't even know that was a card at all," Lex said slowly. "Merce." He let out a breath. "I can't even ask you if you know what you've done because I don't know."

He began to pace, running his hands through his hair. I swallowed hard, trying not to watch the way that his muscles worked as he moved. I had always been attracted to Lexington. And that was the problem. Ever since I had realized that boys were cute and I wanted to date them, Lex had made my heart go pitter-pat. And then I had realized that teenage boys sucked, and I didn't want to ruin one of my best friendships. And even though we hadn't always been in each other's lives, Lex had always been a grounding force.

And apparently, I was the one who was changing the game.

"Okay, so I might have ruined everything. How can I fix this?"

"Well you're going to have to come with me to the damn retreat," he growled.

"Lex."

"No. Because Gia's father is going to wonder where the hell you are if I don't bring you. And then it's going to be the full topic of conversation if you're not there. But if you *are* there, we can just brush by it, and I can talk with all of the developers and estate managers at this thing and work my magic. Which sounds ridiculous, but there it is. You're just going to have to go, pretend you're my girlfriend, and pretend like I know what the hell I'm doing."

"Tell me this, would Gia have made it any easier for you if you were going alone?"

He froze then, before running his hands through his hair one more time. "No. She was here testing the waters. I don't know what she was up to, and frankly, I never know what she's up to these days. I thought her and I were endgame, turns out we weren't. Same with Carly. By the way, if you want to have a real marriage eventually, just date me, and then your next guy will be your number one."

"What?" I asked, confused.

"Every woman that I date finds her husband right after we break up. Or, in some cases, while we're still dating. But I digress. Gia was probably just testing the waters to make sure that I'm just as miserable as always."

"Lex. You're not miserable, are you?" I asked, feeling just as miserable.

"No I'm not." He paused, letting out a breath. "I'm not. I have plenty of time to find the woman of my dreams. But right now I want the job of my dreams. And Gia's family is standing in the way of that."

"So I'll help you get there."

"Why on earth would you do that?"

"Because I just sort of made everything worse."

"There's no sort of about it," he said dryly.

"Hey. She was being mean, and I wanted you to not look all alone."

"Because pity always makes me feel better."

"That's not what I meant. I'm alone too." I paused, not feeling great about that sentence. "It's fine being alone. I'm good at it. I don't need a husband or happy ever after or anything like that. But I didn't like the way she was acting, and frankly, if you want that job so badly, and you need to look married and happy in order to have it, then I'll help you. Because screw conforming to normalcy. We'll lie our way through it and make plans."

He stared at me for a moment, before he threw his head back and laughed.

"What? What did I say that was so funny?"

"Everything. You are ridiculous. But so am I. Because you know what? Why not. I frankly wasn't in the mood to deal with Gia's pitying looks, because yes, they were pitying. So now I won't have to. Now we'll just have the curious ones."

"And what about your family?"

"They're not going to be at the event, so we won't

have to lie to them. But I'll probably tell them to keep it under wraps. Just in case."

"So we lie to everyone that's not a Montgomery. Which oddly sets aside a large group of the population that will know the truth," I said, trying to make light of a very awkward situation.

"Yes, making fun of the Montgomery monopoly is really where we're going with this."

"You're the one who said the Montgomery monopoly exists."

"We're a cult, or a mafia. Not a monopoly."

"How many times are you going to say that word in a conversation?"

"Okay. We'll do this thing, it's only an overnight event because there's an early morning golf thing, but I don't even know if I want to do that."

"Okay then. Just tell me what to do. And we'll fix this. You'll get the job of your dreams, we'll make sure Gia doesn't get that look on her face again, and this will be my thank you for inviting me to that Christmas party. And well, also sorry for being such a bitch when you first moved in."

His lips twitched, before he leaned forward and brushed my hair back from my face. My lips parted, and I sucked in a breath at the touch.

"You weren't a bitch. You aren't one either. And yes,

we'll get that job. In a way more complicated way than I was planning."

"That's me. Your favorite complication."

He smiled then, and I knew once again I was in trouble.

And it had nothing to do with pretending to be his girlfriend.

Chapter Seven

Lexington

DASH:

Are you sure this is a good idea?

BROOKLYN:

I think it's a great idea.

DASH:

I didn't ask you.

JAMIE:

He's already doing it. And it's not like we can bring another girlfriend into the game.

REECE:

How did I get invited to the family group chat about the company?

BROOKLYN:

Wait. How did you get added? Crap. This is the wrong group chat.

DASH:

Damn it. I knew I needed to name this one. Sorry about that Reece.

REECE:

I'm at the job site and now wondering exactly why you're talking about a fake relationship. Though I hope the girl is real and the relationship is the fake part.

ME:

You don't need to worry about it. Just get to work.

REECE:

Oh no. What the hell's going on?

I pinched the bridge of my nose as the family members that worked at Montgomery Construction proceeded to tell Reece, our fire restoration expert, exactly what the hell I was doing. Not that I knew what I was doing.

The laughing emojis that Reece sent after being told exactly what happened pretty much explained it all.

"The family has decided to butt in on what we're doing."

"Oh? What are they saying?" she asked as she leaned into my side.

I sucked in an audible breath, the vanilla scent of her hitting my nostrils. We were at the JW, hanging out in the open seating bar area of the large resort, waiting on other people to show up that I knew. For now it was just men in business suits as they strolled about, trying to one-up one another. I'd had three productive conversations with other estates and committees looking for companies in the future. The Burson representative had been receptive and while I knew they weren't looking to add anything to their plate as of yet, I thought they could be a good fit for Montgomery Construction in the future. I'd make sure Jamie reached out later since she was fantastic at that part of the process.

We had only been here a good thirty minutes, and this was the first time that Mercy had been close enough to me that I could scent her since we'd changed for the event. The hour drive into the mountains for this resort when Mercy had been far too close to me in an enclosed space, had been long enough.

She smiled up at me and I finally brought myself out of my wandering thoughts. "Wait, do I know Reece?"

I shook my head. "He works for us. Well, the Montgomerys. He's newer to the company, and I'm glad that we got him."

"What does he do?"

"He's a fire expert."

She blinked up at me, and I slid my phone into my back pocket after ignoring the rest of the messages. It wasn't as if my family could stop me at this point, nor could they help me figure out what the hell I was doing at this moment.

"He is great at restoration. If there's fire damage in a house, he's the one that can help facilitate any issues. Because restoring an older building to its once grander, or even updating anything, is completely different if there was fire or water damage involved. You have to deal with the sheetrock, any subflooring, as well as deal with the environmental and health impacts of it."

"I never really thought about that. Your job can get a little scary, can't it?"

"Well there's risks with any type of job, but we as a company hadn't fully dived into projects that would entail such difficult circumstances until we brought Reece along. He's been at it for about twenty years now." I pause, doing the math. "Actually, that number's right. Well, I'm going to have to make fun of him for that later."

Mercy's lips twitched. "Ageist."

"No, if I was an ageist, I wouldn't have hired your friend Cullen or Reece at all. Instead, I hired the men with experience, who don't mind working for a company filled with Montgomerys that are far younger."

Mercy's brows furrowed, and I had to resist the urge to lean forward and rub the little line away.

What the hell was wrong with me? Yes, I had always found Mercy hot, had always been attracted to her in some shape or form, but she had been my friend's girlfriend, then fiancée, and now she was my neighbor. A neighbor who probably saw me and was reminded of the bullshit things my former friend had done.

It was just that damn kiss. That freaking kiss that had only been something to joke about for others, haunted my dreams.

And now, we were standing in a large area surrounded by people, and yet the only person I could focus on was Mercy. And it wasn't lost on me that we were waiting on our room key, and I'd be forced to share a room with her overnight.

Thankfully we had a room with two beds, so it wasn't as if I was going to have to sleep on the floor in order to get away from her, and whatever the hell feeling I was dealing with, but still.

"Lex? Where'd you go?"

I shook myself out of that thought. The thought of exactly how the hell I would be sleeping tonight, knowing she was so close.

I needed to stop letting my mind go down paths that weren't good for anybody.

Mercy was a friend. A neighbor, and someone I hadn't been able to stop dreaming about.

Just the memory of the dream I'd had the night before, knowing I'd have to pull off this farce this evening, had kept me up after I'd woken in a deep sweat at three a.m.

Memories of her hands on my skin, her lips covering my own. The way she would feel as I sank into her.

I tilted away from her slightly, knowing that if she saw the quickly rising hard-on I was about to get, she'd call me a menace. Or run away screaming. Probably the latter.

"Lex? What's wrong?" The urgency in Mercy's voice brought me back to the present once again, and I forced a smile and tried not to think about that kiss once again.

"Sorry. Just drifting. Trying to think about exactly how I got into this situation." A pretty blush covered Mercy's face, and I held back a curse. "Sorry."

"No, it is my fault that we're in this situation. I still can't believe I did that."

I snorted. "Honestly same. It's so unlike us."

"Well, I want you to win, and I wanted to kick her. And here we are. In a ridiculous situation that could only happen to me."

"Why do you say that?" I asked, intrigued.

"I have my head in books all day, imagining odd situations that could possibly never happen in real life, so therefore I apparently made one of my own."

I tilted my head, studying her face. She'd put on full glam makeup—in her words—and wore a dress that went nearly to her knees, knee boots, and thick tights. The dress was long sleeved and cut straight across her collarbone, but she also wore this jacket thing with odd angles, and it just looked damn good on her.

"Well, we're here now. And I guess we should continue to get our stories straight?" I asked as I looked around the lower lobby area and hoped nobody was truly listening.

"What can I say, boyfriend of mine, I just couldn't say no."

A grin covered my face. "Oh yeah? Why is that exactly?"

"Are you searching for compliments?"

I rolled my eyes. "Always. I'm a Montgomery. And a middle child at that."

"I thought you were the eldest of two. I know Silas."

"It's the middle child syndrome of the Montgomerys. All of us were raised as siblings rather than a big group of cousins, second cousins, and third cousins, and I'm in the middle."

"Aw, poor baby."

My lips twitched. "You should feel bad for me."

"Well, don't look now, but I'm not going to feel bad for you in this moment." And with that, she slid her arm into mine and leaned against me.

I swallowed hard, my mouth going dry, then I realized it was all for show.

A damn good show.

"Lex, Mercy! You're here." Gia ran forward, her husband Samuel at her side. "I was wondering when you guys would show up."

"We're just waiting on our room. I know there's two presentations that we're going to head to before dinner as well."

This conference was a large retreat that brought different construction companies, different contractors, and other types of people in the business together with large estate managers that were looking for groups to work with. It was a huge financial tangle, and my parents still didn't do anything like this in their company. Neither did the Denver Montgomerys. But we were trying something different. If this didn't work, then we wouldn't do it again. I was already off to a rocky start considering I had to fake being togethjer with my neighbor that I kept having sex dreams about.

"Samuel," I said as I cleared my throat. "This is Mercy. My girlfriend."

"It's lovely to meet you," Mercy said as she held out her free hand.

Samuel, a man fifteen years our senior, with silver at his temples and a sharp smile, shook Mercy's hand. "It's nice to meet you as well. Congratulations, Lex. She's a beauty."

I bit my tongue at that, wondering exactly why he was being such a stereotypical misogynist, and nearly said something. But Mercy pinched my side, and I figured she didn't want to rock the boat any more than we were already doing just by existing.

"You should sit with us at dinner. It's open seating, I know that sometimes they make it assigned, but they wanted to do a little free for all this time because it's the holidays."

"Oh that sounds fun," Mercy said, smiling up at me. Though I saw the laughter dancing in her eyes.

"Lexington. It's good to see you," Mr. Arnault said as he came forward. I let go of Mercy, reluctantly, and shook the other man's hand.

"Mr. Arnault. It's good to see you."

"And is this the lovely girlfriend I heard about? Mercy Caddel?"

I raised a brow, wondering when he had heard her last name, and Mercy stiffened for a moment.

"Yes, that's me. It's good to meet you, sir."

"My wife listens to one of the books that you narrate. You do pretty good. So much talent out there, and this Montgomery seems to have picked you up. I'm glad that he was able to piece something together for you after him and Gia's relationship didn't work out."

"Daddy," Gia whispered. "Seriously?"

"I'm kidding. You know I'm kidding."

"Sure, sir," Samuel said through gritted teeth, and I lifted my chin at the other man. He wasn't my adversary. I wasn't in love with Gia anymore. And I knew he probably didn't enjoy hearing about Gia's ex-boyfriend just as much as I didn't enjoy what the hell Mr. Arnault was doing.

"Well, it was pretty hard to pin Lex down, but I was able to woo him with ice cream and spreadsheets."

I rolled my eyes, wondering where she came up with those two things, though usually it would work for me, and smiled.

"She knows me so well."

"Well, I'm headed off to presentation one. Are you guys coming?"

"Of course. And I'm excited to talk to you about the estate."

"All in good time, Montgomery. All in good time."

The three of them left, as Mercy and I stood next to

each other. When her shoulders began to shake, I looked down at her. "What on earth was funny about that?"

"I'm so glad that you did not have to do this alone. Because what the hell was that? Did he do some CIA deep dive into my past or something?" I shuddered. "I surely hope not."

"So creepy. But at least I know what I'm working against." She rubbed her hands together. "We are going to get you that bid."

"I didn't realize you were so competitive."

"Oh, Emily and I were always competitive with each other. Good naturedly of course, but I tried to win usually."

"Oh really."

"Of course. Like this one time in high school when we were trying to figure out who to ask to the sophomore Sadie Hawkins dance, we both were fighting over the same guy, even though we were just friends with him, and the pranks we pulled on each other just to see who would win were hilarious. Neither one of us ended up asking him, because we liked each other so much more than we liked winning, but it was a close one."

I frowned at that, trying to remember back in high school. "Didn't you take Ethan?"

"Yes," she answered with a blush. "And Emily took Graham. But the other guy ended up going to the dance anyway. He was asked by a few people now that I think about it."

Her tone seemed a little off, and I tried to remember exactly who I went with. "Why don't I remember the girl's name?"

"Well, that bodes well of her."

"It was me, wasn't it? You girls were fighting over me." I fluttered my eyelashes, teasing, when Mercy's lips pressed together.

"What?" I asked, freezing in place. The person behind me cursed, and we moved out of the way. "Are you serious?"

"Emily had a crush on you, and I was a dork wanting to one up her. It was nothing."

I searched her face, the awkwardness settling in, trying to figure out if she was telling the truth or not.

But before I could dive any deeper into that, she looked beyond me, and we moved out of the way for another group.

By the time we made it through lunch, and two presentations, that conversation was long gone from my memory. I had not only given out the Montgomery information to seven other companies, I had met another large company that had a beautiful estate south of Colorado Springs that I would love to get my hands on.

I just wasn't sure if that was going to come to fruition.

My phone buzzed as we were heading back to the bar area to mingle, and I let out a loud sigh. "Finally. Our room's ready."

"Oh good, I want to go see and freshen up."

"You look fine," I said, my mind wandering to exactly how we were going to make the Montgomerys shine.

"Thank you so much for that. I feel gorgeous and stunning with that praise. You should stop."

I cringed. "I mean you look beautiful, Mercy, you always look fucking beautiful. I was just saying you don't look like you need to freshen up. But what do I know. I'm a dude."

"Well if I knew you were going to ramble like that, I'd asked how you felt earlier."

I rolled my eyes as we picked up our room keys. The bell service said that they would bring our bags up to us later, but Mercy picked up her smaller bag so she could indeed freshen up. Not that I thought she needed to. But apparently saying that only led to more awkwardness.

"So, how formal is dinner tonight? I know you mentioned it, but now I'm worried I don't have a good enough dress?"

I looked down at what she was wearing, my lips forming a smile. "If I say you look fine right now, will I get kicked?"

"Maybe elbowed."

"Seriously though, it's not formal. I'm wearing this." I gesture down to my pants and button up shirt. "Nothing too crazy. Promise. Plus the storm is getting to be a bit much out there so we'll be snowed in no matter what. Being warm matters more than sequins. Thankfully I left mine at home."

She narrowed her gaze at me, though her lips twitched. "Okay then. I won't pull out the ball gown I brought."

I nearly tripped at our door. "You brought a ball gown?"

"Doesn't every girl?" She rolled her eyes. "We are going on with this farce," she whispered. "So if I'm going and I go full out, why not?"

"You in a ball gown would be a sight to see."

"I would have to own one first."

"You're confusing me, woman."

"It's what I live to do," she teased.

Shaking my head, I opened the door and froze at the sight.

"What's wrong?" she asked as she bumped into me. "Oh. Crap."

"They promised it would be two beds. I did not do this. I swear."

We closed the door behind us, and I swallowed hard. Wondering exactly what the hell we were going to do for the evening.

"Okay. We can do this. I mean, we're adults."

"Mercy. It may be a king bed, I may be an adult, but you did not sign up for this."

We stood at the end of the only bed in the single room, and I met her gaze. "I do realize that I'm more likely to get this contract because the groups think I'm well on my way to being married, and you're helping with that, but this is ridiculous. All of this is so stupid. We should just go. I have enough contacts now, we'll skip the dinner, the event in the morning, and we'll just see what happens." Though the snow was coming down and I was a pretty sure we wouldn't make it down the mountain if we wanted to. At least not at night.

"Pull out your phone and tell your family you're doing that right now."

"They'll understand."

"Yes, they will. But frankly, I don't want the others to win."

"Is this that competitive thought?"

"Gia was totally looking down on you. She might've

pretended that she was doing just fine, but no. I don't appreciate it."

"Okay then. I can sleep on that tiny chair over there."

"The way you just called it tiny, tells me neither one of us believes you're going to do that."

I swallowed hard and moved to get out of her way as at the same time, she shifted so she could head to the bathroom. I nearly knocked her over in the process and put my hands on her hips to steady her.

We were so close then, I could feel the heat of her through my clothes, and I swallowed hard.

"Merce."

"We can totally handle this. We're adults."

"Right. Plus, when we have dinner tonight, and the party later, you're going to be in my arms like this when we're dancing. So it's not like this will be new for us later."

"Right. Totally." Then for some reason I did the one thing I had wanted to do all day, and the one thing I shouldn't. I leaned forward and brushed my lips against hers. She stiffened for an instant, and I nearly pulled back, before she wrapped her arms around my neck and kissed me deeply. I groaned into her, my hands squeezing her hips. She tasted of wine, sweetness, and all Mercy. I needed to stop kissing this woman. We were friends after all, but none of that made sense in this moment. Instead I kept my hold of her, one hand slowly moving up her back and gripping her neck. She moaned into me as I tilted her head, deepening the kiss.

When her arms came down to pull at the bottom of my shirt, I realized that my other hand had been at the edge of her skirt. Pushing all thoughts of worry out of the way, I tugged up her skirt, finally meeting bare flesh.

"Are these stockings?" I growled against her.

"I wanted to feel pretty."

"You're so fucking sexy." And then I kissed her again, nearly ready to push her on the bed, shove up that skirt, and taste the sweetness between those thighs.

A knock sounded on the door.

I cursed, both of us freezing in our actions. "It's our bags," I whispered against her lips.

"I know."

We pulled away, staring at each other. Her lips were swollen, her eyes dark. And all I wanted to do was ignore the bell service and take her.

But this was just a fake relationship. And fake feelings could get in the way.

Though I adjusted myself, watching the way that her eyes widened at the act, and went to open the door.

Carrie Ann Ryan

And hopefully by the morning, I would be able to forget what had happened.

Even though I knew I was clearly lying to myself.

Chapter Eight

Lexington

"So you see, when I brought my daughter into the business, we truly catapulted ourselves into the next generation. Without family, without knowing where you came from, how can you ever know where you want to go?"

I nodded along as the man who held the future of a major part of our business, droned on and on about family without his family in the room. Gia and Samuel had gone off to dance on the patio area, with fires and fairy lights warming and lighting up the place. Snow drifted from the sky, not quite accumulating over time. Maybe overnight we'd get an inch that would be melted by mid-afternoon. Just enough time to get through an early morning conference and head home.

And as I stood there, drink in hand, I tried my best not to look at the woman beside me.

And yet, I couldn't help but do so.

"He said a whole lot and yet nothing at the same time," Mercy whispered beside me. I leaned down so I could hear better, since she was over a foot shorter than me, even in high heels. Doing so meant I could feel the heat of her more, and I swallowed hard, reminding myself that I was an adult. And I could handle being close to mercy. What the hell was wrong with me? I had spent most of my life being the brother who smiled and laughed but the one you could count on. I had even been the one to push many of my cousins into finding their perfect match and taking a leap when it came to romance.

And all I had wanted was that of my own. A fraction of what could be.

All I wanted for so long was to settle down like my family had. And then Carly had left, and then, of course, Gia.

Well, it wasn't as if I was against relationships.

I just knew if I gave in, it would be far more complicated.

"He's not wrong about family, but our company doesn't solely base who we work with on the company's relationship status."

"Exactly. However, if this is going to be good for the Montgomerys, I'm here. When will we know about the bid?"

As Gia's father looked over, I reached out and finally let myself touch her. I slid my fingers over her wrist, and she stiffened for a moment. When her mouth parted as it had after I had kissed her, I swallowed hard and prayed that my dick wouldn't betray me right then.

No matter what though, using Gia's father as an excuse to touch Mercy was probably all kinds of wrong.

"Montgomery. Enjoying yourself?"

I slid my arm around Mercy's waist and smiled. Since my other hand carried my drink, I didn't have to bother reaching out to shake his. For some reason, I knew if I did, it would be giving in to something. That man was all about his power games, hence why I had a damn fake girlfriend at my side.

"I've always loved hearing about the Montgomery family. You guys have been strong in your beliefs, and your connections. You truly know your values."

I held back a snarl at that, because I had a feeling his values wouldn't be the same as ours. After all, I had more than one set of aunts and uncles in poly relationships, and those weren't exactly the values that some people liked working with. But our family knew how to say fuck you to the rest. And we weren't hurting for it.

I just didn't know exactly where this man stood. And that meant there was more research to go with. Because Gia hadn't been a bigot. In fact, Gia was bisexual and had been dating a woman before me. And I knew her family had welcomed it. So maybe I was just thinking too hard when he said family values.

"Well, my family likes owning businesses. We just tend to have a wide array of them."

"I hear that. Of course, we tend to do the same. Just, more real estate."

My family did real estate too, but not quite what this man was saying. We weren't worth the multi-millions that he was. However, he took good care of his companies and his people.

I didn't know why he was suddenly rubbing me the wrong way.

"Anyway, I'm really excited about what you have planned for the estate. I've looked over your bid, I think we need to talk a little bit more on it, but you have great ideas. And frankly, my wife who couldn't make it here tonight because of a head cold, is at home listening to your girlfriend's voice, and loves the books. So that helps too." He winked as he said it before walking away to talk to someone else.

My hand squeezed Mercy's hip, and I let out a deep breath.

"Did that just happen?"

I thought I heard a soft laugh escaping her mouth, but I could be wrong. "I think it's time to call it a night. Before he realizes that my day job consists of me sitting in sweats and talking to Mr. Darcy."

My lips twitched, but I nodded, then drained my drink before setting it down on one of the empties trays. We made our way upstairs, and my mind went in a million different directions.

I pulled her to the side of the room where no one could overhear. "Mercy, we nearly have the project. I can feel it. This account could catapult us into where we wanted to be as a company. Every single one of my core members wanted to work on some part of that estate. And I have the numbers of multiple other projects that could cement us into our future. Because while we are in the black, we aren't as solid as the rest of the companies in our family. We are younger, newer, and still figuring things out. But this would be a huge milestone."

I hadn't meant to spill all of that but it had been going on repeat in my mind for days. Months if I were being honest. Because the team needed this.

She gave me an odd look as she studied my face. "You put so much pressure on yourself, Lexington."

"Merce..."

Someone called my name, bringing us out of the moment, and we went back to the reason we were at the JW to begin with. The reason we were here. Together. Afterward, we made our way into the room, my mind going far too quickly. My mind focused solely on the bid, when I realized that we were now alone in the room once again. The same room where we had just kissed with so much heat that I had nearly ripped her clothes off, only a few hours before.

A second bed hadn't magically grown out of nowhere.

I turned to look at her then, at her wide eyes. She had taken off her jacket, her dress riding up slightly. When she sat down at the edge of the bed, I swallowed hard and wished for that drink right now.

She went to take off her boots, and the zipper stuck. Without another word, I moved forward and knelt in front of her. When she froze, I swallowed hard, slid my hand over hers, and gently worked the zipper. It came down slowly, and I met her gaze, wondering what the hell I was doing.

"We've been drinking, Lex," she whispered. "And..."

"I know. I know." But I leaned forward and kissed her knee. She shuddered and slid her hands through my hair. I closed my eyes and rested my forehead against the side of her thigh.

"I should sleep in that chair."

"No. We can make a wall of pillows. We already had to pretend I was dating you all night, confusing things."

"You're right." I looked up at her then, nodding tightly. "We'll do that one last presentation tomorrow, with that round-robin seating, and then head home."

"Exactly. And we'll, I don't know, deal with it later."

I didn't know what it was, and frankly, I didn't think she did either. But I patted her knee gently, before standing up and going to my small suitcase.

With my back to her, I fisted my hands and willed myself to breathe.

It was going to be a long night. And both of us knew it.

I grabbed my things and headed to the bathroom to change. I wasn't sure how I was going to make it through the night, but I was going to have to. I turned on the shower, slightly colder than I normally would have, stripped off all of my clothes, and jumped underneath the spray. Hopefully, this would work.

Because dear God, I didn't know when it had happened, or how it had happened, but I wanted Mercy Caddel. And I had a feeling I had wanted her from the first time I saw her standing outside her home, a snake slithering towards her.

This was going to be a problem.

I refused to touch myself, to get off while she was in the next room. I was already rude enough, forcing her to pretend to be my girlfriend. So I showered quickly, getting the sweat off at least, and pulled on my long pajama pants and T-shirt. I normally slept naked, but it wasn't as if the whole one room thing had been a surprise. Only the one bed.

When I came back out, she stood there, still wearing her dress, but no tights or boots. She held her pajamas in hand and smiled softly before scooting by me. I got into bed, set my phone on my charger, and wondered how the hell I was going to sleep tonight. So I slid down under the covers, turned off my light, and shifted so my back was to the bathroom door. So when she came out, I didn't say a thing and pretended I was asleep. The bed shifted as she moved in beside me, and I let out a breath as she turned off her light.

But neither of us set up that pillow wall.

And I had a feeling that neither of us slept.

"So how did it go? Tell us everything." Jamie bounced from foot to foot, planner in one hand, coffee in another.

I narrowed my gaze at the coffee in her hand. "What cup are you on?"

"Tsk, tsk, tsk. That's not important now."

"I'll take that," Brooklyn said with a laugh as she took Jamie's coffee from her.

"I'm an adult. I can handle my own coffee intake." Jamie frowned as we all stared at her. "Fine. I'll go drink water."

"I don't know why you're saying it like that. As if you don't have your full water bottle at your desk that you've already refilled once today."

"How many fluids are you getting a day?" Dash asked as he walked into the main conference room of our building, Reece right behind him.

"I don't think that's any of your business." Jamie lifted her nose.

Brooklyn snorted. "Seriously though, how did it go?" Her phone chimed for a text, and she held up one finger. "Hold on. It's Duke."

"Oh yes, let's stop our work conversation to talk about your boyfriend," Dash drawled.

"We have four minutes until the meeting starts, and I promised I would text back right away."

"That doesn't sound controlling or anything," Reece bit out as he headed over to the coffee machine. He pressed a few buttons, and a latte started up. I raised a brow as the man added caramel to it but sighed as I realized he was making a second cup. This one just black coffee.

Without another word, he handed the caramel latte to Brooklyn, who just beamed at him.

"Thank you. Though this does not count as the coffee you owe me."

"You didn't say I had to pay for it." Reece shrugged and met my gaze.

"I lost a bet on a football game, and here we are."

"Okay then. Seriously though, I want to know about the controlling part," I put in, worried.

Brooklyn just smiled widely. "It's not what you think. Promise. He just got his new promotion, and I said I would text back as soon as he told me because I wanted to celebrate with him. But I have to sadly go to work and be an adult. But Duke got his promotion."

Jamie cheered for her as the rest of us made rumblings of happiness.

I didn't know Duke, but Brooklyn seemed happy with him. And from the way that Nash already had his phone out, I had a feeling that one of the many group chats would be doing their own Montgomery search on the man.

You didn't get to date into the Montgomery family without a full background check.

We had principles.

"So how did it go?"

"Yes, how did the fake girlfriend thing go?" Reece asked, the smile in his eyes making me want to punch him.

"Everybody bought it. And Mercy did great. It turns out that Mr. Arnault's wife likes Mercy's work, and so it came full circle."

"Did we get it then?" Jamie asked, clapping her now empty hands together.

"I don't know. I think we pretty much have it settled, but not fully. I was too late last night after we got home going through all of my notes, and I emailed you guys everything that I know so far. There are a few other projects that we could be good for, as well as some I don't think work for us, but I want you guys to go over it too because I'm not actually the boss."

"You say that and yet I don't believe you believe it," Dash said with a flutter of his eyelashes.

"Honestly, I'm with him on this," Reece added as he gestured towards Dash. "Which doesn't happen often."

"You are boss-like," Brooklyn agreed.

"But I want to know if he's bossy when it comes to Mercy," Jamie added, and I rolled my eyes at her as the others whistled.

"Mercy's my friend, my neighbor, and if the Arnaults ask, my girlfriend."

"What are you going to do when they realize you're not together?" Reece asked, worry in his tone.

My mouth went dry. Were we together? I didn't fucking know. Because what we'd done in that hotel room wasn't something two people who didn't want each other would do. I wasn't about to explain that in this office, however—even if Jamie gave me a knowing look. "It won't be a problem. By then, maybe one of you guys will be married and will take the pressure off me." I tried to sound as if I knew what the hell I was doing, but everyone in that room knew the whole gamble had been idiocy at its best.

An awkward silence settled over the group, and I had no idea what the hell to say.

"We'll go over everything that you learned at the event," Brooklyn said. "And we'll table everything for Q1 and Q2 when we're ready."

"Yes, because in addition to this, I guess we do have to celebrate the holidays," I said dryly.

"Are you guys hosting a New Year's party?" Reece asked before he took a sip of his coffee.

I looked down at my now cold cup of coffee and shrugged. "I don't know. Are we?"

"I don't think there's a set one. Everyone's just doing their own thing. The Christmas party was a lot," Jamie answered.

I nodded. "But Reece, if you need someone to celebrate with, you're welcome to join us. We're just going out for part of the night but planning on celebrating midnight at home."

"We'll see," Reece answered.

I rolled my eyes. "I love that *we'll see*. You have it down like my mom did."

"A mom's *we'll see* is the best out there. But thankfully I mean we'll see."

"What are your holiday plans?" I asked as we settled into our seats.

"Nothing much. Same old, same old. Not all of us have a stadium full of cousins."

"Well, you're welcome to come and hang out with us." Brooklyn beamed. "Mom and Dad and the twins always go all out. Not to mention Duke will be there too."

"For Christmas morning?" I asked, surprised. I hadn't heard when he'd met the family, but things seemed to be progressing.

Brooklyn looked like she lived on Cloud Nine as she

bounced in her chair. "Yes! Mom and Dad already love him."

"You don't need to take care of Little Orphan Reece," he said.

Brooklyn rolled her eyes, not taking the man's usual grouchiness to heart. I didn't know if Reece was an orphan, or if he had any siblings, or any family. I knew he was single, just because the man had mentioned it recently, and had no kids from what I knew. But Reece was a co-worker, so it wasn't as if I was going to pry completely.

"Do you know what Mercy's doing for Christmas?"

I shrugged, though I'd already had the idea on my mind. Trying not to think about Mercy at work was starting to become a full-time job. One I was clearly failing. "I don't know. We didn't talk about that."

"So what *did* you two talk about?" Dash asked.

I flipped him off, ignoring his laugh. "Enough. Let's get to work."

"I have questions," Jamie teased.

I ignored the group calling after me as I headed back to my office. I answered phone calls, went through paperwork, and worked on a few sketches. But the phone never rang with the one I wanted. Not a single call from the Arnaults. I knew it was the holidays, and I probably wouldn't hear anything until after the first, but still, I wanted to know if all of that lying, and stress, got us our dream bid.

I made my way home, before the others did, to finish working on sketches, and I knew it was not that big of a deal. It was rare that we all worked underneath the same roof anyway in this line of business. Music blaring, I tried figure out exactly what the hell I was going to do.

Because all day, while trying to think about the stress of the project, and the actual projects we had on hand, I couldn't help but think about that kiss.

And Mercy.

Damn it.

I pulled into my driveway, only to see the object of my traitorous thoughts standing in her front yard, frowning at her mail. I got out of the truck, and I knew if I went inside and ignored her, I'd be a dick, and frankly, I didn't want to ignore her.

I moved around the truck and came to her side of the yard.

"Hey there."

Mercy looked up, her frown disappearing. "Hey. Why do they send so many bills that I have on e-delivery and automatic payment? It scares me that it's like they're going to shut off my heat or something."

"I think they enjoy the stress, even if they can't see it."

"They're probably watching us right now," she teased.

I stood too close to her, and we both knew it, but instead of moving back, I brushed her hair back from her face and then cupped her cheek.

"Hey," I repeated.

She blinked up at me, mouth parting. "Hey."

And when I leaned down and captured her lips with my own, she didn't push me away. Instead she put her hand on my chest, and just let it rest there as I explored her mouth, and her taste.

It wasn't until I realized that probably every single neighbor in the cul-de-sac was watching me make out with my neighbor, that I pulled away.

"Hey."

"I think we've got that down." She frowned at me. "What was that?"

"I have no fucking clue. But I want to do it again."

"So do I. And I think that should scare me."

"Does it?"

"Not as much as it should."

A wide smile spread over my face before I leaned down and kissed her again.

Chapter Nine

Mercy

How did one go through life wondering exactly what we come to next? Of course, I had no idea what the heck I was doing. In one moment, I was trying to understand exactly how I was going to pull off a fake relationship with someone, the next, I'm running my hands up and down Lexington's back as if we had been doing that for our entire lives.

Now it was nearly Christmas day, and I was trying to get ready for the holiday season. The holidays had crept up on me when I hadn't been looking. I'd been so focused on my projects, getting my house together, and whatever the hell was happening next door, I hadn't let myself think about what the holidays would mean to me

—let alone what I'd be doing on my own. Even though I had gone to a Christmas party, it still hadn't clicked until just now.

Because I would be spending Christmas day alone. Not for the first time, not technically. Because Emily had died before Christmas, but I had been in such a haze, a zombie, walking through life, that it hadn't truly hit me that I would be alone.

We'd had our own traditions. We would open up all of our gifts but one on Christmas Eve because that's what my mother had done as a child. My father had been aghast at the thought but had eagerly joined in at the look of pure bliss on my mother's face for their first Christmas Eve. So when Emily and I had been born, they had added to the tradition.

Eggnog and cookies next to the fireplace. Stockings over the couch so they didn't catch fire like that one time we had actually put them on the fireplace mantle.

We would make nachos and guacamole and random food for Christmas Eve, anything that was super easy to make so we would have more time as a family of four. And then, on Christmas morning, we'd have one large gift each. But it wasn't the sole purpose of the day.

No, we would have a large breakfast, filled with French toast, omelets, fruit, homemade whipped cream. Anything you could imagine for breakfast. Going on walks, covered under blankets, and watching movies by the fire as the Christmas lights on the tree sparkled.

Maybe it wasn't the fantastical Christmas that some people had, but it was our tradition.

And then Mom and Dad had died, and Emily and I had tried our best to keep up with it. We had done the exact same things we had always done, just the two of us.

When Justin and I had been together, we had followed both sets of traditions, always making sure Emily was part of it. She had a serious boyfriend at the beginning of my relationship with Justin but had been single by the time I had gotten engaged. But no matter what, my twin and I had been together.

The first Christmas after the wedding we had been in a hospital room, the sounds of the machines beeping through my mind. Emily had contracted pneumonia, and had been on bedrest, hooked up to IVs and dozens of wires. But she had been alert and smiling as we opened up a single gift. Notebooks for each other. We hadn't even talked to one another about it, but we had bought nearly identical notebooks.

Maybe it was the idea of the twin bond. Perhaps we were following Hamilton's very existence and writing like we were running out of time.

The doorbell rang before I could let myself wallow

too far into my thoughts, and I walked past Mr. Darcy so I could answer.

Brooklyn and Mrs. Montgomery stood there, bright smiles on their faces, and I couldn't help but feel the pang of what I'd lost. I wasn't this person. The one who let those angry memories wrap around me so I couldn't breathe. And yet in that moment, I couldn't do anything but stand there and hope to hell I could keep a straight face.

To hope to hell I wouldn't crumble in a heap at their feet.

Eliza Montgomery smiled at me again, before leaning forward, and hugged me tightly. Without thinking twice, I wrapped my arms around her and hugged her with every ounce of my soul. In that moment, I wasn't Mercy. The orphan. The woman with no family.

I was held by a mom who loved her children and all those connected to her boys. Tears filled my eyes, and I had no idea why. It wasn't as if she'd even spoken to me. But with that one hug, everything had changed, and I couldn't breathe.

I took a step back and realized I was crying. Lexington's mother wiped away my tears and smiled.

"Sometimes I just need a good hug too."

"You're just going to have to deal with a hug from

me as well," Brooklyn put in as she wrapped her arms around me. I hugged her back, but this time we both laughed, the tears happy ones.

"I'm sorry about that. I don't know where that came from."

Eliza shook her head. "The holidays are always stressful, and they bring up memories and emotions that you might not think about on a daily basis. However, we are always here if you want to talk."

I shook my head. "I'm fine. I was just going through the traditions I had with my parents and sister and realized I'm not sure if I want to do them this year. Christmas is in a little over a week, and I don't even have a tree up." It was more that the concept was just occurring to me now. There had been Christmas lights and decorations all over the JW the entire time we had been there. But it had just clicked that maybe my house needed a little more cheer.

"We might be able to help with that," Eliza said with a wink.

I blinked. "What do you mean?"

Mr. Darcy wound his way through my legs, and butted up against Brooklyn. The other woman picked up my cat as if she had been doing it forever and nuzzled my only family member. "I think I'm in love."

Eliza slid a finger down Mr. Darcy's nose, a smile on

both women's faces. "I told you that you should get a pet. Though maybe a dog would be better for you so you can bring him to your project sites."

I smiled at the mother-daughter pair. "Would a puppy dig in your flowerbeds?"

Brooklyn narrowed her gaze. "Oh, there would be training. I love pets. We had so many growing up, and my parents still have a few. It's just so hard to say goodbye." She looked at me and winced. "I'm sorry. That was insensitive of me."

I shook my head. "No. It's good to talk about loss. Whenever I bury those feelings deep, they come out in random crying jags as people come to my door. I haven't even let you inside yet." Embarrassed, I took a step back, and the other two women walked inside.

"Don't worry about it. We were just happy to see you. In fact, we are about to kidnap you." Eliza smiled.

I blinked. "What? Where are you taking me?"

"Shopping of course!" Brooklyn said as she held Mr. Darcy as a baby, rocking him back-and-forth. The cat purred so loudly I could hear it from a few feet away.

"Shopping?"

Lex's mother nodded. "We still have a few gifts to buy for those in our immediate family. We do a secret Santa for everybody else. That way we're not giving hundreds of gifts out every year. The list gets long."

Eliza reached forward to pet Mr. Darcy's stomach, and while I almost reached out to stop her, the cat just nuzzled into her, and I glared at the traitor.

"First, that cat never lets me touch his stomach."

"He loves me already," Eliza teased. "What's the second?"

"Second. The secret Santa idea is utterly fantastic. I don't have gifts for anyone." My eyes widened. "I didn't even think about it."

"Well, we have time. And we're taking you anyway." Eliza held my hand and squeezed. "I'm sorry, but you're about to get adopted into the Montgomerys. And we're going to make sure you get the holiday you want. It might be different than what we do as a vivacious family, but I'm not going to let you hide in your home. I'm sorry. I'm not wired that way."

"You don't really have to do this," I whispered, an odd warmth spreading through me. This family...I just couldn't keep up. Whatever Lex and I had didn't even have a label and they were acting as if I were already part of them. Then again, that kiss...*those* kisses. There was nothing fake about those. And in the twenty-four hours since that kiss, we hadn't spoken about it. Work had been in the way, but then again, I knew we both needed time to think.

Only I hadn't let myself think about him at all.

"We don't. But Lexington is not about to let you be alone on the holidays either," Brooklyn said with a sly smile on her face.

My cheeks heated even as I glared at the woman next to me. "I'm not sure that's his business."

The other woman just beamed. "Oh we're going to be best friends. Just you watch. And you might not think you're his business, but since you're his fake, I'm sorry, I mean *real* girlfriend, you're sort of out of luck here." Brooklyn continued before I could say anything. "Now go get ready, and I'll stay here with this lovely man."

"Duke has someone to watch out for it seems," Eliza said with a chuckle.

I snorted but knew there would be no stopping them. I knew the Montgomerys. Had known them my entire life. It didn't matter that I'd been away for two years. They weren't letting me go now.

Even if I didn't want to think about what that would mean with my fake-but maybe not so fake-boyfriend slash neighbor.

I knew if I kicked these women out and said I wanted to be alone, they would leave. Of course, they would come back as quickly as possible, perhaps sending other Montgomerys or reinforcements to try to either get me out or remind me that I'm not alone.

Sometimes I wasn't sure how I had gotten so lucky with this group of people. I didn't know why I was able to do certain things. To be here. But I had come back to Colorado for a reason. Maybe I had no blood family, but the Montgomerys were damn good at becoming a found family.

I already had on cute leggings, so I switched from my tunic to my long sweater, and stuffed my feet into knee boots, and called it a win. It was chilly out, but not heavy coat chilly. Of course if I was from another state, I would probably be wrapped up in a parka.

That thought made me smile, and I ran back downstairs to see both women taking turns cuddling with Mr. Darcy.

"That's a very spoiled cat," I said with a snort.

"He's just misunderstood," Brooklyn teased. "But now I really do want a puppy."

We said our goodbyes to Mr. Darcy before we all clambered into Brooklyn's SUV.

"I'm so glad that you were able to get a new car this year, Brooklyn," Eliza put in from the back seat. She had forced me into the front seat, and one didn't tell Eliza Wilder-Montgomery no.

"Me too. It worked out that the work truck should just be for work. It's covered in dirt and other raw materials constantly, and sometimes I want to be able to go out to dinner and not end up with mud stains on my pants."

"That wouldn't be awkward at all," I teased and Brooklyn shuddered. "I can't believe that you are a landscape architect. I can't even keep a plant alive."

"Your gardens look really great for winter. But if you ever want any help, just let me know."

"You work more hours than I do from what I hear."

"Maybe. But I like helping friends. And that's what we are. Friends."

"So did you always want to be a landscape architect?"

"I always loved playing in dirt, so yes. I love creating and figuring out what to do next to make someone's dream home or business a true dream. I could ask you the same about being a voice actor."

Eliza and I laughed, but I let out a breath. "I was always great at drama and being on stage as a kid. I enjoyed math and science, but history and English were where it was at for me. And then moving into the arts was where everything clicked. But I realized that I liked making voices and using my voice for good over wanting to act completely. If that makes sense."

"So community theater isn't for you?" Eliza asked.

I shook my head. "No. I thought about it when I was

in college, but we had to work long hours in order to afford college, so it really wasn't my thing."

As we pulled into the parking lot, Brooklyn squeezed my hand. "I'm still sorry about Emily."

I swallowed the lump in my throat as we piled out of the SUV. "Thank you. Every day is terrible without her, but the holidays may get worse."

"I understand." Eliza moved forward and gripped my hands. "Loss changes a person." Something crossed her eyes, but I didn't ask. Everybody had their own secrets, their darkness. Their loss.

"So back to you, were you always good at growing things?"

"Actually yes. My dad is an architect for the Montgomerys, since you know he is one," Brooklyn said with a laugh. "And my aunt Megan does what I do. So I would follow her around, and things just clicked for me."

"And your mom owns a bookstore, right? Downtown?"

"Yes. Beneath the Cover. It's still going strong, and I loved hanging out there as a kid. Hell, I still love hanging out there now." She winced. "Sorry, Aunt Eliza. Didn't mean to curse in front of you."

Eliza did her best to look offended, but the laughter in her eyes spilled the truth. "I mean how dare you. An actual curse word in front of me. I've never heard it before."

We each laughed as we walked through the outdoor mall, stopping for lunch halfway through, and shopping to our heart's content. There were carolers, a small string quartet, and decorations everywhere that just breathed life into the holidays. And it wasn't just Christmas of course. Hanukkah started the day after Christmas, and there were plenty of other holidays that happened within this three-week period. So watching everybody, even a little stressed as they walked around, was entertaining.

"So did Lexington always want to become an architect?" I asked Eliza and could have rightly bit off my tongue.

The other woman's gaze brightened, even as her cheeks pinked with excitement. "He was always good at drawing. As an art teacher myself and somebody who takes time to paint every once in a while, it always made me smile when he would draw alongside me."

"Takes time to paint my ass," Brooklyn said, pausing. "That did not sound right at all."

"Not even a little," I said, holding back the loud laughter that would probably bring attention to us.

"Seriously though, you are an award-winning artist

who just happens to teach at the local community college when you can. You are brilliant, Aunt Eliza."

"Oh stop. I'm good at what I do, and I'm grateful for it, but it wasn't the only thing in my life. Raising the boys and making sure that their father didn't end up falling off a roof or something as the construction lead was a little too much for me."

"So I guess watching his family thrive in their respective jobs led him down that path."

"I think so. Brooklyn's father, of course, is an architect, same as my sister-in-law Annabelle. We have a few more in the family, or at least ones that went along a parallel path. And it just worked out that they were able to find their way. And I'm so grateful for it."

"And he's great with working with others, meaning we get more projects and bids and we can grow over time. But not so quickly that we fall behind." Brooklyn looked at her phone and winced. "We should probably be getting back soon. I still have a few invoices to finish up so I can call it a week and actually enjoy the holidays."

"And I suppose it has nothing to do with you wanting to meet Duke?" I teased.

"I have no idea what you're talking about," she said primly, her cheeks pink. "But, we should probably get home, because I know Lexington will be home soon."

She sing-songed the latter part, and I flipped her off. Of course Eliza caught me, but she just burst out laughing.

We sang along to pop rock and oldies on our way home, and for the first time in forever it felt as if I was finding my place. Finding friends.

When we pulled up to my home, I frowned as Lexington's truck was already in my driveway.

"Did he forget which house he lived in?" I asked, even as my stomach tightened.

He got out of the truck, and I did my best not to watch how his jeans hugged his thick thighs as he did so. After all, his mother was less than a foot away from me. I needed to control my hormones. Maybe.

"No, he's right where he needs to be," Eliza said as we scrambled out of the car.

"Good timing," Lex said with a grin. "I have one of your presents right here."

I stumbled, my throat tight. "A present?"

Of course I had gotten Lex a present, not that I had told the others who it was for. No, I had just been doing it because he was a great neighbor. And I really liked his kisses.

Lex smiled, and awkwardness settled in. Was I supposed to go to him, touch him, hold him, run away? I didn't know. But then Lex Montgomery did what he did best and took control of things. He rubbed his knuckle against my cheek and leaned forward, brushing his lips against mine. "Have fun shopping?"

I blinked at him, wondering if he realized that he had just kissed me in front of his mother. But nobody said a damn thing, instead they opened the back of Brooklyn's SUV and proceeded to pull out my bags.

"What are you doing here?" I asked, my voice soft.

"I remember when you were growing up that you always had two trees in the house, if not more. And well, the front bay window seems a little empty right now." That's when I realized the back of his truck wasn't completely empty. A medium-sized fir tree lay there, and my throat tightened.

"Lex," I breathed.

"It's not the best tree in the world, it's a little straggly since we're so close to the holidays, but we need to let the tree live to its full potential."

"I don't know what to say." Tears filled my eyes, and I blushed, ducking my head.

Lex cursed under his breath before he wrapped his arms around me.

"Did I mess up? I can put the tree in my house. I don't mind having two."

"No. You did good. I was just focusing on so many things that I was trying to let the holidays pass me by. But it seems your family's not letting me."

"We Montgomerys are a little stubborn like that. So I did okay?"

I looked up at him then, and my eyes filled. "You did great. I love it."

"Good," he said, letting out a relieved breath. "Well let's get this inside, and I have a few things for you to decorate it with, I wasn't sure what you wanted to do with it."

This time the uneasiness in his tone outweighed the happiness, and I went to my tiptoes and kissed his cheek.

"I have a few things, but let's look at what you have. Starting new traditions is good."

"Yeah, it is."

And I took a step back before I did something silly like kiss him again in front of his family.

"Okay, how can I help?"

"We've got this," Dash said, and I hadn't even realized the other man was there. He just winked at me, playful as always, and the two of them wrestled the tree into my house. Eliza went down on her knees, crawling underneath it to make sure it was settled, despite all of our protests.

"Dad is going to kill me if he sees you there, taking care of things with me not helping."

"I'm an adult, I can handle it," Eliza said.

"Why the hell are you letting your mother do the hard work?" Beckett Montgomery said, and I jumped.

"Sorry about that," Beckett said as he grinned. "The door was ajar, and nobody heard me knock."

"Oh, it's okay. Come on in, Mr. Montgomery."

"Call me Beckett." He gave me a tight hug and kissed the top of my head.

"It's good to see you home, Mercy."

I met Lex's gaze, and he just winked at me. Then I rolled my eyes and got to work on decorating.

When Silas joined in, the four Montgomerys of their tiny branch laughed together, as if them standing in my home trying to make my house full of joy was a usual thing. Brooklyn had left soon after dropping us off, because she did have work to do and I didn't feel out of place. Even in my own home. Silas carried Mr. Darcy around, surprising me, and I just looked at the family of four and how tight knit they were.

No, the boys didn't look like their parents since they had been adopted when they had been babies, but they still had the same Montgomery mannerisms, and I knew that they had always felt like Montgomerys by blood.

Just like this family was trying to make sure that I wasn't alone for the holidays.

My heart clutched, and when I tried to lean back into the wall, I realized it wasn't a wall, instead it was

Lex himself. I sighed, letting myself relax against him as he squeezed my hip.

"You like the holidays yet?" he whispered.

"A new kind of holiday. But yes."

So I settled in and watched how his family drew me to them.

Even as I had no idea what to do with the man currently holding me close.

Chapter Ten

Mercy

The next day, after working for four hours when I probably should have been cleaning my house or trying to relax, I stood in my bedroom, hands on hips, partially dressed, wondering what the hell I was going to wear later. Brooklyn would be over any moment to pick me up, and somehow I would have to look presentable.

And by any moment, I meant an hour away from now, but it didn't give me a lot of time to get ready. My hair was already done, my makeup partially done, I just needed to figure out what lipstick to wear, and I would settle on my jewelry once I had my outfit.

Seriously though, I had no idea what to do for a girls' night out.

It's not like I was used to girls' nights out. I hadn't

done them since Emily had been alive. I put my hand on my stomach, letting out a breath.

"Em, babe, you were so much better at this," I whispered. And it was true. My sister was great with people. She had been a little quieter than me, but always fit in everywhere she went. She made people happy. I was usually the more outgoing one, or at least I had been before, well, everything had changed. So, with the two of us together, we always found the perfect middle. Only now it was me alone. Trying to find a way to settle down and be normal. Not that anything felt normal these days.

My doorbell rang in that moment, and I froze. I was still wearing sweats and a tank top, but no bra, and looked like a mess. However, when I checked my phone, it wasn't Brooklyn.

I put my hand on my stomach once more and let out a breath.

"You can do this," I whispered.

I ran downstairs, nearly tripping to my death as Mr. Darcy darted forward to win the race I wasn't aware we were in, and tried to calm down as I opened the front door. Lex stood there, hands in his jeans pockets as he rocked back on his heels.

"Hi," I said.

"Hi." He shook his head. "If we start down that hi

and hey path again, I'm never going to be able to actually say a proper hello."

The idea that he was just as nervous as I was should have soothed my nerves. Not so much. "I never used to get flustered around you, Montgomery. It's worrying."

"Talk to me about it. I'm usually good with words."

"I'm going out with a few of your cousins tonight."

Lex winced.

A ball formed in my belly, and I frowned. "Did you not want me going out with your cousins tonight? Because I know things are weird and we haven't talked about anything, but I'm trying. Trying to live again. So if you think that you can bar me from hanging out with your family because things will get too complicated, well no. I'm just not going to do that." Suddenly his finger was over my lips, a single brow raised.

"Shush." He lowered his hand, a smirk on his face that made him look far too handsome for his own good.

"Did you just shush me?"

"Damn straight I did. Woman. The only reason I even reacted at all was that I was annoyed that Brooklyn got to you first."

I blinked, confused. "What?"

In answer, he rolled his eyes so hard I was afraid he was going to hurt himself before he reached out, gripped the back of my neck, and crushed his mouth to mine.

Surprised, I stood there silent and awkward for a moment, before I finally gave in and kissed him back. Damn it, Lex was too good at kissing. Why hadn't I known this when we were younger? I mean, this talent took effort. When had he learned it? And why did I suddenly feel as if I should have known this long ago?

When he pulled back, both of us were breathing slightly heavier, and he looked like a cat who had caught the canary.

He slid a piece of my hair behind my ear. "I am annoyed that she got to you first because I wanted to take you out tonight. But I was too slow apparently. She got you all day yesterday as did my mom, and apparently, I'm now fighting with my cousins for your time. I don't appreciate that."

Warming, I played with the button on his shirt. A man in a button down and jeans just did something to me. Okay that was a lie. It was Lex. Always. And that was something I would have to think on more later. "Oh. Well, she asked first. And you didn't ask at all."

He winced. "The only reason I didn't ask you to dinner or to see you or anything was that Brooklyn had already said your time was claimed. And I know when a man loses. Mostly because she's a Montgomery woman, and they're scary."

I snorted as I walked inside, him following me. Mr.

Darcy sniffed at Lex for a moment, before he pranced away and over to the catio. I had left the screen door open so he could have his way. It was mostly guilt though, because I would be leaving soon, and he'd be trapped inside all alone. That mom guilt was a real thing.

"Can we have a talk before she gets here?" I blurted. Well crap. I hadn't meant to say that.

Lex tilted his head, studying my face. "Do we need to? I like kissing you. I like spending time with you. Let's just figure things out."

This time I snorted. "We both know that I'm not good at going with the flow and figuring things out."

"Neither am I, that's why we're going to be good at it together."

This man. "I don't think that's how it works. But you're right...maybe we don't have to make things too complicated and we can just...be."

"That sounds about right. Though I'm not good at going with the flow so you might have to keep me in line." He kissed me again and my knees nearly went weak. "Have fun tonight. And then I'm taking you out tomorrow."

"Oh?" Bossy man. Why the hell did I like it?

"Yes. Oh. On a real date. Not a fake girlfriend date."

"You're not even going to ask you're just telling me?"

But even as I said it, my stomach tensed. Because I really wanted to go out with him. Call me a glutton for punishment, but I liked this side of Lex.

"Also, while we're here, is that what you're wearing? Because it's sexy as hell."

I looked down and realized that my white tank top was perfectly see-through, and he could see every inch of my hard nipples. I put my hands over my chest and scowled.

"Lexington Montgomery."

"What? I'm just saying. I really like that shirt."

"I am just trying to figure out what to wear."

"I can go upstairs and help you."

I gasped. "You haven't even taken me on a real date, and you want to go upstairs and strip me naked?" I paused. "Okay, do not answer that."

"I'm just saying, you would really like the answer. Trust me."

I shoved at his shoulder but didn't go upstairs. Because for some reason I knew that if I went upstairs with him, clothes would be coming off, and I would be very late hanging out with the girls.

"Have you heard anything about the project status?"

Storms clouded his eyes, and he shook his head. "Only rumors that he's wooing other companies too."

"Bastard. I thought you had it."

"We will. Damn it. I want that estate. No matter who owns it. It'll be great for the company, and frankly, I want to get my hands on those plans and just dive deep."

"Well, your fake serious girlfriend is ready to help. Even though that layer of complication is going to be interesting."

"So we'll have two camps. My fake serious girlfriend that goes with me to schmooze my ex-girlfriend's father, and then my childhood friend turned woman that I really want to kiss again and take out. What do you think?"

"I think it's so simple that it doesn't even need labels. And it's totally not going to blow up in our faces."

"I believe in you." He leaned forward and brushed his lips against mine. "Go get ready. And I think you should wear that maroon dress thing you have with the black boots."

I shook my head. "How do you remember that?"

"You looked really hot in it. We were at a party, remember? And Jusitn couldn't come, so I had to be your date. Oh look, a pretend date. I guess it's not our first time."

My mind whirled, memories hitting so quickly it was if I'd lived countless lives within a single breath. "I remember that. And it was a really good time. And I do happen to have that dress still."

"Wear it. With a long coat so that way you don't get cold."

"Okay. I can do that."

"By the way, if you didn't know, you're going to be spending Christmas with the Montgomerys."

"Lex..." I said, exasperation oozing out of my tone.

"Mom's going to give you the full invitation soon, but we're running out of time, and I want to make sure you knew. It doesn't have to be anything scary, but we were friends long before I wanted to kiss you." He paused. "Okay, scratch that. I wanted to kiss you before, but then we were friends and then well, life."

"You confuse me so much," I said as I put my hands over my face.

"You confuse me just as much. This is why it's going to be fun. And totally not insanity wrapped in a bow."

"Exactly."

He kissed me, leaned down to pet the top of Mr. Darcy's head as my cat had decided to make another appearance, and then he stood up again.

I swallowed hard, watching as he moved. He was good at moving.

"I'll see you tomorrow, okay? Have fun tonight. Be safe. And well if you get a little tipsy and want to drunk text, I'm here."

"You're a menace, you know that?"

"I've always been a menace, Mercy. I'm glad you're figuring that out."

And with that, he left my house, pressing the button on the door so it locked itself.

Always keeping me safe that Lex Montgomery. Indeed a menace.

Knowing I was running out of time, I ran upstairs and slid on that maroon dress, black boots, and thick tights. Should it worry me that he remembered this outfit so much?

Or should it worry me even more that dancing with him that one night even though I had been seriously dating Justin at the time, had been one of my favorite nights in my life.

It just hadn't clicked that it had been because of Lex.

I gripped the edge of my vanity and let out a breath. Going any deeper into whatever this kind of relationship was with him would be a serious mistake. Our lives were already tangled enough. But maybe it was okay that I was living a bit. Maybe it was okay to be reckless.

Maybe it was okay to let Lexington Montgomery seduce me.

I shook my head, finished my makeup, and was just sliding on a thick black knee-length coat as my doorbell rang again.

When I answered, Brooklyn stood there, dressed to the nines, looking sexy as hell in a red dress, brown knee boots, and a similar jacket to mine.

"You look amazing. Are you ready for tonight?"

I shook my head. "Maybe. You scare me."

"That's what all of her friends say," Daisy Montgomery said as she leaned forward and hugged me tightly. Daisy was a couple of years older than us, older than the rest of us, and another one of Lex's many cousins. She worked in the Montgomery security branch of the family and was such a badass that I wanted to be her when I grew up.

And when I told her that in the restaurant later, she had thrown her head back and laughed.

"You don't really want to be me when you grow up. You end up with a lot of bruising."

"I end up with bruising too, mostly because I trip over things," I said with a laugh. "And you actually know how to protect yourself."

Shivers ran up my spine, and I looked behind our booth but shook my head. Nobody was there. I was just imagining things. Of course, I couldn't help but remember that time in the grocery store, when I had overreacted because a man had dared to shop at the same time as me.

"If you want to take self-defense lessons, I can help."

"She's great at it," Brooklyn put in as she poured us more wine.

We were a large group tonight, but I didn't know the other women very well. They weren't Montgomerys, but friends of Brooklyn and Daisy. Sasha, Mercedes, Clarisse, and Justine had introduced themselves but were all quieter than the Montgomerys. I was grateful to meet new people, but I worried I'd forget names by the end of the night.

Jamie, one of the others who worked with Lex had wanted to come out, but she had a last-minute emergency. She was fine but hadn't been able to make it. And my bestie Posy hadn't been able to come either because she was out of town with Cullen on a road trip to see each of their families. I knew there was a story there, and I would have to wait until she got back until I heard it.

"Maybe self-defense training would be a good thing. It's weird being a woman living alone. And I only have a cat to protect me."

"Mr. Darcy is amazing, but yes, you should. And we can put in an alarm if you want?" Daisy answered. "You can go over and look at Lex's and see what we did. It's subtle."

"So does everyone know that Lex and I are neighbors?" I asked, putting emphasis on the word neighbors.

Sasha laughed. "As in the two of you are maybe dating? Yes, word spreads fast in the Montgomery network."

"That's a little jarring. I forgot about that aspect."

"We're a small town in ourselves," Brooklyn answered. "It's annoying, but sometimes it's nice. Because you always have someone to lean on." Her gaze brightened as her phone buzzed. She looked down and started to text back quickly.

"I thought we said no phones," Daisy teased. "I'm not allowed to text my beautiful British husband with the accent that makes me want to faint, and you're not allowed to text Duke. The man that puts that look on your face."

Brooklyn nearly swooned in her seat. "I'm just texting him an update. I won't be long."

"I'm going to need to hear all about this Duke," I said, finally leaning into the whole girls' night thing.

"Oh, don't get her started. She's going to go on forever," Sasha teased, though her eyes were filled with laughter.

I sat back and listened to Brooklyn talk about every aspect of the man that she was falling for. In her own words, she usually dated losers, but Duke was in finance, worked his ass off, and was actually a good guy. And the more I asked about Duke, and Hugh, Daisy's sexy British husband, maybe they wouldn't ask so much about Lexington. It was a win-win for me because I had no answers for them. Let alone myself.

We went to three different bars for tapas and wine. While the others had all gotten rideshares to bring them here, Brooklyn had only had one glass of wine, and then water for the rest of the night since she'd be driving us home. I felt a little buzzed, a lot happy, and was ready to call it a night when someone slid his hand over my mouth. I screamed, kicking out, but the guy shoved me to his chest.

"Quiet."

I stepped on his foot with my high-heeled boot, before he let out a groan. And when he pushed me to the ground, roughing up my knees as my tights tore, I tried to get up.

Only, the man wasn't there anymore. Instead, Daisy was there, and in a blink, he was on his stomach, arms pinned behind him, her knee pressed tightly between his shoulder blades.

"Are you okay?"

Brooklyn helped me get up as I leaned into her, my eyes wide.

"I'm fine."

"Your knees are bleeding. Is someone calling the

cops?" Daisy asked, her voice no longer slightly buzzed, but all business.

"On it," Brooklyn said.

My hands shook and my tights were torn, blood oozing from the slight wounds, and I just ran my hands over my arms, wondering what the hell had just happened.

By the time Brooklyn dropped me off, we had already given our statements to the cops, and the man who refused to speak was in custody. I didn't know what would happen then, as I didn't understand the justice system at that point, but I was exhausted and just wanted to be home.

"Thank you for driving me home," I said after a moment, and Brooklyn just squeezed my hand.

"Don't worry about it. I'm just glad that you're okay."

Daisy's husband had picked her up since he had been close by, and I was grateful that I wouldn't have to explain that I was fine to anyone else.

Of course, I had spoken too soon.

As soon as I got out of my car, Lex was there, his hands on my face. "Are you okay? What the hell happened?"

"How did you.... What—who told you?" I blurted.

"Well, *you* didn't," he ground out.

While it was nice that someone waited for me at home and was worried, I didn't like the tone. "I'm fine. They got the guy. It was just a weird mugging, I guess. Who called you?"

"The Montgomery phone tree is really good," a deep voice said from the shadows, and I jumped.

Reece moved forward, hands up. "Sorry. I was at Lex's house when his phone started blowing up, letting us know what happened. And I'm the one that held him back from driving out there and trying to murder someone."

"Lex," I said, exasperated.

"Don't Lex me. Why didn't you call me?"

"Because we were handling it. And I was going to tell you, I promise. It just didn't occur to me to text you right away. I'm sorry."

"Lex, ease up," Brooklyn ordered before wrapping her arms around herself. "Daisy was really good at her job."

"I don't like it," Lex growled.

"Well, I don't like it either, but I'm sorry that you're offended I didn't call you. But it seems like your family took care of it for me. I'm not used to having an emergency contact anymore. Sue me," I spat.

Reece whistled between his teeth before he moved forward. "Brooklyn, can you take me home?"

She raised a brow. "Where's your car?"

"Doing just fine in his driveway, but you're not driving home alone."

"Okay, Daddy."

"Don't call me Daddy, girl. Or I'm going to call Duke and have him deal with the fact that you were nearly attacked too."

Brooklyn blushed. "Don't you dare."

The two began to argue as they got into Brooklyn's car, and she drove off.

I finally let out a breath and turned to Lex. "Did you guys plan to ambush us to make sure the women weren't alone?"

Lex slid a finger down my nose like I did with Mr. Darcy. "Of course we did. Come on, you're sleeping at my place."

"I'm not."

"I have a better alarm system. Mr. Darcy won't mind it."

I merely sighed.

"I'm fucking scared, okay? Just please? I'll sleep in the guest room. My bed's better anyway. The mattress helps your back and all."

"Lex, I just want to go to bed."

"You can. Come on. Let's get your cat and your

pajamas. I promise not to make a move on you. Unless you ask," he added, and I heard the stress in his tone.

Frankly, I didn't want to be alone either, he'd just gotten on my nerves.

I wouldn't give in later, at least that's what I told myself.

So with a sigh, I walked inside and threw a couple of things into a bag. Lex had already grabbed Mr. Darcy, the two looking as if they had been best friends their whole lives, and had a small bag for him.

"I got some food and things. Wasn't sure what else."

"It would make more sense if you just stayed here."

"I have an alarm system. Sue me."

"It looks like I'll be trying to budget for one soon."

"I know a guy," he teased.

I leaned in into him for a moment, tears threatening. There was still a slight bit of shock running through me, and it was the only thing allowing me to stand straight.

We turned off all the lights, locked the doors, and headed into Lex's place. Tomorrow I would pay more attention to it. Tomorrow I would notice the details beyond the construction mess. But he took me to his bedroom, instead of something sexy and sweet and romantic, I went to his restroom, changed to my pajamas, the comfy ones that covered every inch of me, and slid into bed.

Mr. Darcy jumped next to me, cuddling on my hip, as Lex stood at the doorway in his pajamas.

"Good night, Mercy."

"Don't go. I know I'm being a brat. Just come hold me?"

Without an answer, Lex moved forward, lifted up the blankets, and I turned, disrupting Mr. Darcy, so I could snuggle into Lex's hold.

My hands against my own chest, I tangled my legs with his and let myself be enveloped. He rubbed his chin over the top of my head, and I finally let out the breath I hadn't known I'd been holding for hours.

"You're safe, Mercy. I promise."

"I know. I know."

And even though I hadn't thought I would be able to sleep tonight, I closed my eyes and let the sound of Lex's heartbeat lull me to sleep. Because in his arms, I didn't have a care in the world.

At least for now.

Chapter Eleven

Lexington

It had taken me for too long to fall asleep. With Mercy in my arms, all I could do was watch her chest rise and fall as I tried not to freak the fuck out.

Some man had put his hands on her. He had touched her, scared her, and I didn't know why.

A mugging gone wrong? Something *worse*. Just the idea of what could have happened sent a mixture of rage and horror warring through my body. I was so damn grateful that Daisy had been there. Daisy, my cousin who was good at protecting those in her charge as well as herself. I shuddered to think what would've happened if she hadn't been there. Not that I wanted my cousin harmed. Hell, I wanted to keep everyone I cared about wrapped in cotton wool and safe at home, but I knew that wasn't feasible.

I lay on my side, my face resting on my fist as I looked down at Mercy as she slept.

Without thinking, I reached out and traced my fingers along her jawline, her cheekbone. When she opened her eyes quickly, I winced.

"I didn't mean to wake you up like a creep."

"Always slightly creepy," she whispered before she put the back of her hand to her mouth and yawned. "How long have you been awake?"

"Not that long," I lied.

Did it count when I hadn't fallen into a deep sleep?

Mercy reached up then and traced her fingers over what had to be the dark circles under my eyes. The ones that matched hers.

"Liar," she whispered.

I leaned down and brushed my lips along hers. I couldn't help it, I just needed her touch, needed to ensure she was safe. "Good morning," I whispered before resting my forehead along hers.

"I have morning breath."

"So do I, so we'll just ignore it. We're adults after all."

She smiled after I kissed her again. "Is it weird that I'm waking up in your bed? I don't even know exactly what we are, and here I am, feeling far too comfortable in this bed."

"Because it's a comfortable bed," I hedged. I opened my mouth to say something, anything, since we hadn't defined our relationship, and seemed to have skipped a few steps, when something nudged on my elbow.

I turned quickly, sitting up as Mr. Darcy walked across my legs, then right over my stomach, and I was grateful he hadn't pressed his claws against something far more sensitive.

Mercy let out an oaf as the cat proceeded to try to knead her stomach and then walk over her neck. "Mr. Darcy, I think, is hungry," she said with a laugh as we both reached out to run our hands along the black cat's back. When our fingers tangled, I just looked into Mercy's eyes and wondered what the hell I was doing.

This had only started as a fake date, right? A fake relationship to get through an evening, a weekend with an overbearing business owner. A fake relationship, so that way I wouldn't have to deal with Gia's patronizing looks.

And yet here we were, in bed together. Maybe not sleeping with one another, but it sure felt real to me.

"We brought his food and everything. I'll go take care of it."

Mercy shifted so she could sit up. As Mr. Darcy

popped off the bed, he looked over his shoulder, chirped, and ran to the door. Then he began to pace in front of it, as if impatiently waiting.

"I've got it but thank you. He's very particular."

"I hear cats are that way."

Mercy scowled at me. "Excuse me, I know for a fact that some dogs are the same way. Mr. Darcy, however, is in a strange and new environment, and he just needs something that's a little normal."

It didn't take an expert to realize the subtext of that thought.

Because there was nothing normal about what we were doing in this moment.

Before I could say anything though, she got off the bed and practically ran out of the room.

I could hear her soft murmurs to the cat as she fed him, but I wasn't sure what I was supposed to do.

Somebody had attacked Mercy, and yet, she was in my house right now and that seemed to be the more pressing matter.

I looked down at my cock, and the way that it tented the sheets.

"Well, we won't be taking care of you," I muttered.

I got out of bed and walked to the bathroom, knowing that today was going to be a weird day. Christmas Eve was right around the corner, and I wasn't sure what the hell I was going to be doing that day, let alone with Mercy.

When the woman who centered my thoughts walked back into the bedroom, I gestured towards her bag.

"Your things are in there, and you can use this bathroom. I'll go use the guest one."

She shook her head. "That doesn't make any sense. I have everything in one place, so I can make it to the guest bathroom. Or I could go home."

"Don't," I blurted.

She frowned at me. "Don't? Don't what? Go home? I'll be okay."

"I just, we don't know if that guy knows where you live or something."

"It's not like that." She let out a breath. "And don't tell me I'm underreacting. Seriously, I'm fine. I'm going to go home, shower, get dressed, and try to go about my day. Thank you for letting me sleep underneath your roof so I could feel safe for the evening, but I'll be okay, Lex."

Scowling, I paced towards her. She didn't move, in fact, she stiffened as I leaned forward and cupped the back of her neck.

"Stay. I don't want you over there without a security system."

"You don't get to tell me what to do, Lex."

"Fine, *please* stay. How's that?"

"It still feels like an order," she mumbled.

"It's not." Though I wanted it to be. "Just, Daisy's going to be over later to go over things. Can we just wait for her? I'll make breakfast. You have all you need to shower, right? Just stay, okay?"

"And does that mean you're actually going to talk to me about what the hell we're doing?" she asked, her brows raised.

In answer I squeezed the back of her neck and used my thumb to tilt her chin up. When her mouth parted, her pupils dilating, I held back a growl. "Maybe. Just let me have this, okay?"

"Fine. Just for now."

I nodded and pressed a hard kiss to her mouth. Before I could deepen it, or press her back to the wall and have my way with her, I pulled back, my chest heaving.

"Go shower. Before I join you."

Her brows raised. "And you think I'm just going to let that happen?"

"From the way that your nipples are pressed against your shirt right now? I think it's a possibility."

Her hands moved to cover herself before she froze

and dropped her hands. "I didn't realize you were such a jerk."

"I'm not. I'm just moody. What can I say?"

She rolled her eyes before she leaned down and picked up her bag.

As she walked out, Mr. Darcy flicked his tail at me, and I hadn't even realized the cat had followed her in. Then the two turned down the hall, leaving me standing there, my cock hard, and wondering what the hell I was going to do with that woman.

She was my friend.

And yet friends didn't want to do exactly what I wanted to do to her. It was only supposed to be a fake relationship. And yet, I could still taste her on my tongue. I still remembered exactly what had happened in that hotel room. So no, things weren't simple. And I wanted more.

I jumped into the shower, grateful for the cold temperature at first. As the water began to heat up, I poured soap into my hand before wrapping my fist around the base of my cock.

I imagined Mercy on her knees in front of me, her tongue sliding into the slit at the tip of my cock. I'd pulled her by her hair, keeping her steady as I ran my cock over her lips, tapping them to tell her to open them. Then I'd slide between those pump lips of hers, all the way down to the back of her throat. She'd gag, but she'd take it. Then I'd keep moving, sliding in and out of her as she bobbed her head, taking more and more of me with each thrust. I'd make her show me how wet she was by sliding her hand between her legs and then lifting her fingers for me to taste. One hand would be in her hair, guiding her head as she sucked me off, and the other would be playing with her nipples, loving the way that her breasts would overfill my hands.

Because Mercy had amazing tits, and I couldn't help but want to paint them with my cum.

Groaning, I moved my hand faster, imagining her bent over in front of me in the shower as I slid my cock into her ass. It would be tight at first, and she'd whimper, but then she would relax, pressing back into me.

My fingers would be in her pussy, my thumb over her clit, as I fucked her ass, taking her as we both craved. And when she finally came for the first time, I'd fill her with my cum, licking up her spine as both of us stood in the cooling water, panting, and not nearly sated enough.

And at that thought, I came, spurting on the bathroom wall. I held back a groan, trying not to whisper her name so she wouldn't hear as I had the hardest orgasm of my life.

All with just thinking about Mercy.

Disgusted with myself since she was in the damn

house, I quickly finished my shower and turned off the water.

I wrapped a towel around my waist and walked into my bedroom to get my clothes.

Mercy stood there, eyes wide as she traced every inch of my bare and wet chest.

When her tongue darted out to lick her lips, I couldn't help but smirk.

"Need something?"

Then her gaze went lower, to where my recently sated dick was now hard once again, tenting my towel, threatening to peak out.

"Well, I want to ask about your tattoos."

I grinned and looked down at the dragon inked on my side from Leif, my cousin, and then the tree that had been hollowed out, filled with jagged shards of glass, that Sebastian had added last year.

"I still have the rest of my chest and back to go. But my rib cages are done. Thankfully."

"That had to hurt," she whispered. I didn't even realize we had moved closer to each other until her fingers traced along the dragon's spine. I'd groaned, swallowing hard.

"It wasn't easy."

"I've always wanted a willow tree down my spine,

down my rib cage, the branches wrapping underneath my breasts. But I've been afraid."

I tilted my head. "Afraid of the pain? Or of the artist?"

"Maybe a little of both?"

"You know my cousins. They're brilliant at what they do, and they'll make you feel safe. You don't have to be topless for a chest tattoo. No matter what another artist might say."

"I learned that the hard way."

I scowled, rage zipping up my spine.

"Excuse me?"

"Oh, I didn't let them ink where I wanted. I wanted an upside-down heart locket between my breasts and over my heart. One that looked worn and rusted to match my own when I'd lost Emily. But the man wanted me topless for it."

I froze. "Is he alive? If so, I can fix that."

She snorted. "I went with a different person who let me wear a shirt and made sure everything felt safe. The other guy even handed me tiny little pasties that wouldn't even cover my entire nipple."

I couldn't help but look down at her bra and T-shirt covered breasts, imagining those nipples.

"Eyes up here," she said, snapping her fingers.

"So says the woman that was just staring at my

cock."

"Your cock is currently pressing against my stomach, so I don't think you have a leg to stand on."

"Maybe a third leg."

She let out a groan and rolled her eyes. "Seriously, that's the joke you're going with?"

"My cock is touching you right now and it's really hard to think." I leaned forward, sliding my hands through her wet hair, and brushed my lips against hers. "Want to see more of my tattoos?"

"I thought we both had work to do today before we take time off for the holidays."

"We do. But I can't help but want to taste you."

When Mercy's head fell back, I licked up her neck, biting her jaw. She shivered, and when I went to slide my hand up her shirt to feel those nipples she kept talking about, my doorbell rang.

With a groan, I cursed my cousin's timing.

"Do you think that's Daisy?" Mercy asked as she took a step back.

My cock and I wilted in disappointment. "Most likely. Let me get some clothes on."

"I really like what you're wearing right now," Mercy said with a laugh.

"See? I knew this would work."

"This..." Mercy asked, her eyes wide.

But before I could explain or even think about what this was, my doorbell rang again. I opened up the app on my phone and spoke through the camera microphone. "You have the code. Come on in."

"Is the deadbolt not on?" Daisy asked.

I cursed. "Damn it. Yeah, I locked us in to be safe. Like usual. One second."

"I've got it," Mercy said as she scrambled away from me, her cat on her heels.

I closed the app on my phone and quickly shoved into jeans, not bothering with underwear. I pulled on a dark blue Henley and padded downstairs barefoot, hating the fact that my cousin was so prompt and good at what she did.

Because my morning of having breakfast by eating out Mercy and then making her a real breakfast was no longer happening.

Daisy stood in my kitchen, her husband Hugh at her side. "I hope it's okay that I brought Hugh. The kid is with my parents." The kid being her adorable stepdaughter we all loved.

"It's no problem." I tipped up my chin at Hugh, who just smiled.

"Did you find anything out on who that man was?" Mercy asked. I moved forward, nodding my head in thanks as Mercy handed me a cup of coffee. Then I tangled my fingers with hers and didn't miss the knowing look in Daisy's eyes.

"Why don't you take a seat?" Hugh said, his British accent soothing, though I heard the undertone of worry in it.

I let go of Mercy's hand reluctantly and pulled out a seat for her in the breakfast nook.

"Thanks," she whispered.

I took my seat next to her and wrapped my hands around my warm coffee mug. "Talk to us."

"Is it okay that I say all this in front of Lex?" Daisy asked. "It's not proprietary information, and it's good for him to know, but I also want you to have the choice."

I scowled at my cousin. Because of course I was going to fucking know. I needed to know what the hell was going on in Mercy's life.

Mercy squeezed my knee before nodding at Daisy. "You can talk in front of him. I know the cops said they'd call today to get in touch, so I wonder what you must have found so quickly. Did the guy say anything? Or was it just a mugger?"

Daisy met my gaze, then turned to Mercy. She shook her head, and my whole body stiffened as Mercy's shoulders fell.

"The man has ties to a loan shark."

I blinked, leaning forward. "I'm sorry, what?"

Mercy cleared her throat. "He works for a loan shark? Why the heck would he follow *me*?" She turned to me. "I don't even do scratch off tickets."

"Denver isn't pristine, and there is an underworld out there. And the guy we picked up is one of the enforcers who tries to use family members in order to get what they want from clients. Namely clients who are in debt to them."

"I have no idea why he would be targeting me though. I don't have any family."

"But you almost did," Daisy said slowly, and I pushed back from the table, my chair falling.

"What the hell did Justin do?" I growled.

"Is he right? Is it the man I almost married? That ass-wipe who cheated on me?"

If I was going to love her, if that was an option in whatever relationship we had, this moment was probably where it would've begun. Because that look on her face? It was *everything*. And it was probably the least likely time for me to even pretend I wasn't falling.

"It seems that Justin owes money, a lot of money. We're talking six figures. The loan shark that he worked through has mob ties and happens to be a cousin of a cousin or something like that to the head guy. It's not good."

"But why would he come after me? It's been two years. I don't even know where he lives."

"Florida," I growled.

Mercy looked up at me. "What?"

"Justin lives in Florida. With his brand new wife," I spat.

"You're right. He does. However, it seems that our least favorite person made a connection with another guy in Justin's new home, and Justin explained that he didn't have any money, but he knew who did. Justin believes you got enough insurance money from your family that it can cover his debts. And while I don't know if whoever loaned him the money truly believes that, they're going to take it out on whoever they can until they get paid."

Mercy pulled back from the kitchen table and began to pace. "That small-dicked, little piece of shit, cheating asshole. What the hell was he thinking? Why would he need money?"

"He's not great at gambling and picked up a lovely pain pill addiction," Hugh added.

Mercy froze, her hand going to her chest as she blinked. I didn't blame her. Because what the fuck?

"No, Justin didn't even like taking Advil."

"There was a reason for that," Daisy whispered.

"You know what happened with his aunt." I

nodded, remembering everything my former friend had told me about his family. "She OD'd. It started with just normal pharmaceuticals and turned into something worse. Is that what's happening with Justin?"

Mercy came back to sit next to me and I slid my hand over her shoulder, running my thumb along the back of her neck. She was so tense I was afraid she was going to break something. But after a few moments of my touch, she relaxed. Marginally.

"We're still looking into it. It's only been a few hours, but this is what we could scale off from the top. We have good people on our team." Daisy shook her head. "I'm sorry. I'm going to let the authorities know exactly what we found, because I'm sure they found something similar. But, please let us put a security system into your home? You work from there, you're there often. Just let us help."

"I can't afford that," Mercy said, looking down at her hands. "All of that insurance money went to Emily's debt for all the medical bills that we had. I'm still in debt."

My hand squeezed around her neck for a moment before I forced myself to relax. "Money isn't an object here," I whispered.

"You can't do this for me," Mercy said as she looked towards me, and my hand fell.

"Then let us do it for you," Daisy said calmly. "A Christmas gift from the Montgomerys. And if I need to break into your house in order to keep it safe, I will," she added with such a bright smile that it took me a moment to see the edge underneath.

"I cannot believe that asshole. Are they really going to keep coming after me?" Mercy didn't sound scared. She sounded *pissed*. And I didn't blame her.

"I'm sure the authorities are going to do what they can to make sure that doesn't happen, and so will we. I just need you to be safe for now. Okay? Take the security system."

"It's way too much," Mercy said with the shake of her head.

"Don't be stupid. Let us help you."

She scowled at me. "And don't call me stupid. Fine though, as long as it's from all of the Montgomerys." She was speaking to Daisy as she said it but looking at me. So I knew exactly what she meant. We had no idea what we were to each other in that moment, no idea what would happen next, but I'd be damned if anyone put their hands on her again.

Chapter Twelve

Mercy

It wasn't every day that you found out your former fiancé/worst nightmare owed money to a loan shark with *connections*. Or was it the Mafia? I had narrated a few mafia romances, and it was always the innocent bystander who'd gotten in the way who ended up hurt or dead. I was not going to let myself dwell on that however, at least in this moment. Because it was Christmas Eve, and I was taking a full day off work. I was not going to dwell on the concept of my imminent doom, demise, or downward spiral. Because if I did, oh, there would be spiraling.

Justin was such a punk-ass bitch that he couldn't even stand up for himself two years later. I didn't know when he had stolen that money. Because not paying back a bookie was pretty much stealing. If he had done it after we had ended everything, then he was truly reaching far back in time to find a scapegoat.

But him and his perky wife, the woman I had trusted with my wedding, were safe and sound in Florida.

And I was apparently being mauled on street corners in Denver.

After Daisy had gone over everything, I had also explained to the group about the uneasy feeling that had washed over me in the grocery store as well as the random phone calls. While I had told the authorities that, the Montgomerys hadn't known. Lex had paced his kitchen, my cat oddly pacing right along with him. At one point, Mr. Darcy had tripped Lex, but the man I was slowly falling for had merely caught himself, growled, and continued to mumble.

I didn't know what the Montgomerys were planning, or how the authorities were going to fix this, but I was so damn annoyed that the person I truly did not think of often, thought of me enough to throw me under a bus.

And now here I was, dwelling on it when I said I wouldn't dwell. Frustrated, I flipped my mascara a little too hard and ended up with black on my eyebrows.

"Son of a bitch."

"Here you go. I do that too many times to count," Brooklyn said as she handed me a tissue.

I wiped at the black smear that was slowly starting to seep into my foundation and growled.

"That's it. I'm just going to draw on my face and call it a day. Can we have it as a costume party for our dinner tonight on Christmas Eve?"

A group of us were all heading to a nice restaurant that was owned by a friend of a friend and were going to celebrate as couples for Christmas Eve. Later I would open my gift underneath the tree, slightly different than when I was younger, but it would just be me and Mr. Darcy, unless Lex wanted to stay.

I warmed at the thought of that, because the two of us were sure acting like we were in a real relationship, and we hadn't even slept together yet.

Yes, we had slept next to each other but we hadn't had sex. We had been close enough a few times, but distractions and interruptions truly were the bane of my existence. No, Justin was the bane of my existence. Distractions were just hindrances. Maybe my Christmas gift would be an orgasm. That would be wonderful.

"I would love to know what you're thinking," Brooklyn said with a laugh. "And don't worry, I'll help you get that streak right off, and we won't have to draw on your face like that one *Friends* episode when they went to Vegas."

Laughing, remembering the ridiculousness of that particular show, I let out a breath.

"You really don't want to know what I was thinking."

Brooklyn, one of the most gorgeous women I had ever seen with her honey-colored hair and freckles that covered most of her face, winced. "I really don't want to know about your sex life with my cousin. It really sucks when people that I've become friends with or people that I've known all of my life start to date my family members. Because then we can't have the normal talks. I don't want to know about bedroom antics or the size of his dick." Brooklyn let out a shudder. "I can't believe I just said that aloud."

Laughing, I turned back to the mirror and sighed. "Thank you for the mascara help. And don't worry, I wouldn't even know what to say about that certain aspect. I mean, I think we're dating. Lex sort of alluded to it, but it's not like this whole time together has been any form of normal."

"Life isn't normal. That's the whole point of it."

"So wise."

"I think I heard it on a TV show once. Or I'm just making up words. Either way, I have many questions.

But first, if you think it might be a real relationship, are you just going to bypass the whole it started as a fake relationship thing?"

I threw my hands up in the air, grateful I didn't toss the lip gloss with the motion. "I have no idea. It's not like we talk. And the holidays have been busy. I mean, it's already Christmas Eve. And this is not exactly how I thought I'd spend my day."

"How did you think you would?" Brooklyn asked with a tilt of her head.

"Reading a book next to the fire with my cat on my lap. I mean, it's not a bad night."

"Not at all. That sounds like a lovely evening. But now you have a tree, lights, decorations, and Montgomerys invading." She cringed. "I can leave if you want. If you want that time. And I'll drag Lex away too."

I shook my head, guilt setting in. "No. I was fine being alone. I really am. I mean, now that Emily's gone, I *am* alone." I swallowed hard, ignoring the tinge that always hit with that thought. Brooklyn reached out and squeezed my hand.

"I'm still so sorry. I know that memories can be difficult, but I'd love to talk about her."

"That's sort of why I moved back. Because people knew Emily. I want to talk about her. I want to talk about her laugh, how she was outrageous sometimes but was the quiet one of us too."

"She was a hoot. Did I tell you that one time when we were young you were out with Lex doing something, and so Emily and I snuck up behind you guys and tried to spy on you, but instead we got caught by another one of my cousins and were chased around with paintballs. The soft kind that didn't hurt, but still."

"I did not know that. I wonder what Lex and I were doing?" I paused. "It's weird. Because Lex and I were friends before, close friends. And then I started dating his other friend, and things just changed."

"Okay, we're going to circle back to the first part of our conversation if that's okay. That way I can get it all out there. First off, you look lovely. We're going to go out tonight and have fun. And I'm sorry that we're kidnapping you. And, you and Lex haven't had sex yet?" she blurted.

"I'm very confused about the circular conversation, but no, we haven't. When would we have time?"

"I don't know, when you guys were snowed in for an evening at a very beautiful resort?"

"Well, we sort of got close." I blushed.

Brooklyn grinned like the Cheshire Cat. "Don't tell me all but tell me enough."

"There's not much to tell. But it was close. And

that's when it went from I'll be your friend just to annoy Gia and make sure that you guys can get the contract, to whatever this is. Like the fact that we spent so much time together, and I'm texting him more than I'm texting Posy, and I text Posy all the time."

My best friend was currently on a road trip of mass proportions that I did not even want to think about, but she was happy, safe, and I couldn't wait to hear her story with a certain friend of hers, all alone in a cabin. But that meant I would have to tell her what was happening with me and Lex. And I had no idea what that was.

"Well, I guess this means once the holidays are over, maybe you and Lex can just talk about it. Which is funny coming from me, because I'm usually the worst when it comes to talking about men and relationships."

I leaned against my vanity, folded my arms over my chest, and looked at the other woman that was slowly becoming a close friend.

Like I had told her, I had moved here for a reason, but I hadn't realized another reason had been needing relationships like this. I was still trying to figure out how to break out of my shell, but the fact that I could just have a moment of getting ready for a dinner while I put on makeup with another woman, felt wonderful. I was like a sponge soaking up all the interactions I could get. After spending the past two years trying to heal and yet grieve at the same time, maybe this was me stepping into the light.

"What do you mean by that?" I asked, shaking myself out of my thoughts.

"I usually date the worst guys. Not the bad boys, you know the ones with tattoos and motorcycles."

That made me laugh. "Um, your family is the tattoos and motorcycle crowd."

"Too true. No, I dated the guys with the polo shirts and the tan slacks and the ones that you could take home to mom and be happy about. Well, maybe not my mom. My mom's a little more discerning than that." Brooklyn shook her head. "But they never stood up for me. They were just easy. You know? You just got along, the sex was fine, you went out to dinner, and no matter what, it just was. Ever since middle school, the guys I would date would be not quite boring, but boring enough. Weak in some aspects."

"But Duke isn't like that?"

She shook her head, her whole face brightening. "No. I know it's only been a little while, but he is fantastic. He listens to me. He holds the door open for me and doesn't growl when I open the door for him. And when I walk, sometimes he'll lead me by putting his hands at the small of my back. He texts for no reason, and sometimes just shows up with a cup of coffee, making sure that we know we're on the same page even though our schedules don't always align. I mean, I work with dirt for a living, I'm messy, my hands are never beautiful. I am hell on a manicure. And he loves it."

"And you love him," I said, my heart practically sighing at the look of happiness on her face.

"I think I do. I mean, I think I really do. And well, I'm really glad that you and him are both coming to dinner tonight. Because I want him to be friends with my friends. And I realize that a couple of work friends are coming as well, so it's not just a double date, but going out on Christmas Eve is nice."

"You sound so freaking happy."

"I am. And I want you to be happy too. Not in the condescending I'm in love so I want you to be in love sort of way that some people are. It's because I love Lex. He's one of the best people in the world. And I like the way you two are around each other. You butt heads, and yet you just melt into one another."

"You really think so?"

"I know so. So, we're going to pretend he isn't my cousin for a moment, and I'm going to tell you to ride that man for Christmas Eve. Enjoy yourself. And now he's my cousin again, so blech." She gave a full body shudder, and I laughed as my phone buzzed.

POSY:

Merry Christmas Eve!

ME:

Merry Christmas Eve to you. Are you having fun?

POSY:

Oh yes. I have so much to tell you.

ME:

Maybe about a certain man named Cullen?

POSY:

You'll see.

She sent a photo of the two of them, and I let out a sigh.

"Wait, is that Cullen and Posy?" Brooklyn said as she lifted her hands into the air and cheered. "Finally."

"I know, right? The two of them have been dancing around each other forever." Cullen worked at Montgomery Construction, and Posy was one of my best friends. Another reason I had moved back to Colorado. They hadn't been dating at the Christmas party, and now a little over a week later, they were spending Christmas Eve together.

And I couldn't even comment on that because it seemed that Lex and I were on the same path.

Before I could say anything however, the doorbell

rang, and I picked up my bag and practically ran to go answer.

I might not know what the hell I was doing, but I was going to let it happen. For now.

Because there was enough to be fearful of, especially when it came to whoever the hell was after Justin, and therefore me. But I wasn't going to let any other fear enter my life.

At least for the night.

I LEANED INTO LEX, laughing at something Dash was saying when I noticed a couple walking toward us. I squeezed Lex's leg, and he looked down at me, his eyes dark. Well, I *had* squeezed a bit high on his thigh, but thankfully he must have seen the panic on my face because he looked up and put on a broad smile.

Gia and her husband walked past and waved, not saying a word. But the lines between her brows deepened as she took in the group enjoying themselves on Christmas Eve. Friends and family and warmth.

And Gia wasn't part of it.

Lex waved back, though the others didn't notice the couple walking past, and I turned my head to kiss his cheek.

Gia met my gaze, and I wanted to growl *mine*. But we were in public, and I wasn't *that* possessive.

Okay maybe I was. But still.

Lex looked down at me once again, ignoring Gia and her husband as they walked away—probably to tell dear old dad that the couple who wanted the contract was indeed a couple out on the town for the holidays—and kissed the tip of my nose.

Neither one of our gestures were fake.

I knew that.

He knew that.

And part of me wondered what we'd do now that the base of whatever relationship this was happened to be based on a lie.

I just hoped that base wouldn't crumble.

A laugh broke me out of my thoughts, and I turned back to Dash's story, immediately caught up in the warmth of the table.

Gia long forgotten.

Though the lie still lurked beneath.

"No really, green hair," Dash said as he leaned back into his chair, wine in hand. "With purple stripes."

I looked over at Lex, grateful for the distraction, and raised a brow. "How did I not know this?" I asked, warm with my single glass of wine and full after a wonderful dinner.

"It was only for a weekend, and it was very, very temporary dye. I lost a bet, and the rival colors of our college team were apparently Barney colors."

"Are there photos?" Reece asked, his grin wide, the lines at the edges of his eyes wrinkling.

I didn't know everybody at the table, but we were a party of fifteen on Christmas Eve. As it was a friend of a friend's restaurant, Lexington and the others had longtime reservations. And everybody who worked here not only got double their normal rate, they all had plans later as a group to celebrate their holidays.

"There are no photos," Lex said primly.

"I don't know if I believe you," I said quickly.

"I'm telling you, there's none."

Brooklyn looked over at me, eyes bright. "You're just going to have to take his phone later. Distract him."

"And how am I supposed to do that?" I laughed.

"Just show him your boobs, and he'll give you anything," Dash said deadpan, and I blushed so hard I could feel heat radiating from my cheeks.

"You're lucky I don't throw food in public, Dash," Lex growled. "And I thought everybody knew I was an ass man," he said so primly, that I snorted into my wine.

"You know, I'm learning so much about the Montgomerys, I'm a little worried," Duke said as Brooklyn leaned into him, looking so happy that I could practically see stars and hearts popping above each of their heads.

"You know, it's getting late, and I should probably get home," Reece said after a moment, and I turned to the man I didn't know as well as the others. Mostly because he wasn't dating a Montgomery and just happened to work with them. Honestly, I was surprised he'd even come tonight, but Dash had apparently dragged him.

Lex ran his fingers along my arm, rubbing back and forth as little shivers slid down my spine. I clenched my thighs together, wondering why just a simple touch would do this to me. But as he looked down at me, his pupils dilated, I swallowed hard.

Apparently, I wasn't the only one wondering how tonight would end.

"You're right," Lex said after he cleared his throat. "Let's head out, let the staff have this table, and call it an early night. It is Christmas Eve after all. I know we all have plans tomorrow."

We all stood, said our goodbyes, and headed out to our cars. Each of us had only had a single glass of wine and mostly water all night. So even though snow was slowly beginning to fall, we were all okay to get home.

Reece looked over at us, then at the others who had

slowly left the table, and then turned towards his car, the one parked the farthest away.

"I know many of the people who came tonight were your friends, but I was surprised Reece was here," I said, voicing my thoughts from earlier.

"He likes to keep his personal life close to the vest, so I don't know why he came, other than Dash probably forced him into it. My cousin's good at that."

"Brooklyn pretty much dragged me out too. Not that I'm not having fun," I added quickly.

"But a quiet night at home would've been nice too," he whispered before brushing his lips along mine.

I shivered, and it had nothing to do with the cold, but Lex pulled away anyway and led me to his truck. He helped me into it, since I was too short for it, and we headed back to our subdivision. When he pulled into my driveway, I raised a brow.

"Really?"

"The snow is coming down pretty hard, and I don't want you to have to walk home. Mr. Darcy misses you."

This man...he just did something to me. And honestly, I was done waiting. "Are you coming in?" I asked, my voice tight. I really wanted him to say yes, but I wasn't sure if he should say no.

"As long as you want me to." He paused. "And I have your Christmas gift."

"Oh, I have yours too." I shook my head.

"Well, let's get inside before we're trapped in here." He pulled out his phone and frowned. "A blizzard warning? What the hell?"

"Snowed in on Christmas morning? Well, that's going to upset a few people. Are you going to be able to make it to your parents?"

A frown covered his face before he shook his head. "We'll see. Let's just get inside first."

The snow had truly started coming down in earnest, the wind turning it sideways as we made our way inside, and I shivered. I set up the new alarm, grateful Daisy had sat me down to learn each button, and let out a breath.

"I am freezing," I said.

Mr. Darcy wound between my legs, and I bent down to pick him up, nuzzling him to me. "You're warm. Thank you, Mr. Darcy."

"I've been replaced by a cat. I knew it was only a matter of time," Lexington teased. He turned on my fireplace, and then my Christmas tree, before gesturing to me.

"Come sit next to me."

"I love that you just made yourself at home," I said dryly.

"You make coffee in my kitchen every day."

I blushed, shrugging. "Well, you need coffee in the middle of the day, and I don't mind making it for you. And I like your coffee maker more than mine." I set down Mr. Darcy before I took a seat next to Lex. I pulled his gift out from underneath the tree and pressed my lips together, feeling oddly awkward.

I sat cross-legged, the small, delicately wrapped box on my lap, and let out a breath. "It's not much, but well, I'm really not good at this."

In fact, most of the gifts under the tree were for Mr. Darcy. The two others were gifts for me, from myself. But one was a bath bomb kit, and the other was for work so I would be comfortable after a long day in the booth. But the fact that I even had a tree at all was a testament to the love of the Montgomerys.

"Mine isn't too grand either. I didn't have a lot of time, but I saw it and I thought of you."

I blinked, my throat tight, as we exchanged gifts. I didn't open mine, afraid of what it would mean, a sense of urgency and nervousness, compounding on one another.

"I guess I'll open mine first, I'm better at gifts when it comes to family than I am when it's other people that are important in my life." He shrugged as he said it, as if he hadn't just called me important. As if I was more than a fake girlfriend and neighbor. But I knew I was.

Thinking that I wasn't, was just living through denial once again.

He slowly unwrapped the gift, being far more careful than I thought he would.

He looked up at me and shrugged. "Sorry, I used to save the paper like my mom taught me."

"I vaguely remember that from a birthday party long ago."

"It's funny that we have so many shared memories, even though our lives diverted from each other so often."

"I was thinking about that earlier."

"Life comes at us fast, doesn't it?"

When he opened the box though, a wide grin spread over his face. "This is amazing." He pulled out a leather notebook, one with a soft and supple texture, one that I had pet far too often before I had wrapped it. "This is gorgeous, babe. You had it stamped with my name."

"Your initials. It's a very long name, but they were able to make it work. And the Montgomery Iris."

He pulled up the side of his shirt and pointed to the tattoo on his side. I tried not to swoon. "I love the fact that all of us Montgomerys, every single one, including my grandparents, have this brand, this logo, this tattoo on our bodies."

"I mean, one would say it's a cult, but I do appreciate the tattoo," I said as my gaze went to his rock-hard abs.

He winked at me, and I blushed.

"So the notebook is so you can draw while on the go and constantly add papers or photographs or inspiration pieces to it. And also in the box should be pencils that the lead is special or something for that kind of paper. I know you do a lot of your things digitally, and you can fit a tablet in there easily, but I also know you like drawing."

"Thank you." He leaned forward and brushed his lips against mine. I sighed into him, knowing what was coming next.

At least after I opened his gift.

"Well, now I hope you like mine," he mumbled.

I frowned at him, but slowly unwrapped his gift, giving him a knowing look as I ripped the paper. "Oops."

"My mother won't be pleased," he teased.

But I ignored him as I looked down at the large black velvet box in my lap. My heart raced as I traced the edge with my finger. "I don't know what to say."

He tilted my chin up with his finger so I met his gaze. "You haven't even opened it yet. I promised I didn't go overboard." His cheeks pinked and the part of me that had tensed at the idea of something so serious relaxed.

Nervous, I slid open the lid and smiled wide, tears threatening. The leather charm bracelet was gorgeous, lying on black velvet, and was the perfect mix between luxury and simple. I lifted up the jewelry piece and met his gaze.

"I see we were both on the same page when it comes to leather."

"Well, if you would like to wear leather at some point so I can try to peel it off you, we can try that."

I burst out laughing. "Really?"

"I'm just saying, you in a leather corset with your boobs up to your chin. Amazing."

"Didn't you just say you were an ass man?"

"Maybe. I can like both. I like every part of you," he said with a shrug, as if he once again hadn't thrown me off kilter. This man.

I shook my head and froze as I looked down at the tiny charms.

He cleared his throat, nervousness sinking into his tone. "I know you don't like too much jewelry, but this one you can add or take them off as you like."

I slid my finger over the first one, a tiny gold snake. "I'm never going to live down screaming over a venomous snake, am I?"

"I would've been screaming right along with you if I hadn't been blown away by seeing you again."

I looked up at him, mouth wide. "You are very good at that."

"Very good at what?"

"Lines that aren't lines and are from the heart that just make me think. Make me swoon. And I don't use the word swoon often."

"Well, I think you should," he whispered.

I swallowed again and looked down at the second charm, a tiny musical note entwined around a tree. A tree of life. I frowned, wondering how he could have found this. "They just had this charm? It's so perfect."

"I was lucky to find it, but yes. I know you and trees. You would have them tattooed all over your body if you could."

"And you already do," I said with a laugh.

"True. But the musical note is for you. I love when you sing to me. Honestly, I was surprised you went into voice acting and not singing."

"Because singing is personal, just for me. But I like using my voice to bring others' works to life."

"See? I learn something new every day."

I smiled even harder, and then looked down at the third charm, one that was slightly bigger than the others.

"If I made a mistake with this one, let me know."

I frowned before opening the tiny locket. My breath caught and tears threatened as I ran my thumb over one side filled with the image of my sister, smiling wide, and the other of my parents, not looking at the camera, but at each other.

"Damn you. I went with practical, and you went with *everything*," I rasped.

"I'm the practical guy, and you are the one who brings in the creative part, so it's only right that we switch off on this."

"I think we're a mix of both."

"You might be right."

I set his bracelet gently to the side and put it back in its case so Mr. Darcy wouldn't get to it, before I moved slowly and crawled over to him.

He raised a brow, but didn't say anything as I sat on his lap, wrapping my legs around him. "Merry Christmas Eve, Lex."

He swallowed hard, running his thumb over my cheek. "I never expected you as my gift. But I don't mind it. If I kiss you now, please know it has nothing to do with being a fake girlfriend. I promise. Because when I kiss you, I don't want to pretend anymore. I don't want to pretend for Gia."

I nodded before he pressed lips against mine once again, and I was lost. The warmth of the fire radiated off my back, as the Christmas tree to my right blinked out of the corner of my eye, but in that moment, I was all for him.

"If anybody interrupts us this time, they're just going to have to stand and watch. Because I'm done waiting," he growled against my mouth, and I couldn't help but smile at him.

"I hope they're in for a show then," I teased as I slid my fingers along his bearded chin.

"You're letting your beard grow."

He frowned. "I can stop and just shave if you'd like. Though, I don't think I can wait any longer. You're just going to have to deal with beard burns on your thighs."

My eyes widened and I opened my mouth to say something, but then Lex *moved*.

I found myself on my back with Lex's mouth on mine.

I groaned, sliding my hands up his back. I couldn't help but arch into him as he caressed my breasts over my sweater, pinching my nipples.

"I fucking love your tits. I cannot wait to see them covered in my cum."

"Did I know you were a dirty talker?" I panted as he continued to play with me.

"You're going to learn now."

Before I could say anything, he slowly kissed his

way down my body, shoving up my sweater so he could press his lips to my skin.

I writhed beneath him, wondering how I was already so wet with just a few kisses. But when he tugged on my boots, I pointed my toes so he could slide them off quickly, and before I could say anything, he had my leggings and panties off too.

Now my sweater was above my bra, and I wore nothing beneath.

"You work fast," I said with a laugh.

"I would say something about that, but now I'm just looking at your pussy and I cannot think about anything else.

"Damn, look at you, all swollen and wet for me." He knelt between my thighs, his thumb parting my swollen folds.

"And look at this little nub, all pert and waiting for my mouth." He leaned forward then and sucked my clit into his mouth. I shot up off the floor, but then he put one hand out and pressed me back down. He continued to suck, squeezing my folds and rubbing them in turn, nearly sending me over the edge. When he slid one finger inside me, teasing, I wiggled, wanting more. Then, he curled that finger, pressing against that soft bundle of nerves, and I came right then and there, clamping around his finger.

But he didn't stop, instead I looked down as he continued to suck on my cunt, and we met gazes. I nearly shot off again, but then he pulled out, leaving me wanting.

"Take off your bra and sweater. Now," he ordered.

Swallowing hard, I did as he said, my breasts falling heavy in his hands. He molded them, squeezing them hard in between his fingertips.

"Look at these, so pretty and begging for my mouth. You're so fucking hot. How am I supposed to think or work when I know that you're just next door, these breasts waiting for me." He sucked one into his mouth, squeezing the other nipple so hard that I tried to press my thighs together. Only he was kneeling in between me, and the feeling of his dark jeans on my inner thighs made me shiver.

"I'm going to fuck these tits one day. And when I do, you're going to ride my thigh, and then suck my cock. What do you think?"

"I think you're saying a lot of words, and I haven't seen your dick yet."

Lex threw his head back and laughed, before he pulled back and stood up. I tried not to blush at the damp spot on his pants, that I knew had come from me as I had indeed rode his thigh, and he just met my gaze and smirked.

"Damn you."

"Oh, fuck you."

"Oh don't worry. I'm going to fuck you. Are you ready?"

"You say that as if I'm not the one naked on the floor right now," I whispered. In answer, I held one breast and slid my hand in between my legs. My clit was swollen, the rest of me so hot and wet I could barely think straight. It didn't take much for me to nearly go over the edge, but then Lex was there, stopping me. He had shoved off his shirt and pants, and that's when I realized he hadn't worn any underwear, damn the man. But I didn't have time to pay his cock the attention deserved before his mouth was on me again, and he was finger-fucking me so hard that the sounds were indecent.

"That's it, ride my hand, move those hips, Mercy," Lex ordered as he knelt between my legs, sliding three fingers in and out of me so quickly that my dampness coated his palm and my thighs.

With a gasp, I came again, my eyes rolling back and my toes curling. I tried to sit up, tried to do anything, but instead I just lay there as Lex squeezed the base of his cock.

"I thought about this. While in the shower, in bed, even at work. How it would feel to have you beneath me, begging for my cock. But then I found myself the one wanting to beg for that sweet pussy of yours. Think you can do that?"

"Think I can do what?" I ask, not really tracking his words.

"Do you think you can take me?" Lex asked, and that's what I realized the true size of him. He was thick, long, and I couldn't help but lick my lips. He winked before he moved over to his pants and pulled out a condom. "I have more in my bag," he teased.

"And I have some upstairs. I wasn't really expecting to get fucked in front of the fireplace and my Christmas tree."

"Merry Christmas to me," Lex said before he used his teeth to tear open the wrapper. He met my gaze as he slowly slid the condom down his length, covering himself.

"Now. What do we do here?" Lex asked as he lifted one of my legs so my ankle was on his shoulder. He guided his cock to my pussy and slid the tip through my folds.

"You're already so tight after coming. Tsk. Tsk. We're going to see how well you can take this teasing."

"Stop teasing and fuck me already. I want this to be my Christmas gift instead."

"Next time I'll tie you up just like a little Christmas present and see how well you like it."

"I have so many questions with that, but I can't think straight."

"Frankly, neither can I. Now, look between us and see how greedy your little cunt is. Look at it taking me. It's begging for me."

I looked down as he slowly slid into me inch by inch. The pressure was nearly too much, his cock thick, stretching, but I couldn't help but suck in a breath as I did indeed take him in. He paused for a moment, not quite fully deep inside, and let out a shuddering breath. "I'm about to come like a teenager." He sighed. "You're so fucking beautiful."

I swallowed hard, trying to breathe. "You are the one that takes my breath away. How the hell do you have an eight pack?"

"You can use your tongue to count the muscles later," he teased.

"Promises promises," I said on a gasp as I tilted my head back. He pushed then, hard and fast, so he was fully seated in me, his heavy balls pressed against me.

"Look at you, you took all of me. That's a good girl." My leg was still up high, but he leaned forward slightly, stretching me as he ran the back of his hand over my cheek.

"Are you okay? You tell me if anything hurts, okay?"

"I'm really okay, Lex. Please. Just *move*."

"That I can do."

He kissed my ankle before he slid out of me slowly, oh so slowly. I opened my mouth to complain, but then he slammed into me to the hilt, and there was no more thinking. He kept moving, hard and fast, and as my leg fell he leaned over me, taking my mouth.

I tried to hold back, but the orgasm came once again, and I was groaning his name as I clamped down around him.

Lex pulled out of me, and I curled into a ball, my body shaking from the aftershocks, but then he gripped my hips and flipped me to my knees. Before I could say anything, he slammed into me again, fucking me from behind with such ferocity that we moved with each thrust towards the Christmas tree.

Afraid I was going to end up underneath the tree, I pressed back at him, arching.

"That's a girl, you're so fucking hot. So beautiful," he muttered, continuing to say words that I wasn't sure either one of us understood.

When I was close to orgasming again, I whimpered, not sure I could take it, but then he was moving us once more. He sat down and pulled me on top of him as we had been by the tree to start with, when we had been both fully clothed.

"Slide on top of me, Mercy. I want to see your eyes when I go over. When I fill you."

I shuddered, nodding.

"And one day, I'm going to fill you completely. I'm going to go bare, and fill you up with my cum. What do you think about that?"

This man was a menace. And I was falling far too quickly. "I think you're once again all talk."

I practically panted the words, and he smiled before sliding me down over his cock. I wrapped my arms around his waist as he slowly rocked into me, and we held one another, our gazes meeting.

"Merry Christmas, Lex," I whispered against his lips.

He held the back of my head, my hair fisted in his hand, and he just smiled. "Merry Christmas, Mercy." And then we were both moving, hard, fast, and when he came, I followed, loving the sound of my name on his lips.

"Nothing fake about that," he muttered, and I grinned, feeling steady for the first time, and yet completely tilted off my axis. But maybe, just maybe, that was the Christmas gift we both had needed.

Chapter Thirteen

Lexington

Every year, there is a certain week in which you weren't exactly sure what day it was, nor if you were supposed to go to work, relax, eat a special meal, or celebrate with family.

No matter what though, you were filled with cheese.

And in this special case, you didn't even have to be a Montgomery to be filled with cheese.

"Okay, this is the best thing I've ever had in my life."

I couldn't help but grin over at Mercy at her words.

She sat cross-legged on my bed, wearing only an old button-up flannel of mine and her panties. She'd piled her hair on the top of her head with some form of scrunchie or hair tie. It wasn't really a scrunchie I didn't think because it had long bandana-like strings to it, or maybe I was thinking too hard about her hair.

"So, do you like the cheese, the pastry dough, or the homemade cranberry chutney jam thing?"

I popped a bite of the homemade dish into my mouth, the buttery pastry mixing with the sharp yet buttery taste of Brie decadent underneath that sharp cranberry. I'd even gotten a tiny piece of rosemary that just sent the whole bite to pure bliss.

I hadn't meant to groan out loud, but I couldn't help it. The week of cheese was currently the second-best thing to happen this week.

The first best thing was Mercy wearing my shirt in front of me.

"I like it all. I mean, what could be wrong with this? It's perfection. And I can't believe how easy it was to make."

"It was only easy because I bought premade pastry." I shook my head. "If we'd had the time, I would've gone through the whole process of layering and folding and chilling, but it was either do that, or eat you out." I held up both hands as if weighing the options.

She choked on her wine and set it down on the side table behind her. "You're ridiculous."

"Well, you did enjoy the fruits of my labor."

"Considering I paid you back by choking on your cock to the point that my eyes watered, I think we're even."

I threw my head back and laughed. Every time I tried to shock her, she met me word for word. "If we were to count orgasms, I don't think we're even."

"One of the best things about being a woman is a multiple orgasm. So in reality, there needs to be some form of algebraic equation. You know, the number of orgasms for a woman must have must equals $3X + 4$. Where X is the number of orgasms a man has, and 4 is just a number I came up with because sometimes having to deal with men in general requires an extra little flair."

And now I was about to fall in love with her. "Did you just make a math joke for me? I think I just got hard again."

"If math is what gets you off, I'm sorry, that was the best I could do. And I'm pretty sure I got that wrong."

"I don't even care if it makes no sense. However, it seems that if that's the case, you may be owed a few more orgasms. Should I go get my tablet so we can write everything out?"

"Oh yes. And watch you accidentally show your family orgasm math."

"We could start a whole new thing. Write books about it. The world would want to know."

"I'm totally going to believe that men are going to read a book about a woman's orgasm. Some of them can't even find the clit."

"Really? So now we have a math textbook, and it seems we need a geography one too?" I asked, tilting my head.

Mercy's eyes widened, but I moved slowly, taking the food tray that we had shared everything on and setting it on my nightstand. Now there was nothing between us, and I couldn't help but notice the blush on her face. And the fact that that blush slid down her chest, the peak between her open buttons tantalizing.

"Now, we have the beginnings of an algebra book. Let's see what I can do with geography."

"If this is your version of adult schoolhouse rock, I'm in."

"We'll have to write down everything later." And then I jumped on her, loving the squeal that escaped her lips. I had her on her back, her legs spread, my body nestled between her thighs and felt as if I was home.

We had only left her house or mine once since Christmas Eve. And that was only to see my parents the day after Christmas. The blizzard had let up for a single day, as we had ended up being snowed in. Then after we had gotten home celebrating a late Christmas, the snow had returned, and it didn't make any sense to leave the house. So we each worked, and I was pretty sure we were going to have sex on every piece of furniture in both of our homes. I might end up with rug burn, but it was a sacrifice I was willing to make.

"You taste like Brie and croissant," Mercy mumbled against my lips.

"Hold on, that's the sexiest thing you've ever said to me," I joked before I deepened the kiss, tugging her hair slightly.

We alternated between hard and fast and leisurely, and it felt as if we were in some form of bubble. One where whatever reality was at the end of this would hit us, but I thought I could possibly be ready for it.

Or maybe it was just me wishing I was ready for it.

I pushed all thoughts of what would happen after the holiday bubble burst and lifted myself to lean on one arm as I met her gaze. She licked her lips as I undid each button, letting the flannel fall to each side. Her breasts were the most beautiful breasts I'd ever seen in my life. And they were covered in my marks, as I was covered in hers. I cupped her breast, letting it fill my hand. I squeezed a few times, idly taking my time.

"Now let's see, this part of geography is more of a mountainous region."

"Oh really?" she asked, her eyes dancing.

I pinched her nipple hard between my fingers, and she gasped, her body arching. "And look at that. Was that an eruption?"

"Not quite," she said, her body shaking with laughter.

I leaned over her, taking her other nipple into my mouth, loving the way that she squirmed beneath me. I lazily licked and sucked my way down her body, before finding myself face deep between her thighs and grinning.

"Now what do we have here?"

"I'm pretty sure you've licked every part of me at this point," she said as she leaned up on her forearms.

"Well, I don't know, if I'm going to write this geography book, I better explore." I moved her panties to the side and grinned.

"And look at that. Somewhere new, at least for the day."

I leaned forward, licked at her folds, and she moaned.

"No, that's not your clit there."

I teased her entrance with two fingers before spearing her quickly. She gasped, her inner walls clamping down around my fingers.

"No, that's not your clit there either. However, there seems to be a spot in here that we might need to explore later." I let my fingers rub against her G-spot, and she nearly came. However, I eased off, keeping her close to the edge.

"Now, what is this?"

I wrapped my free arm around her thigh so I could reach around her mound and spread her for me.

"Now look at that. Is that what I think it is?"

"Are you going to use that prim and proper voice all day?" she asked. "We do have plans later."

"Well, if we have plans, I better see what I can do with this."

With two fingers still deep inside her, I used my thumb to rub over her clit.

"What do you think about that?"

"Can't think, can't thought. Can't talk."

Laughing, I leaned down and lapped at her cunt. When she shot up off the bed, I used my hand to press her down and continued to fuck her with my fingers, licking and sucking every taste of her. And when she came, I continued to eat her out, needing that orgasm on my face.

Her body still shaking, she sat up quickly, and I removed my fingers from deep inside her. Knowing exactly what she wanted, I spread her wetness over her lips and as she opened her mouth, I shoved my fingers deep inside.

"Lick it, suck it."

She did so, eyes on me, before she pulled back and licked her lips.

"My turn."

My brows rose and I let out a laugh as she shoved me to my back. As I was only wearing boxer briefs, it wasn't that hard for her to strip me naked. I kicked off my boxers so she would have easy access and watched as she knelt between my legs.

"Now, what do we have here?"

"A new geography lesson?"

"You're going to have to explain it later, because I don't think I'm going to be able to talk soon."

With a wink, she opened her mouth and swallowed me whole. I groaned, nearly blacking out as my head fell back. The tip of my cock reached the back of her throat, and she swallowed, taking me deeper. I nearly came right then and gripped her hair tightly.

"Are you ready for me?"

She nodded, humming along my cock. I began to lift my hips off the bed, making sure to keep it gentle at first. I wouldn't hurt her no matter what.

Her fingernails dug into my thigh, even as she gripped the base of my cock, keeping us steady.

We moved as one, having learned our rhythm, and when I was nearly ready to come, I tugged on her hair.

"I want inside that pussy. As much as I want to paint those pretty breasts, or even your face, I want your pussy."

"How am I going to hang out with your family today, knowing you say the dirtiest things?"

"Please, do not mention that right now."

She opened her mouth to say something, but instead I just crushed mine to hers.

We tumbled on the bed, each of us vying for who would be on top.

I reached for the condom, quickly sheathed myself, and before she could say anything, I had her on her stomach, her whole body pinned, and shoved into her.

We both groaned, the sensation familiar, and yet not at the same time.

When she tried to arch up, I shook my head and pinned her legs together.

"No, we're going to try this way."

"I'm so full this way."

"Exactly."

I leaned over her, kissing at her neck, her shoulder, as I slowly rocked my hips. When she finally came, as she had been rubbing herself against the bed, I pulled out of her and rolled to my back.

"Ride me woman."

"Is this your New Year's Eve gift then?" she asked, and I just smiled.

"Well, if we're giving gifts, I better work on that math problem again."

She slid down my length, and we both groaned.

I pushed her down towards me, so I could lap at her breasts, paying extra attention because I couldn't help but taste every inch of her. We rocked into each other, slowly at first, then hard and fast.

And when I flicked my thumb over her clit and she finally came again, I followed, groaning into her neck. Spasms shocked us both, and we just lay there, my cock fully embedded within her, and neither one of us wanting to end the afternoon.

"Well, I have to say, you've just passed math *and* geography."

I smacked her ass, loving the way that she gasped. "Good thing I'm an overachiever."

"Gold stars all around."

We rolled so I was on top and I rocked my hips in and out of her, still slightly hard.

She was swollen, a little sore, so I knew I should be gentle.

Because I was just getting to know this Mercy, the woman that I had been falling for without knowing. The woman that I had tried not to want all those years ago.

And now she was in my bed.

And nothing could go wrong.

"Why are we back at the JW?" Sebastian asked with the shake of his head. My cousin, a man fully covered in ink and piercings, didn't look like a man who would usually stand on a golf course on New Year's Eve, but we were taking a family trip for golfing, because apparently the others had lost a bet.

"I didn't choose it," Dash said. "It was this one over here."

"What? I had points. This is free. I'm not quite sure why you're complaining."

"I like the word free," Crew said as if the man wasn't a millionaire and could probably buy out much of the land around here. However, we didn't talk about that.

"Well, I can't believe that Harry fixed this."

"So what are your plans for the night?" Sebastian asked as he watched Dash set up for a hole.

"Mercy and I are just going to take it easy."

"Look at that. You settling down?" Crew asked, tilting his head as he studied me.

"Well, I don't know about that," I sputtered. "But since you're taken, I kind of had to move on."

"Really? That old joke?" Sebastian said with a roll of his eyes.

Crew and I had never dated. Though, most of our family and friends had assumed we had. Instead, Crew had dated my cousin Daisy, before he had eventually ended up with Aria, Sebastian's twin.

Now the two were engaged and happy as can be.

Considering I knew both of them had gone through hell, I was glad for Crew. Even the darkness that had usually settled into his gaze wasn't there anymore. Sometimes a grayness settled in, but not always.

It was like the world was no longer on his shoulders, pressing him down into the ground.

And considering Sebastian had literally walked through hell, like Orpheus, I was just glad that my cousin was no longer looking back.

In fact, the man was so happy, it was a little startling.

But he and Raven not only had Sebastian's daughter from his first love, who was now eight, they also had a three-month old at home.

It was a little ridiculous how quickly my cousins were out there breeding.

"Hey, you and Aria ever think about having kids?"

"We've been engaged for like a minute. So no." Crew shook his head. "And frankly, I don't know if we're planning on having kids at all."

"Aria is always good at being the auntie, but she never played with dolls as the mom as a kid. She played the cool aunt," Sebastian explained.

"Aunt Autumn and Uncle Griffin never had kids,

even with the rest of the family breeding like bunnies so we have forty-nine cousins or some shit like that. They kept it real," Dash explained.

"You and Aria are already the best aunts and uncles that the kids could have, other than me of course," I added.

"So should I ask about you and Mercy then?" Sebastian asked, being far too nosy.

I blinked, my throat suddenly going dry.

"Not so nice when the shoe is on the other foot, is it?" My cousin grinned.

"Seriously, you are the most meddlesome of all of the cousins when it comes to our relationships, so we need to hear about you and Mercy," Crew put in.

"Wait, are we talking about Lex and his new true love?" Dash asked, drawing out the word love.

Once again, my mouth went dry, and I dropped my club.

"What? No, it's not like that. I mean, what? Fuck. Or just, you know."

"No, we don't know," Crew said slowly. "One minute you're neighbors, the other minute you're spending the entire week together, and I have to hear about it because you didn't spend as much time with the family over the holidays that you usually do. And I'm not even a Montgomery."

"You're as good as," Dash corrected. "Seriously, though. I thought it was all fake. I mean, so that way you could tell off Gia, and make sure her dad knew that you were a nice family man. You know, ready to settle down and make sure the company's good. Not that I agreed with it. It was an idiotic move, but it was real, right?"

I opened my mouth to say something, anything. Because I wasn't quite sure when it had gone from fake to real. Because it wasn't as if we had been fake fucking for the whole week. And even just calling it fucking seemed rude, demoralizing. Because I wouldn't have gotten her that charm bracelet, wouldn't have been thinking about her for practically all hours of the day for the entire month, if it was fake.

However, I wasn't able to say a thing.

Because the blood drained from my face as I realized we weren't the only people on this part of the course.

I turned slightly as Dash cursed under his breath.

Because Gia, her husband, her mother, and her father stood there, faces stone, and Gia's bright red.

"Fuck," Crew whispered under his breath.

And I was pretty sure that that was just an understatement.

Chapter Fourteen

Mercy

I wasn't technically a workaholic for getting some work done on New Year's Eve, but it couldn't be helped. I needed to get a few chapters in and answer the dreaded email. My producer was thankfully off for the week because they were smarter than me, so when they got back they would have things to work on and not feel rushed. Because if I did my part, everybody else wouldn't be behind with their part. It was just common sense.

And focusing on work would help me clear my thoughts of exactly what had happened this past week.

Because I had fallen for Lexington Wilder Montgomery.

I wasn't sure exactly how it had happened. But here

I was, head over heels in love with a man when I wasn't sure what he felt for me.

Yes, the sex was great, but it had been a whirlwind to say the least.

It hadn't even been a month, or really, now that I thought about it, it had been a month to the day since I had been out in the partial winter weather and a snake had decided to ruin my day.

And now Lex wasn't just my neighbor. Wasn't merely the man who had been standing near me on one of the worst days of my life.

Wasn't the man who had held Emily as she had coughed up blood, the first indication that we were going to lose her.

I let out a breath, knowing I wasn't going to be able to work anymore for the day. I put everything away, trying to focus on anything but Lex, but that wasn't going to happen.

"How the hell did this happen, Emily?"

She didn't answer back. She never did. Sometimes I would have those dreams where she would be sitting next to me and everybody would be talking to her, as if nothing had happened. As if she had always been here. And she wouldn't judge me for being with Lex. For wanting to be part of the Montgomery family once again. She would just be part of it with me.

And yet I would look at her and I would know she shouldn't be there. I would know she would leave at any moment, and if I truly believed that she was by my side, that my best friend, twin, other half was alive, then I would break once she left again.

Because if she was alive in my dreams and I had given up far too early, then I had moved on and left her behind.

The guilt that crept through my system every time I woke up from one of those dreams still made my chest ache.

Because Emily was gone. And I wasn't sure what I was supposed to do with the rest of my life. I had friends, at least I was learning to allow myself to have friends. I had a job I loved. A house I was slowly making mine.

And I hadn't expected Lex.

Maybe I should have. After all, he had been such a key part of my middle school years and beyond. But once I met Justin, things had changed.

I had thought I loved that man with every ounce of my soul. But it turned out, I had loved the man I thought he was. The man that Lex seemed far closer to being. And how odd was that?

I set the kettle on for tea, as it was oddly warm outside for New Year's Eve, but it still wasn't summer.

The fact that Lex and the guys were out golfing confused me. But if that's what they wanted to do for their man time, I would let them. I knew that Brooklyn and the others had said I could hang out with them for the day, or they would come over to me, but I had wanted some time alone to think. And once again, maybe I was thinking a little too much. But that's what I did best.

My phone buzzed, and I answered it, the unknown number making me frown. But these days, with so many clients and industry people that I worked with, I wasn't going to always know their number.

"Hello?" I answered.

"Mercy Caddel?" a deep, crackling voice asked.

I blinked, not recognizing the voice.

"Yes, and who's this?"

"It doesn't concern you. All you need to know is that we're looking for our money. And if you don't have it by tomorrow, we'll make sure you regret it."

Ice slid up my spine, and my palms went damp.

"I don't have your money. I'm not with Justin."

"That's not what he says. And well, we'll just see about that." The click at the other end of the line, followed by silence, echoed through my head as I ended the call and tried not to drop the phone with my shaking hands.

I immediately texted Daisy what had happened, before I pulled out my notes app and looked up the number for the detective I had spoken with.

This wasn't my life. Organized crime and bookies? Threatening calls? No, this wasn't me. How could I have been so wrong about Justin?

Well, maybe my judgment wasn't as great as I thought. After all, I had chosen wrong once before. And I knew Lex wasn't Justin, but for some reason, everything felt a little off.

I told the detective what had happened, and though he was off duty, he said he would look into it. I had given him the number, but I wasn't sure it was going to lead anywhere. And when I assured him that my security was all in place and I was locked up tight within my home, with only my cat for company, he had offered to send by a cruiser, but I had declined. It was New Year's Eve, and there was enough to deal with out on the roads. I was fine, I lied to myself.

And Lex would be here soon, and then I wouldn't be alone.

There. I was going to rely on someone. Trust someone. And that was good for me.

An hour passed, my tea long cold, when Lex knocked on the door. I let him in, quickly doing the security up again, my hands chilled. I turned to say something to him, to tell him what had happened, but then I realized that Lex hadn't said a word to me. He had just walked inside, hands in his pockets, and didn't even bother to kiss me.

"What's wrong?" I asked, feeling oddly out of my depth.

He met my gaze then, and the bleakness there hit me like a two-ton truck.

"Is it your family? What happened?" I asked as I moved forward. He took a step back, and a single crack reverberated through my chest. Just a slight one, not a full break, just a tiny sliver that could be mended with a kind word or a touch.

Only I didn't think I knew how to do that.

"Lex?"

"We fucked up. We fucked up so bad." He slid his hands out of his pockets and put his palms to his eyes.

Alarm shot through me and I moved forward. "What are you talking about? Talk to me."

"We were golfing, and we were just bullshitting around, and next thing I know, Gia and her entire family are next to us, and they overheard us talking about us being in a fake relationship."

I stood there, the distance a deep cavern that I knew I couldn't cross without taking a deep breath and possibly breaking.

Because he said *in* a fake relationship. Not *had started* or *had begun*. But currently *in* a fake relationship. And perhaps that was just a slip of the tongue, but perhaps it was the forefront of his mind. And yet I didn't think that was the important part to him in this moment.

"What happened?" I asked, and I surprised myself with how steady my voice was.

"It all blew up in our faces. Gia's dad was so fucking mad. We're not getting the contract, and well, it doesn't matter. Everything's just fucked up."

I held out a hand without thinking, but he didn't reach for me, didn't touch me.

"Okay. I'm so sorry. Lex, I don't know what to say. It's disappointing, but there are other jobs, right?"

"This was *the* job. This was the job that mattered," he said, his voice rising.

I took a step back, his voice angrier than I had ever heard. "And there's no way you can fix it?"

"No. Because I lied. I should have just gone to that stupid event alone and used my merit and not a lie."

"I'm sorry." Guilt ate at me, because it was partly my fault. I was the one who lied, because I hadn't wanted to let Gia have the last word, as she was hurting Lex, but instead it looks like I had done it anyway.

"What are you going to do?"

"I don't know. Fuck. This whole fake thing. It was a mistake."

Another jagged shard. This one larger. Emptier.

"What was a mistake? The fake girlfriend thing? Or everything?"

"What, no. I mean, it's not that. I just, I'm so off and I shouldn't have let you do this to me. I shouldn't have let this happen."

My eyes widened and I took a step back. "*Me.* Just me."

"I should have just ignored," he began as he paced, not listening to me. "I should have just joked with you and then gone to the event alone. Gia would've forgotten about it, and none of this would've happened."

"I'm sorry. I thought I was helping."

"Well you weren't," he snapped, and I blinked at him, wondering what the hell was happening. Because that wasn't anger in his voice, no, it was hurt.

"I made a mistake," I said. "But you went along with it."

"Damn it, Mercy. I'm sorry. For all of this. But damn it. I shouldn't have gone through with the whole thing." He shook his head. "I need to fix this. Somehow."

"Because it was all fake," I said, hoping he would correct me.

Instead he just stood there, staring through me.

Maybe he was thinking too hard, trying to come up with a plan, but he didn't tell me that it was real. Didn't say a single thing. And this time another piece of me shattered.

"You need to leave," I whispered. "Just get out."

He blinked as if coming out of a trance, confusion etched on his face. "What? Mercy. What? What did you say?"

"I need you to leave." I would not cry. I would not break down. Maybe he was stressed out about more than one thing, and yes, I had been the one to blurt something stupid, but he wasn't denying anything. "You said I did this. That it was my fault. That it was a lie."

Something seemed to shift in him, and his eyes widened. "That's not what I meant."

"But that's what you said."

"Mercy—"

"No. This job was important to you, I understand that." More important than me. "You should go. Fix that. What I fucked up."

"Mercy. Please. I promise that's not what I meant."

"Just go. You clearly have a lot to think about, and I am to blame. So leave. And I'll stay here. Because you need to deal with this." I shook my head. "Alone."

His face fell and I wasn't sure what I was supposed to feel. But with just a few words he'd already hurt me. I didn't want to chance that again. Not when this already hurt so much.

"I'm just...I just need to think."

He reached out for me then, but didn't move forward. Instead, I turned, opened the door, and stood there, not looking at him.

Because I had been wrong. So wrong.

And when he walked past me, his hands once again in his pockets, he didn't say a damn word. So I locked the door behind him, turned on my alarm, and realized I hadn't even told him that I had been threatened once again.

I guess it didn't matter. He had already broken me. And I had let him.

I stood there for far too long, Mr. Darcy weaving through my legs, when my doorbell rang. Part of me hoped it was him. For him to apologize, for me to do the same, and yet, when I looked through the peephole and saw Brooklyn there, part of me shattered.

I opened the door and shook my head. "I don't think I can be with a Montgomery right now," I said, my voice shaky.

"Fine. I'm not a Montgomery right now. I'm your friend. And I have ice cream."

"Brooklyn," I whispered, but I couldn't say another word. Instead I burst into tears, and my friend, one of the few friends I had let myself have in this new life of mine, closed the door behind her, and held me in her arms.

I hadn't truly cried in far too long. I hadn't cried at the saying goodbye to Emily until later. I hadn't cried at the wedding. Because I had been so busy trying to make sure everyone was okay, that I hadn't broken into tiny pieces. I hadn't let the tears come. But I couldn't stop them now.

So I let Brooklyn hold me, and then as the tears wracked my body, not just for what I had nearly lost a few moments ago, but for everything in the past few years, I let my friend hold me.

Later, Brooklyn drew me a bath, gave me a pint of ice cream and a spoon, and kissed my cheeks. She didn't say a word, and I knew that was probably for the best.

Brooklyn should be with her boyfriend right then. With her family. With her friends. But instead she was helping sad little Mercy who had probably overreacted and broken everything, and yet, he had just left. Walked away without a fight.

Maybe I wasn't worth fighting for.

Self-pity was new for me, and I didn't like it, but the tears I had been holding back since Emily had first coughed up blood, broke through.

And I laid there in the tub, scraping at my cookies

and cream ice cream, and knew I had broken a promise to myself.

I had lost the second family I had ever had. But it wasn't just because of a single lie.

No, because we could have come clean or changed everything in a heartbeat.

I had broken everything because I was scared. And if I had just let myself tell him that I was falling for him, maybe he would've fought.

Or maybe it would've hurt more in the end. Only with the way that my chest ached right now, I didn't know if it was possible.

The thing was, he had left. He didn't fight. So maybe, maybe it was all for nothing.

And maybe I had lost them all and had broken myself anyway.

Brooklyn came into the bathroom later and sat by the tub. She held up her phone, and showed me the countdown to midnight. I just stared at her, wondering what right I had for this woman to be so kind even though I didn't know if I was worth this type of friendship, this type of caring.

The clock struck midnight, and I might not be alone in this room, but yet, I had never felt more lonely in my life.

And it was all my fault.

Chapter Fifteen

Lexington

Give her space.

Give her space.

Those were the three words that Brooklyn had whispered to me when I had gone over to Mercy's place right after the ball had dropped. Because I was such a fucking idiot, that I had waited too long.

And that meant I couldn't see Mercy. She didn't want to see me. Because Brooklyn had opened the door, shook her head, and said to give Mercy space. So I hadn't walked back over there. And she wasn't answering my calls.

Fuck.

I paced my office, trying to pretend I could focus on work, but nothing was coming to me. Not only had we lost out on the estate with the Arnaults, but I had also been avoiding my family and their most likely obvious displeasure about the fact that I had lost such a potentially huge contract for us.

All because I hadn't been able to stand up for myself. Or keep my personal business out of what the hell was going on at work.

Or even stand up for Mercy.

I ran my hands over my face and looked down at my work board. My desk, usually pristine and organized, was a mess. Crumpled up pieces of paper, charcoal pens, everything was sprawled about, and not just in my workspace.

My gaze landed on the leather binder that Mercy had given me for Christmas, and I let out a breath. I needed to fix this.

Only I didn't know how.

I had always been the one who watched as others walked away from me.

Or broke me.

Never the other way around. And yet, here I was, making mistake after mistake when it came to the person that I hadn't even realized mattered the most. I was falling in love with Mercy, and in the end, it wouldn't matter because she wouldn't be able to love me back. Not when I had hurt her.

Why had I said those things? It was my fault. I was an adult.

I hadn't even thought about the words escaping my mouth until it was too late.

"How am I supposed to fix this?" I asked myself.

"Lex?"

I turned to see Jamie standing there, her face void of expression. She had her hair pulled back, her sweater buttoned up to her neck, and her outfit looking far different than she usually did. I wasn't sure what was going on with Jamie, but it wasn't as if I was allowed to ask. Because I would probably be the one who fucked it up. It wasn't my place. Right?

"Jamie? What's going on?" I asked, stiffening. Was that my voice? That hollow excuse for whatever the hell I was thinking? There were so many things wrong with this. And I wasn't sure how I was supposed to fix it. Let alone move on. Because I did not want to move on. I just didn't know what I wanted. And that was the crux of the situation.

"There's someone here to talk to you. They don't have an appointment, but I figured you might want a distraction."

"Oh. You know who it is?" My heart beat rapidly in my chest, and part of me hoped it was Mercy. Maybe she would come back. And I wouldn't feel like I was such a fucking idiot for ruining everything.

"A man named Mr. Burson? He said he met you at the resort."

My stomach fell, and I swallowed hard. "Oh. Send him back."

"I can do that." She paused, studying my face.

"What is it, Jamie?" I asked.

"I know this isn't a great time, but I might have to leave for a little bit."

I blinked. "What? Are you okay? What's wrong?" I moved forward, unsure of what to do. Jamie was always the steady one of us. Of course, that's what they used to say about me. So what did I know?

Jamie just smiled softly. "Everything's okay. I just need to do a few things."

"Do you want me to call Leif?" I asked, speaking of her eldest brother.

My cousin snorted before throwing up her hands. "For the love of God, every time that I need to do something that might seem out of character doesn't mean you have to call my big brother to save me. Seriously, I just need to take care of something. Okay?" she asked, her voice a little more energetic than it had been all morning.

"Okay. If you need anything from me, I'm here, though."

Her face softened. "I know that. Just like I know you have a lot more on your plate. We love you, you know."

"Jamie," I began.

"No. Yes, this is a place of business, but a lot of us are family. You're just going to have to deal with it. Now, I am going to let Mr. Burson back, and I will talk to you later."

And with that, she turned on her heel and left, leaving me confused as hell. Maybe I *would* talk to Leif about his little sister. But she might hate me for it. Maybe I'd talk to Cullen, one of her other older brothers. He and I hung out the most whenever he was in town. Because if something was wrong with Jamie, they would want to know. Or maybe I was just thinking too hard on it.

A Black man with wide shoulders, a wide smile, and an expensive suit walked into my office. I held back a frown for a moment, until his name finally clicked with the face and when we'd spoken last. My brain clearly wasn't firing on all cylinders if it had taken this long.

"Mr. Burson. It's good to see you." I held out my hand, and he shook it, nodding.

"It's nice to see you, too, Mr. Montgomery."

"Call me Lexington. There's more than one Montgomery underneath this roof and it gets confusing."

"So I hear. We're a family business, as well. Well, we have been for the past one hundred years."

"You guys do great work in the furniture building sector. And well, every other sector you've moved into in the past few years."

"My grandmother wanted to take over the world, and we're just trying to follow through." He grinned as he said it, but I had a feeling he wasn't being too hyperbolic.

"My family was the same way. We're just following along in their footsteps."

"And you're doing a damn good job." After a moment, the other man shook his head. "I'm going to be blunt with you. I am not a fan of Mr. Arnault."

I blinked and gestured towards the couch on the other side of my office. "Here, take a seat, that way we're not on opposite sides of a desk while we talk. Can I get you something to drink?"

"No, I'm okay. But I will take you up on sitting down. We went skiing for New Year's, and I've found out that being forty means your body starts to wear down over time. Who knew?"

My lips twitched. "My cousins and parents have said the same thing."

He pointed at me. "Mark my words, as soon as you hit thirty, it's all downhill, and then you go uphill and downhill. Or you fall on your face skiing as I did most of the weekend." He shook his head. "Like I was saying, I know you were gunning for the old Arnault estate. A lot of people were, and you would've been the best for the job. I'm not surprised, though, that Arnault went another way."

I winced. "What's he saying around town?"

He raised a brow. "He likes to badmouth everybody. Even if he's doing it with a Cheshire cat smile. So most of us don't tend to believe a word he says. So it doesn't matter what lies he's telling. Even if some of them might be true. Because he doesn't matter in the end."

I sighed. "I have a problem believing that his opinion wouldn't matter in our field."

"*He* believes his opinion matters. And he owns a lot of strong businesses that I know overlap with both of ours. But he's not the only one in the game. I have four estates that are of historical reverence that I had been waiting to work on for a while now. And I want to work with you. We talked a little bit at the JW, but I want to talk more."

My whole body stiffened for a moment, wondering how the hell this windfall had just fallen on my lap. Because Mr. Burson's properties were legendary. And nobody outside of their family was allowed to work on them. I hadn't even bothered to put in a proposal because I hadn't known they were on the table.

"I wasn't aware that you were searching for a company. I'm sorry that I didn't know."

"We're always searching, we just don't tell anyone." The older man smiled softly. "But I like your family business. And well, I like Mercy."

My throat went dry. "She doesn't work with us. She's a family friend." And that was a damn lie. She was so much more and yet I wasn't sure how to make sure she understood that. So it wasn't as if I was going to mention that to this near stranger in my office.

The other man just raised a brow. "Yes, I know she's a family friend. Whatever happens in your personal life is not my business. Just like what happens in our personal lives is not your business. But she made my wife laugh hysterically when others were ignoring her, and I know your work. You're one of the best in the business. And I want to see what you and your family can do with my family business."

I rolled my shoulders back, knowing I once again owed Mercy everything. Just like I owed my family everything. "I'm honored. Now what can I do for you?"

"Let's talk."

"I'm all yours."

If I couldn't fix anything else in my life, I could at least fix this.

I hoped.

By the time the other man had left, Dash, Brooklyn, and Reece were in my office, shaking their heads at me.

"Can you believe that just happened?" Brooklyn asked. "Fuck the Arnault estate. This is a huge thing."

I couldn't help but smile at her enthusiasm. If anyone ever needed a moment to breathe and find joy, it would be Brooklyn. "It is. I can't believe he just walked in and offered it."

Dash grinned. "We're going to have to work our asses off, but dammit, Lex. This is brilliant."

And it sure as hell didn't feel real. "Yeah. I guess it is."

"And if you don't stop blaming yourself for whatever happened with Arnault, you can just fuck right off," Brooklyn said so politely, that I blinked when her words finally caught up to me.

Reece barked out a laugh, and I narrowed my gaze at the other man. "What she said. I realize that I'm not part of the leadership of the company, so I'm grateful I was invited to this meeting."

"Excuse me, you have tons of experience, and one of the estates is pretty much going to be under your purview with the damage to it," Brooklyn explained.

Reece tilted his head. "Again, I'm grateful to be part of this, and the Arnault estate was going to be a pain in the ass to work with anyway. You know they micromanage more than even you do." He gestured toward me, and I held back a laugh.

"That is very true," Brooklyn added.

I resisted the urge to flip them off because we were in an actual work meeting.

Reece gave me a look that told me he knew *exactly* what I was thinking. "And on that note, I have work to do, and we should leave Lexington alone to brood."

"He's really good at brooding," Brooklyn said with a wink.

"Come on, kids," Reece said, gesturing for the door.

"Not a kid," Brooklyn sing-songed before she stomped out of the office, leaving a laughing Reece in her wake.

Dash just grinned at me, shaking his head. "This is good for us, you know. You did good."

I winced. Perhaps, but it didn't feel real. Nothing felt real until I figured out what the hell I was going to do when I got home. That was more important. "This was an accident. Everything I was working toward got fucked up."

"So you say, but I think for once you should probably give yourself a break. And I don't know, go see Mercy?"

"Dash."

"No, no, I'll go deal with real work. You mope in here, or brood, or whatever we want to call it."

Dash held up both hands before walking out of my office backwards, nearly running into Jamie. Before I could even comment on that or wonder what the hell I was going to do next, my office was filled once again. I looked up, ready to growl, and froze.

"Mom? Dad? Silas? Why are you guys here?"

My younger brother closed the door behind him, leaving me alone with my immediate family.

"I think it's time to talk, son," Beckett Montgomery said, and I slid my hands in my pockets.

I frowned. "About what? I'm sorry I wasn't around too often during these past couple of weeks. I'll make it up to you."

Mom shook her head. "That's fine. We see you often. And I got to see my baby on the holidays. Everything's okay. At least with us." My mother moved forward, cupped my face, then said, "Well, what the fuck are you doing, Lexington Wilder Montgomery?"

Silas barked out a laugh, while I just stared at my mother. "Did you just curse at me?"

"Why are you acting as if I don't curse as much as the Montgomerys? I'm a damn Wilder."

"And I love you more with each passing day," my dad said as I stared at my parents wondering what the hell was going on.

"I don't understand why you guys are here."

Mom took a step back and put her hands on her hips. "You put so much pressure on yourself, that you don't see what's right in front of you."

"I don't know what you're talking about." My parents always saw too much and frankly, I was a little afraid right now.

"Yes, you do," my dad corrected. "I know how much work you put into that proposal. And I'm sorry it didn't work out, but from what I hear, you're kicking ass in everything else—other than your personal life."

Heart racing, I held up both hands. "Stop it. Please. That's none of your business."

"I beg to disagree," my little brother said.

I narrowed my gaze at him. "That's enough out of you."

Silas just shrugged and went to go sprawl on my couch.

Mom gripped my hand, pulling my gaze back to her.

"You try to carry the world on your shoulders, Lex. Why can't you see what's right in front of you?"

"I don't know what you're talking about." I repeated the lie.

"You know exactly what we're talking about," my dad added. "You keep thinking you need to do more than we ever did. That you don't want to stand in our shadow. But you couldn't be further from the truth."

I stood there, wondering how the hell I was so surprised that my family understood me. We were close for a reason. But I didn't want to hear these words.

"Baby," my mom continued, "we need you to be healthy. That's it. And I want you to be happy."

"I am happy," I lied.

She gave me a look that spoke volumes. "You have already done so much for us. With everything that you do. But you put so much pressure on yourself for things that aren't as important."

"I...I'm fine. I've got this handled," I said softly.

My mom let out a breath. "I know you wanted this contract. I know that Mercy worked with you on it, but there's so much more out there. *She's* out there."

"Mom."

"No, listen to me. Do not break the one thing that could be amazing for you, that could be everything, because you're scared. And you hurt that girl,

Lexington Montgomery. You hurt that girl, and you need to fix it."

My mother, the one who would stand in front of a bear, a gun, or an angry mob for me, narrowed her gaze at me, and I stood there, confused as hell. And knowing I'd fucked up even more than I'd imagined.

My dad moved forward. "I hurt your mother once because I was scared too. I'm not going to ever do that again. But I don't want you to do it either. Don't follow in my footsteps there."

I blinked at him. "What? I don't know this story."

My mom rolled her eyes. "Beckett, that was a long time ago. And I love you." She turned to me. "Frankly, your dad might have bruised my heart just a little bit, but we both healed each other in so many ways. And we put up walls around ourselves because we put so much pressure on each other. Before your dad, I married a man who, in the end, I couldn't trust. Who broke his word and broke me. But that was not your father. And you are so much like your dad that sometimes it surprises me that you don't have our genes. But baby, you are loved. You don't need to lean on the image of what you think you need to be. You need to realize who you are. You are brilliant, you are caring, and you were worth everything. Now go stand up for what you could have with Mercy."

"How am I supposed to do that?" I asked.

"Grovel," Silas said as he stared at his phone. "Say you're sorry, do something about it so she knows you're sorry, and fix it. You gave her time, you gave her space, according to Brooklyn. So now fix it."

I stared at my younger brother, wondering how the hell he could think that would work, but my parents just tangled their fingers together as they leaned into one another.

Mom leaned forward and took my hands. "I don't know why you thought pretending to be in a relationship would work, but from what I've seen, it was real. The timing at first might've been off, but it was real. Make sure she knows that," my mom ordered.

"And go fix the best thing that could ever happen to you," my dad added.

And just like that, I knew what I had to do. And I would hate myself later for it being my little brother's idea.

Chapter Sixteen

Mercy

As I finished my final epilogue for the project that had taken me through every emotion I could possibly think of, I let out a deep breath. Because there wasn't a sound from next door.

Even though the holidays were over, Lex could have begun his construction again at any point. The addition was almost done, in fact every time I had been at his home, there hadn't been any construction going on at all. The calendar from before had said there would be construction going on today. But he had kept everything silent, calm, stagnant since I had kicked him out of my house.

I pinched the bridge of my nose before forcing myself to put everything away and get out of my booth. Because I should have let him speak. Or maybe I should have said something other than to get out. I had been so ashamed in my part of him losing that job, that I had let every lash of his words slice into me—however his words had been a mistake he hadn't meant to speak.

And I hadn't called him back. I was going to today though. It was time for me to finally fight for myself.

I didn't fight for myself when it came to Justin, but in the end that was a good thing. Not only had he cheated on me, embarrassed me, and ruined what we had, he had sent a bookie after me.

I had been so wrong in my judgment before, that I couldn't help but worry that I had done it again.

But placing my worries about what Justin had done on Lex was wrong.

So I would tell Lex that.

If he ever came home so I could see him again.

Mr. Darcy meowed at the back door, gesturing towards the catio, and I sighed, letting him out on his own.

"Lex put a new lock on the back door that you cannot open. Do you understand me? I need you to stay safe inside. While it's too cold for snakes, it is also too cold for you to be out for too long."

My cat blinked at me as if he understood me, or maybe that's just what I wanted him to do, and I closed the sliding door behind him. He stretched, and I resisted the urge to say good stretch, and went back to his little bed. He curled up, a little black void of poof, and I couldn't help but smile.

I wasn't the greatest cat mom in the world. I was still learning. But he was my everything. And I could tell from the way that he frowned at me, and pouted, that he missed Lex as much as I did.

I was going to fix this. Because there wasn't any other option. Was there?

My doorbell rang as I tried to think of how to approach Lex other than just going over to his house, and I froze, slowly pulling my phone out of my pocket. He stood there, hands in his pockets, looking as lost as I felt.

Part of me wanted to reach out and trace his face with my fingers on the screen, but that was ridiculous.

Because he was here now. And I would hear what he had to say. And then figure out what I needed to say along the way.

I opened the door, heart in my throat, and he stood there, looking so handsome that it was hard for me to breathe. But that was usually the case with Lex. He always made it hard for me to breathe.

"You answered," he said softly, and I nodded.

"I'm sorry for not answering my phone yesterday. I

was in the booth, and then I didn't know how to call you back. I just needed time to think."

"I understand. I wouldn't have blamed you for never answering your door. I was such an asshole."

"Maybe, but I didn't listen either."

"Can I come in? I can stand on the porch if you'd like, but I'd like to come in. If you'll let me."

I took a step back, my heart aching. I didn't know what I was supposed to say. But looking at him? It was as if every moment that I had been trying to forget slammed back into me, and I couldn't breathe.

"I shouldn't have blamed you. I know you were just trying to help with the Gia thing, and it was exactly what we needed."

My eyes widened, but I didn't say anything.

"Gia was trying to rub her relationship in my face. She cheated on me, dumped me, made me feel like shit. And she was trying to lord it over me. I hadn't realized how many times she had tried to do that. And you stood up for me. But Mercy? The moment I held your hand at the JW? It was real. Everything was real to me."

"I'm still sorry for lying. But you're right, it was the both of us."

"And it was real. And frankly? If we would have had more time, it would have been real from the start."

My eyes widened. "What are you saying?"

"Mercy. I wanted you when we were teenagers. When we were out of college, I wanted you, and was ready to ask you out and stake my claim in that growly way that we both joked about, but then Justin did it first."

"So he staked his claim?" I asked, my voice dry.

"And I thought you loved him."

"I thought I did too."

"So I stepped back, and then as soon as I saw you here again, it was like I had a second chance. Only I wasn't sure how to take it, and then the facade happened first. I don't regret anything that happened. Other than the fact that I hurt you."

"You did hurt me. But I should have listened. I should have taken a moment to just figure out exactly what we were doing."

"You didn't owe me that. You should have yelled and thrown things and called me bad names. I said shitty things. And I'm sorry."

"I wasn't looking for you, Lex. When I moved here. I was trying to figure out how to live again without my twin. To be alone. And I don't know how to do this."

He moved forward then, cupping my face. I sucked in a breath, his touch warm, familiar.

"I love you, Mercy. I didn't mean to fall this fast. But I don't regret it. It would have been inevitable because I fucking love you. And I know I'm not the easiest man to be with. I work too hard, I'm sometimes too far into my head, and my family's ridiculous, but I love you. And I want to be with you. I want to figure out how to live in this new world of ours together. And I don't want to forget where we came from. I don't want to forget Emily. I don't want to forget what we've lost. I love you. So please, take me back? Forgive me? I'm an asshole. An idiot. A stupid man. But this stupid man loves you."

I hadn't realized that a tear had fallen until he wiped it away, and I shook my head.

His eyes went wide in that moment, and I realized he took the shake of my head wrong.

"I'm sorry. And of course you're forgiven. I was going to forgive you as soon as I saw you next. Because we just needed to talk. Something that neither one of us is very good at when it comes to each other. We're both great at listening to others, but not ourselves."

"Damn straight. But I'm figuring it out. With you. I love you. And it was always real to me, Mercy. You have to believe that."

"I do. And I love you too."

He smiled so wide then, I couldn't help but kiss his chin.

"I hadn't realized how long I'd been waiting for those words."

"Well, I'm just going to say it, and you're going to have to deal with the fact that I am ridiculous sometimes."

"Same. And my family's even worse."

"I don't mind."

Something scratched at the glass door behind us, and I turned to see Mr. Darcy there, on his back feet, meowing loudly at us.

"I guess we should let him in. And I know he thanks you for fixing the door," I said with a laugh.

"Ah. I get it. You just love me for my handyman skills?"

"Well, that's part of it."

He brushed his lips against mine, and then we went to let Mr. Darcy in, and I couldn't help but laugh as the cat wove his way around Lex's legs before nearly tripping us both.

"I see how it is. I'm not forgiven by him, am I?"

"Probably not. But I don't think I'm forgiven for breathing either."

"Again. Sometimes I feel like I don't know what I'm doing. So you're just going to have to coach me with this whole falling in love and wanting to be with someone thing, okay?"

"The last time I loved somebody, it turned out they were a lying snake who decided to send people after me.

So yes, let's work on this whole being together thing together."

"Deal."

And when he crushed his mouth to mine, I melted into him.

Because I hadn't meant to fall for Lexington Montgomery. But if I was honest with myself, I knew it had always been inevitable.

Because he had always been the one there for me. Even when I hadn't expected it.

And now there was truly nothing fake about this.

And there was never going to be again.

"Why is it that you wearing my shirt and nothing but my shirt while cooking me brunch is the sexiest thing I've ever seen in my life?"

I moved the eggs off of the burner and turned to Lexington, raising a brow.

"I feel like you telling me you like me barefoot in the kitchen means you want to get slapped."

He rolled his eyes and then moved so he pressed his front to my back, hands on my hips. I groaned—I couldn't help it, considering what exactly was pressing against my lower back.

"I just like you near me. Sorry. I can't help it. You do know I'll cook for you anytime you want. As long as you're naked."

"Oh. That's nice." He licked up my neck, biting down gently. I shivered, grateful that I had already turned off the stove.

"Brunch is going to get cold."

"I think we'll be okay."

He slid his hand between my legs and froze. "You're not wearing any panties."

"You just said you liked me wearing only your shirt. When was I supposed to put on panties?"

He groaned. "Woman."

Before I could say anything though, he speared me with two fingers, and I let out a gasp. "So fucking wet for me. Do you hear yourself? Do you hear the sound of your wetness on my fingers? Your pussy is just calling my name."

Before I could even think, he had me twisted so my back was to the other counter, and he was on his knees.

"Lex," I gasped.

But he didn't say anything, instead he lifted one of my legs, set it on his shoulders, and licked up my cunt.

"Sweet. Tart. A perfect appetizer to brunch."

My head fell back as he continued to lick and suck, biting down on my clit ever so gently with his teeth.

And when he continued to finger fuck me, licking at my clit, I arched into him, pressing my pussy to his face.

When I came, he laughed at me, sucking every single ounce of my orgasm, and I barely kept standing.

"I need you," he growled.

"Lex," I moaned.

And then I was pressed over the counter, ass in the air, and he slammed into me. No warning, just his thickness stretching me as I went to my tiptoes, pressing back into him.

"Mercy. I...I can't think. Every time I'm inside you my mind goes blank and all I can do is go deeper. Harder. Mercy. Tell me you want this. Tell me you *need* this."

I could have said something sarcastic, something funny, anything to lighten the moment, and yet all I could do was lean back and ache. Because this was Lex. *My* Lex. And what else could I say? "I love every moment of it."

"That's my girl." He leaned down and bit at my shoulder after he pulled his shirt back. With a crack of sound, he slapped my ass, sending my eyes rolling to the back of my head, before he moved.

We arched for each other as I met him thrust for thrust, but it was hard to keep up as he pounded me into the counter. We would probably both end up with bruises, considering how we had continued to use every flat surface in both of our houses for the past couple of days. But it didn't matter. I just needed him. When he flicked his fingers over my clit again, I came, clamping down on him.

"I love you," he whispered, and then he came, his hips rocking. Warmth spread deep inside and it was so different than before. "Fucking you bare might break me, Merce. I don't think I could go back."

I looked over my shoulder and he kissed me softly before pulling out of me. "I love you too. And you're right. It was...*different*. I liked it."

He kissed my shoulder before pulling his pajama pants back up his hips, though he was still not wearing a shirt. Then he kissed me softly on the mouth. "Go shower first. If I go in there with you, we'll take forever. I'll figure out how to save brunch."

My heart ached, but I kissed him once more before heading to the back of the house, Mr. Darcy finally coming out of his hiding place. He hadn't been a fan of the sounds we'd made.

But things...things were good. I was in love with Lex Montgomery. I didn't know when it had happened, but I had a feeling that it had been a long time coming. Longer since I had been back in town. Knowing that both of us were trying to figure out how we fit into each other's lives while never letting go made everything worth it.

I quickly showered, my inner thighs sore and covered in beard burn, and I couldn't help but smile.

We had plans with his family later today, so we had to look at least somewhat respectable.

And me being sticky with the evidence of what we had been doing all week probably wasn't the best impression.

"You almost ready? I sort of saved the eggs," Lex called out.

"I'm sure we'll make do," I called back.

The doorbell rang, cutting through the moment. Knowing Lex's family, honestly it could be anyone. My phone was back in my office, so I didn't bother checking the readout to see who it was.

"I've got it," he said, and I just shook my head at the fact that it was so easy that he could answer my door. As if he belonged here.

Because he did.

Lex had pulled on a shirt, and I frowned at the way his shoulders stiffened.

"Can I help you?"

"Mercy Caddel?"

That deep voice. I knew that deep voice.

"Lex!" I called out.

But it was too late.

Though Lex had kept the chain on the door, it wasn't strong enough. Two men kicked it down and pushed at Lex. Lex staggered back as I moved forward and he ducked at the first fist that came at him.

"Get out of here, Mercy. Call the cops."

"Lex!" I'd have to pass them to get to my phone, but I couldn't just leave him like that. I had never seen Lex move so quickly, nor did I know he had any of those moves. Because he punched out, getting the first guy with a fist to his chin.

"You don't have to make this hard. We're just here for the money from that dumb bitch," the second man said. "There's no need to get your face broken. Just sit still."

The bookies.

They'd found out where I lived. Or followed me. Or...I don't know. I wasn't a criminal mastermind, and I could barely think with the pounding in my head. Justin was a dead man when we got out of this. Because we would. There was no other option.

"We don't have your money," I screamed as Lex punched the first guy again. But now there were three of them, and Lex was severely outnumbered.

I did the first thing that I thought of and picked up the egg pan. When one guy got free of Lex and came at me, I shot out, slamming it over the man's head. He groaned and went down to his knees.

"Get out. We have nothing for you."

"Bitch!" He grabbed my ankle and pulled. My legs went out from beneath me, and I fell back, slamming my head to the tile.

Stars shattered behind my eyes as Lex shouted from in front of me.

There was another grunt, a scream, and I tried to scramble out of the way. But the guy had me by the ankles and was pulling me towards him.

I reached out for the pan again, but I couldn't grip it. Instead the guy nearly on top of me slapped me hard in the face.

Blood trickled from my mouth, and I kicked out, finally connecting my knee to his groin.

"You're a fighter. I like that."

"Fuck you." I turned to my stomach and tried to crawl away, even as the man reached for me again.

Even as I turned out of the way, Lex knocked a third guy to the ground but grunted as another slammed into him.

The knife slid through flesh, a knife I hadn't seen. It was if time stood still as I watched Lex stagger back for a brief moment. Blood spurted, and I screamed. Lex, however, didn't make a sound. He just pushed the man backward, slamming him into the wall hard enough he slithered to the floor.

Mr. Darcy jumped out from beside a corner and split his claws into the man who had attacked me.

"Fucking cat," he growled, lifting his arm to slap Mr. Darcy away.

I gripped the cutting board that I had finally been able to reach and slammed it over the man's head. Mr. Darcy hissed, and ran to the other side of the room, as the man fell to the ground in a heap, blood covering his forehead.

I tried not to think too hard about that, as I tried to make my way towards Lex. But he stood there, two men on the ground in front of him and his arm covered in blood.

"Cops are on their way," Lex said as he gestured towards the security panel.

I would care about that soon. I would focus on real life as soon as I could breathe. But I could only think of one thing. "Lex. You're bleeding."

He looked down at his arm and shook his head. "I'm fine. I'm fine." But he staggered a bit, and I grabbed a dish towel and covered the wound on his arm.

"Oh my God," I whispered.

"Just a little lightheaded at the sight of my own

blood. But hey, Mr. Darcy saves the day," he said softly as he studied my face.

"They hurt you." We needed to tie these guys up or do *something* but no one was moving and I could only think of Lex in that moment. Honestly I could barely get a thought through the chaos in this moment.

"You're the one who's bleeding."

He uses his free hand to touch my forehead. I grimaced, not realizing that I'd hit my head hard enough to cut myself at some point.

"So are you."

"I'm going to kill Justin," I snapped. At least I could think of that through the fog.

"We're going to have to wait in line," he whispered, and I knew we were both finally coming down from the adrenaline high.

And so as Mr. Darcy stood in front of us, back arched and hair raised, I held the towel to Lex's wound and tried to figure out exactly what the fuck had just happened. The man that I loved was bleeding, and there were three large men knocked out and bleeding on my floor.

And that's when my knees went weak.

Lex caught me, and we sank to the floor, as sirens rang in the distance and the neighbors began to pile into my home. They took in the scene and helped secure what they could before I could even say a damn word.

I just let Lex hold me, my heart beating so loud I could practically feel it in my ears.

"I love you, Mercy. You're okay. We've got this."

"I love you too. Just don't let me go, okay? Because I think I'm going to throw up."

"Deal. Oh, I might throw up with you."

And that's how I found myself laughing as the cops stormed in, and I could only imagine the sight before them. I couldn't think about anything else except for the fact that Lex was bleeding, and both of us could have died.

I could have lost him. We could have lost each other.

And Justin was going to have to pay.

But for now, we were safe. And that was all that mattered.

Chapter Seventeen

Lexington

"Only twenty-three stitches. You're not even close to the world record for the Montgomerys." Dash leaned back in his chair and crossed his ankles, setting his feet on my hospital bed.

I glared at my cousin. "Is there a reason that you're trying to annoy me?"

"You get nearly stabbed and suddenly you're all grouchy? I mean really."

"Would you like me to kick him out of the room?" Mercy asked from the other side of the bed, her voice soft.

Dash immediately put his feet on the ground and sat up straighter. "Sorry, Mercy."

My lips twitched, but it was Brooklyn who spoke up

next. "Oh, I like this. All you have to do to get Dash to not be an asshole is to ask a woman he respects to tell him sweetly what to do."

"Excuse me, I love women. I'm great with women."

"I can't believe you just said that with a straight face," Mercy said deadpan, and I snorted.

"You think I'm going to be able to get out of the hospital soon? It's not like they have to keep me overnight, right?" I asked as I looked down at my newly bandaged arm.

Between the time the cops had come and now, a few hours had passed. We had gone through our statements and made sure that Mr. Darcy was safe with a neighbor. A neighbor who'd come over with the others to make sure Mercy was safe. And the surprise on her face that others had been there to help would forever be in my memory.

Mercy wasn't alone.

And I'd do all in my power to make sure she remembered that.

Now Mr. Darcy was safe instead of being at the house alone—now a new crime scene. Of course after getting to the hospital, getting through all the red tape, authority issues, and stitches, we were all exhausted.

"Thankfully you don't have to stay overnight," my mom said as she walked into the room. "Although, the fact that I'm starting to recognize some of the nurses and staff here because of you and your cousins is truly beginning to worry me."

"You say that as if our generation didn't spend our time in various hospitals around the state." Dad wrapped his arm around Mom's shoulder and kissed her temple.

She just rolled her eyes. "Please don't scare me like that again. Either one of you." Mom went around the bed and instead of comforting me, she cupped Mercy's face in her hands. "I realize you didn't have to have stitches, and you don't have a concussion, but you're still going to have to let us take care of you. I'm sorry, you're family now. And I don't take no for an answer."

I nearly opened my mouth to tell my mom to back off, but when my dad glared at me, I sat back.

Mercy however, just leaned into my mom's hold. That, more than anything, told me I'd be able to sleep at some point. Because if she could lean on my mom, the image of her bleeding on the floor wouldn't be the only thing on my mind.

The love of my life smiled softly up at my mom. "After the day we've had, I'm okay with you guys taking care of me. I kind of miss the whole mom thing."

If possible, my mom smiled even brighter.

"Well, you're stuck with us now. And if I can't step

up to the plate, one of my various sisters-in-law will." She kissed Mercy's temple, and then gently touched underneath her eye. "You're going to end up with a black eye there."

"I know. I'm not looking forward to the array of colors." Mercy cringed. "However, I think the other guy is worse. Which I can't believe I get to say that. I thought I only got to narrate things like that."

"Please don't remind me that you had to fight for yourself," I growled.

"Excuse me," Mercy snapped, though her eyes were filled with worry. "You are the one who took down two guys. I only took down the one. And Mr. Darcy helped."

Dash leaned forward, reminding me that he and Brooklyn were in the room. "You know it took me a really long time to remember that Mr. Darcy was your cat and not the guy with the hand flex in that one movie."

"Oh my god, the hand flex is the best thing that's ever happened in cin-e-ma," Brooklyn said as she clapped her hands with each syllable. Mercy, however, rubbed her temple, and Brooklyn winced. "Sorry. I'll be quiet."

Mom rolled her eyes like she had when we'd all be children. "You should all give them time to rest. Honestly, I'm surprised that Mercy isn't admitted now."

"I'm checked out," Mercy put in. "Now we're just waiting for the paperwork for Lex, and we can go home." She scowled. "Well, *Lex* can go home. I have blood on my carpet."

"We'll take care of it," my dad said, his voice low. "Between our two companies, we've got it down. Hell, I think Reece is already talking with the authorities to see when he can get in there. He's had experience with this sort of thing."

Mercy glanced at me, and I shook my head.

"Not my story to tell."

"I have so many questions." She rubbed her temples and I reached out to grab her hand, running my thumb along her palm. "But mostly I want to know if Justin is going to get in trouble for any of this?" she asked, her teeth digging into her lower lip. I squeezed her hand, annoyed I was still on the damn hospital bed. My stitches were in and we were allowed to go home—I just needed the damn paperwork.

"I don't know if they can do anything about it, but I'm sure they're going to try. I'm not sure they really like having other people send bookies and enforcers to innocent people's homes." I scowled. "And if they don't, well, it's a quick flight."

"Oh, we're going on a road trip? I'm in. I wonder if I'm allowed to bring brass knuckles in a suitcase? Probably not my carry-on." Dash tapped his chin, then winced as my dad gently slapped the back of his head.

Dad glared at him before turning to me. "We are not going to take matters into our own hands. The authorities will take care of it, and your house will be right as rain, Mercy. For now though, you can stay with us or Lex. I'm pretty sure my son's not going to want to let you out of his sight anytime soon."

Mercy blushed, and I finally tugged on her arm. "Come sit next to me. I feel awkward with everybody standing around me."

She rolled her eyes but tucked in next to me.

"That's better."

"Oh, I need a photo." My mom pulled out her phone and snapped three photos before I had a chance to scowl at her.

"Seriously? This is the look that you want to remember?" I asked directly.

"I have a lovely photo of your dad and his brothers all with black eyes for some tussle or another framed at the office. You know that."

"I want to know the story behind that," Dash asked.

"Ask your father," my dad said dryly, and then tilted his head towards the door.

"Come on, folks, let's give these two time to talk. And seriously, we're taking you guys home. Even if it's

Lex's home, you're not getting rid of us anytime soon. You scared the shit out of us. Okay?" Beckett Montgomery just shook his head and practically dragged my mom and the others out of the room after they all said their goodbyes.

Then it was just me and Mercy sitting on my hospital bed, waiting for paperwork, and finally I could breathe.

"I have never been so scared in my life," I said after a moment. I turned in the bed so I could face her. I lifted her hand once more, bringing it to my lips. I pressed a kiss to her palm before we tangled our fingers and rested them on the bed.

Mercy stared at me before closing her eyes. "I can't believe they just broke through my door like that. I didn't know people did that outside of the movies. It was so damn scary."

Guilt swept over me and I could kick myself. "All of that security and I opened the damn door to the people after you. I could have killed you."

"Hey. You answered the door like we always do. You used the chain and didn't let anyone in. And we had no idea they knew where I lived. It was all so...weird. Justin doesn't even have my address so we thought I'd be safe. Even behind a chain that clearly didn't work. My door is broken, but we're okay."

I wasn't going to forgive myself any time soon. "We're going to fix it. Don't worry about that."

"I don't care about that. You could have died. Mr. Darcy could have died. I just—I just can't believe Justin would do such a thing."

That was the part that got me too. Because that wasn't the man I'd become friends with. I didn't know what the hell I was supposed to do about that. I wanted to strangle him though I knew it wouldn't help anyone. "Neither one of us knew him. Or maybe he's just changed even more so over time. But it's over now."

She sighed and kissed my cheek. "Good. Because I never want to see that much blood again."

I looked down at my newly bandaged arm. "It really wasn't that deep."

"It was deep enough. And honestly, I hope that man's wounds from Mr. Darcy gets infected."

My lips twitched. "Well, I can hope that too. Your cat's a badass."

"And he knows it. He gets anything he wants."

"I guess this means I should build a catio when I finish the renovations on my home."

I said it offhandedly, but I couldn't help but to keep my gaze on hers as the words spilled out.

She stiffened for a moment before her face softened. "I think we'd both like that." She ran her fingers over my jaw, her gaze on my lips. "The holidays went by so fast, and I'm so grateful that I finally figured out that we live next door."

Careful of the wound on her head, I pushed her hair back from her face. "You were always the girl next door. I'm just glad that you're mine now. And I'm never letting you go. I hope you realize that."

"Oh? You promise?"

"Damn straight. I mean, we fought off the mob together. You can't break that up."

"Was it really the mob? Or just a couple of bookies?"

"When we tell the story to others, it's going to be the mob or the Mafia. We're going all out."

She threw her head back and laughed, her whole body shaking.

"Okay. If that's what you'd like."

"It is exactly what I'd like. So, you're just going to have to do what I ask. After all, I got stitches for you." Her face shut down, and I could have kicked myself. "I'm sorry. That's not what I meant. It's not your fault."

"No, I know it's not my fault. It's that asshole's fault. And I'm wondering if I could borrow Dash's brass knuckles."

"I'm sure that could be arranged," I said with a laugh

before I leaned down and brushed her lips with mine. "I love you, Mercy."

"I love you too. I was so afraid I was going to spend the holidays alone, wondering why the hell I had moved back, and yet, I'm glad that I was wrong."

"Are you ready to deal with the entire Montgomery clan? You've only met a fraction of us."

"I think I can handle it. After all, we fought off the mob." Her eyes danced, and I wrapped my arm around her shoulder, holding her close.

Because she was my forever. She might not know it yet, we might not be there yet, but I knew she was it.

I had always been the man that you dated before you found your forever. And part of me knew I was running out of chances. Mercy wasn't my last chance though, she was my only chance.

And she was mine.

Complete with fighting off the mob and the Montgomerys. And I knew was whatever happened next we'd figure it out. Together. If we could fight off the world, we could have this moment together.

Where everything was real, and nothing fake could ever touch us.

Chapter Eighteen

Brooklyn

A few months later

"Why do I have so many freckles? I think I have more freckles than everybody in the family combined." I scrunched my nose, staring in the mirror. My freckles had been the bane of my existence for longer than I cared to admit. It wasn't that I truly hated them, but sometimes I wished there weren't so many. They covered most of my face, not just my cheeks and nose like my siblings. No, they were on my forehead, my chin, all down my chest. My dermatologist swore I was doing just fine, and it wasn't anything to be alarmed about. It was just genetics.

And yet, none of my cousins had this wide array of freckles. Not even my brothers. And yes, technically they were my half-brothers, as we didn't share the same father, but still.

Riley snorted at my side. "You do realize that it doesn't matter what kind of freckles we have genetically? Because although I love you with every ounce of my soul, we don't share quite the same genetics. Some, yes, but not all of them."

I frowned at my cousin, or perhaps first cousin once removed (I could never understand what that meant), then conceded the point. "Okay fine. But your siblings don't have any freckles. And you only have like three. Our dads are twins. You would've thought we would've looked a little more alike."

Riley, the oldest of her siblings, just snorted. "My friend. My cousin, near love of my life. We do look alike. We have the same nose, the same chin. Your eyes just happen to look gray and silver underneath some lights. While mine are boring blue."

"Okay, we don't need to go and comment about who has boring eye color, do we?" Mercy said as she leaned back in her chair. She had her e-reader on her lap and was barely paying attention to us. Considering I knew for a fact that our cousin Lex had kept her up all night doing things I didn't want to think about, I was surprised she had any energy left to even join in the conversation.

"Okay sorry, I love my eyes. I love everything about

us. And I love your freckles," Riley said pointedly. "And Duke loves your freckles."

I blushed, that bright pink shining radiantly underneath said freckles. "He does, doesn't he? Once he tried to count them all and kiss them all, and it took all night." I put my hand over my chest, that warmth sliding through me. Then once again I looked down at my left hand, at the new ring twinkling underneath the lights.

"I'm getting married. *Married.* I can't believe it."

"I can't believe Uncle Storm let it happen," Riley said with a snort.

"You know, I grew up with you guys, at least in the periphery. And I know that you guys say that your dads are all overprotective and growly, and yet, I don't think so. I think they're just marshmallows."

Riley and I met each other's gazes before we burst out laughing.

"Oh they are. Especially for their little girls, however," Riley continued, "you don't tell them that. Because if you tell them that, then they get more overprotective just to annoy you. It's sort of how things work."

"Do you think Lex will be like that when he's older?" Mercy asked.

"Duh," Riley and I said at the same time. Then my cousin and I met each other's gazes and burst out laughing.

I loved my family. I loved the depth of it, the immense number. Even though we all saw each other often, we were also smaller units. Meaning many times the only family that I had and got to see every day were my parents and my two older brothers. And Nate and James had that twin thing going on. So sometimes it was just nice to be surrounded by women, the girls I had grown up with. Of all of my cousins, I supposed Riley and I were the closest. We were the same age, had gone through all the same classes, and of course, our dads were twins. And in a family where twins ran rampant, it meant many connections.

I was just sad that Riley hadn't decided to come work with me. Instead, she had gone to organize and practically run the Montgomery Art Gallery by herself. However, our other cousin Jamie, until recently, was making sure that Montgomery Construction didn't blow up.

I frowned, wondering what we were going to do now that Jamie was gone. And not just gone from our job, but from the state.

"What's that frown about?" Mercy asked as she set her e-reader down once again.

"I miss Jamie. And Libby. Why do they keep moving to Wyoming? What's so good up there?"

"Ranchers in tight jeans?" Riley asked.

"And on horses. Knowing what to do with their hands? And with that slight accent that doesn't make any sense because they're from Wyoming?" Mercy put in.

"Okay fine that is all true. But I don't need a cowboy. I have Duke. He's fantastic." I'd grown up surrounded by healthy and happy marriages. I knew love was real and I could scream from the rooftops that it was finally my turn.

"And you're getting married!" Riley said as she twirled around. Her dress, a handmade piece by one of her friends, flowed around her, and I couldn't help but take a quick photo with my phone. I wasn't the photographer in the family but could do decently well with a point and snap.

"So do you think Patrick's going to propose?" I asked, meeting Riley's gaze.

She and Patrick had been dating for a couple of years and really gelled. He was a nice guy who thought Riley walked on air. As long as Riley was happy, I'd be in Patrick's corner. The moment he broke her heart however—if that ever happened—I'd use one of my trusty shovels and show Riley my ditch digging skills from work.

That's what friends were for.

She shrugged. "Maybe. We're doing great right now

though, so if it happens it happens. I don't want to put so much pressure on it that I'm not enjoying the moment. I love him. He loves me. And we've been through so much together. I'm just happy with the way things are."

Mercy stood up then and wrapped her arms around both of our waists. "And I'm glad that you guys have adopted me. Being around you two just reminds me that I don't have to sit in my booth alone all day. Even though I might get behind on my deadline."

"Deadline schmeadline," I teased. "Okay, now do I look okay? Even with all these freckles?"

"Stop talking about your freckles. They're gorgeous. And I'm glad you're not covering them up."

"I'm just glad that I can find a decent coverage foundation that has sunscreen in it that's not actually full coverage." I shrugged. "I may lament my freckles, but they're me. And it did remind me that Duke loves them."

"Okay, go meet your perfect fiancé, and then tomorrow we start wedding planning. I know the moms are going to have fun with it."

"Duke's parents will probably want a say, outside of the Montgomery purview," I teased.

"Maybe, but we still win. We outnumber them," Riley added.

"You outnumber most small towns," Mercy said dryly.

I rolled my eyes and finished getting ready, adding a coat of lip gloss, as well as mascara, and grabbed my bag from Mercy's side table.

We had all piled into her room earlier that day, and I knew that one day soon she would move next door, and this house would go for rent. It was just one more change in the way that our family was growing.

I was ecstatic for Lexington and Mercy. As well as Riley and Patrick. And now I had the man of my dreams.

Before Duke, I'd been the person who dated the wrong guy. All through middle school and high school I dated the guy who wouldn't stand up for me or even himself. I didn't mind being the strong one. The most vocal of the relationship. I didn't mind being the one to always voice my opinions and stand up for us. But just once it was nice when they stood up for me.

And Duke did that.

I made my way downtown, parking behind my mom's bookshop. I was grateful for that space since there was no other parking around, and I walked the two blocks to the restaurant. There were tons of other places to go closer to us, but Duke's favorite place happened to be a steakhouse by his work.

When I got there, the hostess quickly took me to where Duke was seated, and the love of my life stood up and wrapped his arm around my waist.

"There you are. I've been waiting for you." He brushed his lips against mine, and I sank into him.

I loved everything about this man. His kind eyes, the way that they crinkled at the edges when he smiled because he laughed so much. I loved his blond hair, a running joke in our family since most of the men in my life were all brown haired, and apparently the favorite hot celebrities weren't usually blond.

However, mine always had been. I blame Legolas from *Lord of the Rings* when I had been a kid. It just is what it is.

When Duke lifted up my hand and brushed his lips along my ring finger, right underneath my engagement ring, I blushed.

"I'm really enjoying my new jewelry. Though my hand's quite heavy now."

Duke threw his head back and laughed. "That's what I like to hear. Come on, take a seat. I ordered us your favorite sparkling wine. But we can change it if you want."

"That sounds perfect." He knew what I liked and ordered ahead, but never in an overbearing way. I liked being able to just relax after a long day in the gardens.

"I did not order any appetizers, because I have no idea what you want when it comes to food. Wine? I'm your man. Not so much with the apps."

I fluttered my eyelashes. "Considering I change my mind every single time we come here, that makes sense."

"And they have specials. So who knows."

I settled into the booth next to him, leaning against his shoulder.

Things just felt good.

We had new bids at the worksite, and while my hands were covered in minor cuts, and no matter what I did, it felt like I always had dirt under my fingernails thanks to my job, I loved what I did.

Everything was finally coming to fruition, all of our hard work, and all of my hopeful plans.

Life truly couldn't get better than this.

"Well there's a familiar face."

I looked up at that rough, growly voice and rolled my eyes "Hello Reece." My coworker who I got along with but sometimes couldn't stand because he was bossier than my dad and uncles stood there with his girlfriend, Anya. They looked like they'd walked off the runway. Okay, she did. He was a little too rugged and menacing for that.

"Reece, good to see you," Duke said as he stood up. "Thanks for your help on that one project by the way."

"It was no big deal. Haven't seen you in here in a while."

My fiancé hugged Reece and I slid out of the booth to hug Anya tightly. I knew Reece and Anya had been together for a little while, though I didn't know her well. It wasn't as if Reece brought her to work. And she rarely came to work parties as she had a full-time job that took her out of the country often.

"It's so good to see you and congratulations!" Anya said as she held up my hand. "You did good, Duke."

Duke shrugged, a small smile playing on his lips. "I'll have you know that I asked a Montgomery woman for help on this. I am not going to lie about that."

"That makes sense. We women know our jewelry," Anya teased.

Reece blinked at me, then down at my ring finger. "I didn't know. When did this happen?"

I couldn't help the bright smile on my face as I wiggled my fingers so the ring caught the light. "Yesterday. I'm surprised it didn't hit one of your group chats."

Reece snorted. "I'm only involved in one Montgomery family group chat, and every time I try to leave it, somebody adds me back in. And nobody mentioned it in that one, nor the work one."

I snorted. "We enjoy teasing you with family things.

Just because you growl a lot. And I'm sorry we didn't tell you."

"Whatever. Congrats to you both. Seriously. But I have to ask. How many family group chats are there?" Reece asked.

"I'm afraid to know that answer, "Anya teased.

"Would you like to join us?" Duke asked, and I smiled. Because even though we were celebrating our engagement, Duke was never going to let friends walk away without knowing they were welcome.

"We already ate, but congratulations," Reece said, meeting my gaze. "I'll be sure to check the group chat later," he added dryly.

"And just for that I'm adding you to another one. But I'm not going to tell you when. You'll be surprised." I beamed, and he snorted. And as we said our goodbyes, Reece wrapped his arm around Anya's waist, and the two walked away, looking just as in love as ever.

Reece was a few years older than me and had been in the business longer than most of the people on staff, and I was grateful that he was around. Mostly because it was fun to tease him and his taciturn ways, and because he never complained about the youths, as some other older people in our company often did.

"I hope it was okay that I invited them to dinner. I just know there're no more reservations for the night."

I leaned over and kissed Duke softly on the mouth. "I'm glad you did. I would've too honestly. This place has great food, and they're good people."

"You know, I was jealous of him when I first met him."

I nearly choked on the wine that the waiter had brought. "What? Why?"

"Because he's this ruggedly handsome guy who can lift most anything at a construction site and is overprotective with everyone that he works with. I don't know, I just got jealous."

"I should feel flattered about that, right?" I asked, confused.

"Maybe. Or maybe I was just a little insecure when we first met."

"You have nothing to be insecure about. We're getting married. And I can't wait. Reece is...well, he's way older than me so I never thought of him that way. You know?" Not quite a lie. A girl could fantasize, but Reece wasn't in the age range I dated so it wasn't a problem. And the old man would never think of me that way. I held back a grin at calling him an old man and knew I'd have to do it in person later.

Duke leaned forward, kissing me again. "And I can't wait either."

BY THE END of the night, I was exhausted, rung out by one of the best evenings of my life, and had slept through my alarm the next morning. Duke had left, leaving behind a little note on my pillow. Just a Post-it, a J with a heart next to it. I kissed the note softly and set it on my vanity next to his other sticky notes. He was always doing that, leaving me little notes. And one day I was going to collect them all and make some form of art project with it. More than likely I would ask Riley to help. She was far better at that than I was.

I sent him a quick text to tell him good morning and I loved him and got on my exercise bike to work off any extra energy.

Today my mom and the girls were coming over and we were going to start wedding planning. And I would also invite Duke's sister and mother for next time. Today though, was just family. And I couldn't wait for Duke's family to be mine.

After my workout was finished, I showered and made my way to the kitchen to have an afternoon coffee and lunch. My timing was a little off for the day, and I was glad I didn't have to work. I had been out far too late with Duke, but it was the start of our new lives and I was so freaking blessed. My doorbell rang at that moment, and I skipped over to it, wondering if my mom was early.

"Chelsea, it's good to see you," I said as I wrapped my arms around Duke's sister. She didn't hug me back, but then again, I was a little more exuberant than her.

"I'm so excited about the engagement, aren't you? I mean, we're going to be sisters," I said, practically dancing on my toes.

That's when I finally noticed that Chelsea hadn't spoken. Hadn't said a single word.

Instead I looked at her puffy eyes, the way that she stood there, her skin gray, and my smile fell.

"What's wrong, Chelsea? Is it your mom? Is it Duke?" I asked.

But if it was Duke, I would know. After all, I was his fiancée. Somebody would've called me if something was wrong. His sister wouldn't just be at my door. Maybe she didn't want the wedding to happen. Oh God. Was this going to be one of those times where Duke's family finally told me what they truly thought about me, and want me to break up with him?

My chest tightened, and I watched as Chelsea's lips thinned before she let out a breath.

"He's... He's gone, Brooklyn," Chelsea croaked.

I tilted my head, an odd buzzing sound filling my ears.

"What? Who's gone? Come in and sit down, Chelsea. You're scaring me. Let me get you some water."

But Chelsea flinched as I reached out to her, and I stopped moving.

"Chelsea? Who's gone?" I asked, the urgency in my tone frantic.

"Duke. He's dead, Brooklyn. Duke's dead."

And I have no idea what she said after that, or even what I did. Because I stood there, the sun glinting off the diamond in my engagement ring, and I watched as the world fell around me.

This was supposed to be my happy ever after. This was supposed to be our everything.

Because there was no way the love of my life was dead.

And it wasn't until pain radiated up my knees, that I realized that the screaming I heard was me.

And there would be no coming back from this.

Ever.

Next in the Montgomery Ink Legacy series: Brooklyn gets her HEA in Kiss Me Forever

IF YOU'D LIKE TO READ A BONUS SCENE:
CHECK OUT THIS SPECIAL EPILOGUE!

A Note from Carrie Ann Ryan

Thank you so much for reading **LAST CHANCE SEDUCTION.**

I had an idea for Lex and Mercy years ago but I knew it wasn't the right time yet. I had to let them percolate in the back of my mind until I was ready for them. And I am SO HAPPY I finally got to write their story.

And yes...the snake story happened to me.

But I was not saved by a hot Montgomery.

This does remind me to rebuild my cats a catio however at the new house!

Next up we're staying with the Construction crew with Brooklyn and Reece in Kiss Me Forever. I have a few surprises planned and I cannot WAIT to tell you more.

And while we're here...Jamie is heading up to

Wyoming to get her own story in Accidental Runaway Groom. ALL THE THINGS ARE HAPPENING!

Loved this dynamic? Read the first chapter of this second chance, small town, contemporary suspense romance: **The Forever Rule.**

The Montgomery Ink Legacy Series:
Book 1: Bittersweet Promises (Leif & Brooke)
Book 2: At First Meet (Nick & Lake)
Book 2.5: Happily Ever Never (May & Leo)
Book 3: Longtime Crush (Sebastian & Raven)
Book 4: Best Friend Temptation (Noah, Ford, and Greer)
Book 4.5: Happily Ever Maybe (Jennifer & Gus)
Book 5: Last First Kiss (Daisy & Hugh)
Book 6: His Second Chance (Kane & Phoebe)
Book 7: One Night with You (Kingston & Claire)
Book 8: Accidentally Forever (Crew & Aria)
Book 9: Last Chance Seduction (Lexington & Mercy)
Book 10: Kiss Me Forever (Brooklyn & Reece)

Next in the Montgomery Ink Legacy series:

Brooklyn gets her HEA in Kiss Me Forever

**IF YOU'D LIKE TO READ A BONUS SCENE:
CHECK OUT THIS SPECIAL EPILOGUE!**

If you want to make sure you know what's coming next from me, you can sign up for my newsletter at www.CarrieAnnRyan.com; follow me on twitter at @CarrieAnnRyan, or like my Facebook page. I also have a Facebook Fan Club where we have trivia, chats, and other goodies. You guys are the reason I get to do what I do and I thank you.

Make sure you're signed up for my MAILING LIST so you can know when the next releases are available as well as find giveaways and FREE READS.

Happy Reading!

From The Forever Rule
Aston

The Cages are the most prestigious family in Denver—at least according to the patriarch of the Cage Family.

And the Cages have rules.

Rules only they know.

I always knew that one day my father would die. I hadn't realized that day would come so soon. Or that the last words I would say to him would've been in anger.

I had been having one of the best nights of my life, a beautiful woman in my arms, and a smile on my face when I received the phone call that had changed my family's life.

The fact that I had been smiling had been a shock,

because according to my brothers, I didn't smile much. I was far too busy being *The Cage* of Cage Enterprises.

We were a dominant force in the city of Denver when it came to certain real estate ventures, as well as being one of the only ethical and environmentally friendly ones who tried to keep up with that. We had our hands in countless different pots around the world, but mostly we gravitated in the state of Colorado—our home.

I had not created the company, no, that honor had gone to my grandfather, and then my father. The Cage Enterprises were and would always be a family endeavor. And when my father had stepped away a few years ago, stating he had wanted to see the world, and also see if his sons could actually take up the mantle, I had stepped in—not that the man believed we could.

My brothers were in various roles within the company, at least those who had wanted to be part of it. But I was the face of Cage Enterprises.

So no, I hadn't smiled often. There wasn't time. We weren't billionaires with mega yachts. We worked seventy-hour weeks to make sure *all* our employees had a livable wage while wining and dining with those who looked down at us for not being on their level. And others thought we were the high and mighty anyway since they didn't understand us. So, I didn't smile.

But I had smiled that night.

It had been a gala for some charity, one I couldn't even remember off the top of my head. We had donated between the company and my own finances—we always did. But I couldn't even remember anything about why we were there.

Yet I could remember her smile. The heat in her eyes when she had looked up at me, the feel of her body pressed against mine as we had danced along the dance floor, and then when we ended up in the hallway, bodies pressed against one another, needing each other, wanting each other.

And I had put aside all my usual concepts of business and life to have this woman in my arms.

And then my mother had called and had shattered that illusion.

"Your father is dead."

She hadn't even braced me for the blow. A heart attack on a vacation on a beach in Majorca, and he was dead. She hadn't cried, hadn't said anything, just told me that I had to be the one to tell my brothers.

And so, I had, all six of them. Because of course Loren Cage would have seven sons. He couldn't do things just once, he had to make sure he left his legacy, his destiny.

And that was why we were here today, in a high-rise

in Centennial, waiting on my father's lawyer to show up with the reading of the will.

"Hey, when is Winstone going to get here?" Dorian asked, his typical high energy playing on his face, and how he tapped his fingers along the hand-carved wooden table.

I stared at my brother, at those piercing blue eyes that matched my own, and frowned. He should be here soon. He did call us all here after all."

"I still don't know why we all had to be here for the reading of the will," Hudson whispered as he stared off into the distance. Neither Dorian nor Hudson worked for Cage Enterprises. They had stock with the company, and a few other connections because that's what family did, but they didn't work on the same floors as some of us and hadn't been elbow to elbow with our father before he had retired. Though dear old dad had worked in our small town more often than not in the end. In fact, Hudson didn't even live in Denver anymore. He had moved to the town we owned in the mountains.

Because of course we Cages owned a damned town. Part of me wasn't sure if the concept of having our name on everything within the town had been on purpose or had occurred organically. Though knowing my grandfather, perhaps it had been exactly what he'd wanted. He had bought up a few buildings, built a few more, and now we owned three-quarters of the town, including the major resort which brought in tourists and income.

And that was why we were here.

"You have to be here because you're evidently in the will," I said softly, trying not to get annoyed that we were waiting for our father's lawyer. Again.

"You would think he would be able to just send us a memo. I mean, it should be clear right? We all know what stakes we have in, we should just be able to do things evenly," Theo said, his gaze off into the distance. My younger brother also didn't work for the company, instead he had decided to go to culinary school, something my father had hated. But you couldn't control a Cage, that was sort of our deal.

"Why would you be cut out of the will?" I asked, honestly curious.

"Because I married a man and a woman," he drawled out. "You know he hasn't spoken to me since before the wedding," Ford said, and I saw the hurt in his gaze even though I knew he was probably trying to hide it.

"Well, he was an asshole, what do you expect?" James asked.

I looked behind Ford to see my brother and co-chair of Cage Enterprises standing with his hands in his pockets, staring out the window.

With Flynn, our vice president, standing beside him, they looked like the heads of businesses they were. While they wore suits and so did I, we were the only ones.

Dorian and Hudson were both in jeans, Hudson's having a hole at the knee. And probably not as a fashion statement, most likely because it had torn at some point, and he hadn't bothered to buy another pair. Theo was in slacks, but a Henley with his sleeves pushed up, tapping his finger just like Hudson, clearly wanting to get out of here as well. Ford had on cargo pants, and a tight black T-shirt, and looked like he had just gotten off his shift. He owned a security company with his husband and a few other friends, and did security for the Cages when he could, though I knew he didn't like to work with family often. And I knew it wasn't because of us. No, it was Father—even if he had officially *retired*. It was always Father.

And he was gone.

"Can't believe the asshole's gone," I whispered.

Ford's brows rose. "Look at that, you calling him an asshole. I'm proud."

"You should show him respect," Mother said as she came inside the room, her high heels tapping against the marble floors. I didn't bother standing up like I normally would have, because Melanie Cage looked to be in a *mood*.

She didn't look sad that Dad was gone, more like angry that he would dare go against their plans. What plans? I didn't know, but that was my mother.

She came right up to Dorian and leaned down to kiss his cheek. She didn't even bother to look at the rest of us. Dorian was Mother's favorite. Which I knew Dorian resented, but I didn't have to deal with mommy issues at this moment.

No, we had to deal with father issues at this point.

"I'm going to go get him," Flynn replied, turning toward the door. "I'm really not in the mood to wait any longer, especially since he's being so secretive about this meeting."

As I had been thinking just the same, I nodded at Flynn though he didn't need my permission. However, just then, the door opened, and I frowned when it wasn't just Mr. Winstone walking into the conference room.

I stared as an older woman walked through the door following Mr. Winstone, and four women and another man with messy hair and tattered cut-up jeans that matched Hudson's walked behind them.

The guy looked familiar, as if I'd seen him somewhere, or maybe it was just his eyes.

Where had I seen those eyes before?

"Phoebe? What are you doing here?" Ford asked as he moved forward and gripped the hands of one of the women.

"I was going to ask the same question," Phoebe asked as she looked at Ford, then around the room.

Those of us sitting stood up, confused about why this other family—because they were clearly a family—had decided to enter the room.

"We're here to meet the lawyer about my father's death, Ford. Why would you and the Cages be here?" she asked, and I wondered how the hell Mr. Winstone had fucked up so badly? Why the hell was he letting another family that clearly seemed to be in shock come into our room? This wasn't how he normally handled things.

Ford was the one who answered though—thankfully—because I had no idea what the hell was going on.

"Phoebe, we're here for my dad's will reading. What the hell is going on?" he asked. Phoebe looked around, as well as the others.

I stared at them, at the tall willowy one with wide eyes, at the smaller one with tears still in her eyes as if she was the only one truly mourning, and at the woman who seemed to be in charge, not the mother. Instead she had shrewd eyes and was glaring at all of us. The man stood back, hands in pockets, and looked just as shell-shocked as Ford.

But before Mr. Winstone or anyone else could say anything, my mother spoke in such a crisp, icy tone that I froze.

"I don't know why you're acting so dramatic. You knew your father was an asshole. He just liked creating drama," she snapped.

As I tried to catch up with her words, the older woman answered. "Melanie, stop."

This couldn't be happening. Because things started to click into place. The fact that the man at the other end of this table had our eyes, and that everybody looked so fucking shocked. I didn't know how Ford knew this Phoebe, and I would be getting answers.

"We had a deal," my mother continued, as it seemed that the rest of us were just now catching on. "You would keep your family away from mine. We would share Loren, but I got the name, I got the family. You got whatever else. But now it looks like Loren decided to be an asshole again."

"What are you talking about?" the shrewd sister asked as she came forward, her hands fisted at her side.

"Excuse me," I said, clearing my throat. I was going to be damned if I let anyone else handle this meeting. I was The Cage now. "Will someone please explain?"

"Well, I wasn't quite sure how this was going to work out," Mr. Winstone began, and we all quieted, while I wanted to strangle the man. What did he mean how *the hell this would work out*? What was this?

This seemed like a big fucking mistake.

"Loren Cage had certain provisions in his will for both of his families. And one of the many requirements that I will go over today is that this meeting must take place." He paused and I hoped it wasn't for effect, because I was going to throttle him if it was. "Loren Cage had two families. Seven sons with his wife Melanie, and four daughters and a son with his mistress, Constance."

"We went by partner," the other mother corrected.

I blinked, counting the adults in the room. "Twelve?" I asked, my voice slightly high-pitched.

"Busy fucking man," Dorian whispered.

Hudson snorted, while we just stood and stared at each other.

This could not be happening. A secret family? No, we were not that cliché.

"I can't do this," Phoebe blurted, her eyes wide.

"Oh, stop overreacting," my mother scorned.

"Do not talk to my daughter that way." The other mother glared.

"It was always going to be an issue," Mother continued. "All the secrets and the lies. And now the kids will have to deal with it. Because God forbid Loren ever deal with anything other than his own dick."

"That's enough," I snapped.

"Don't you dare talk to us like that," the shrewd sister snapped right back.

"I will talk however I damn well please. I am going to need to know exactly how this happened," I shouted over everyone else's words.

Out of the corner of my eye I saw Phoebe run through the door. Ford followed and then the tall willowy one joined.

"Shit," I snapped.

"Language," Mother bit out.

I laughed. "Really? You are going to talk to me about language."

I looked over at James, who shrugged, before he put two fingers in his mouth and whistled that high-pitched whistle that only he could do.

Everyone froze as Theo rubbed his ear and glared at me.

"Winstone," I said through gritted teeth. "I take it we all have to be here in order for this to happen?"

He cleared his throat. "At least a majority. But you all had to at least step into the room."

"Excuse me then," I said.

"You're just going to leave? Just like that?" my mother asked.

I whirled on her. "I'm going to go see if my apparent *family* is okay. Then I'm going to come back and we're going to get answers. Because there is no way that I'm going to leave here without them."

I stormed out the door, and thankfully nobody followed me.

Of course, though, I shouldn't have been too swift with that, as the woman who had to be the eldest sister practically ran to my side, her heels tapping against the marble.

"I'm coming with you."

"That's just fine." I paused, knowing that I wasn't angry at these people. No, my father and apparently our mothers were the ones that had to deal with this. I looked over at the woman who Mr. Winstone and the mothers had claimed was my sister and cleared my throat.

"I'm Aston."

"Is this really the time for introductions?" she asked.

"I'm about to go see your sister and my brother to make sure that they're fine, so sure. I would like to know the name of the woman that is running next to me right now."

"I'm running, you're walking quickly because you have such long legs."

I snorted, surprised I could even do that.

"I'm Isabella," she replied after a moment.

"I would say nice to meet you Isabella..." I let my voice trail off.

She let out a sharp laugh before shaking her head. "I'm going to need a moment to wrap my head around this, but not now."

"Same."

We stormed out of the building, and I lagged behind since Ford was standing in front of Phoebe who was in the arms of another man with dark hair and everybody seemed to be talking all at once.

"I just. I can't deal with this right now," Phoebe said, and I realized that something else must have been going on with her right then. She looked tired, and far more emotional than the rest of us.

I looked over at the man holding her and blinked. "Kane?" I asked.

Kane stared at me and let out a breath. "Wow," he said with a laugh.

"We'll handle it," Isabella put in, completely ignoring us. "And if we need to meet again later, we will." Then she looked over at Ford and I, with such menace in her gaze, I nearly took a step back. "Is that a problem?"

I raised my chin, glaring right back at her. "Not at all. However I want answers, so I'd rather not have the meeting canceled right now. But I'm also not going to force any of my," I paused, realization hitting far too hard, "*family* to stay if they don't want to."

And with that, I turned on my heel and went back into the building, with Isabella and Ford following me. Everyone was still yelling in the interim, and I cleared my throat. As Isabella had done it at the same time, everyone paused to look at me.

"Read the damn will. Because we need answers," I ordered Winstone, and he shook like a leaf before nodding.

"Okay. We can do that." He cleared his throat, then he began going over trusts and incomes and buildings and things that I would care about soon, but what I wanted to know was what the hell our father had been thinking about.

"Here's the tricky part," Winstone began, as we all leaned forward, eager to hear what the hell he had to say.

"The family money, not of the business, not of each of your inheritance from other family members, but the bulk of Loren Cage's assets will be split between all twelve kids."

"Are you kidding me?" Isabella asked. "What money? We weren't exactly poor, but we were solidly middle class."

"We did just fine," the other mother pleaded.

My mother snorted, clearly not believing the words.

I glared at the woman who raised me, willing her to say *anything*. She would probably be pushed out of the window at that point. Not by me, by someone else, but she probably would've earned it.

The lawyer continued. "However to retain the majority of current assets and to keep Cage Lake and all of its subsidiaries you will have to meet as a family once a month for three years. If this does not happen, Cage Enterprises will be broken into multiple parts and sold." He went on into the legalese that I ignored as I tried to hear over the blood pounding in my ears.

"You own a town?" the other man asked.

I looked over at the one man in the room I didn't know the name of. "Not exactly."

"Kyler," Isabella whispered.

In that moment, I realized that I had a brother named Kyler—if this was all to be believed.

"This can't be legal right?" the tall willowy person said.

"Yes Sophia, it can," their mother put in.

Oh good, another sister named Sophia.

Only one name to go. What the hell was wrong with me?

I forced my jaw to relax. "Are you telling us that we need to have all twelve of us at dinner once a month for three years in order to keep what is rightly inherited to us? To keep people in business and keep their jobs?"

"We don't need the money, but everyone else in our employ does," James snapped. "As do those we work with."

"Damn straight," Dorian growled.

"How are we supposed to believe this?" I asked, asking the obvious question.

"First, only five must attend, and two must be of a different family." The lawyer continued as if I hadn't spoken. "Of course you are *all* family..."

"Again, how are we supposed to believe this?" I asked.

"Here are the DNA tests already done."

"Are you fucking kidding me?" Isabella asked.

I looked at her, as she had literally taken the words out of my mouth.

"Isn't that sort of like a violation?" Kyler asked, his face pale.

"We need to get our own lawyers on this," James whispered.

I nodded tightly, knowing we had much more to say on this.

"There's no way this is legal," the youngest said, and I looked over at her.

"What's your name?" I asked.

"Emily. Emily Cage Dixon," she said softly, and we all froze.

"Your middle name is Cage?" I asked, biting out the words.

"All of our middle names are Cage," Sophia said, shaking her head. "I hated it but Dad wanted to be cute because our father's name was Cage Dixon, or maybe it wasn't. Is he also a bigamist?" she asked.

Her mother lifted her chin. "We never married. And no, your father's name was not Dixon, that was my maiden name."

"What?" Sophia asked. "All this time...are our grandparents even dead?"

"Yes, my parents are dead. The same with Loren's." The other mother's eyes filled with tears. "I'm sorry we lied."

"We'll get to that later," Isabella put in, and I was grateful.

I let out a breath. "In order to keep our assets, in

order to keep the family name intact, we need to have *dinner*. For three years."

The small lawyer nodded, his glasses falling down his nose. "At least five of you. And it can start three months after the funeral, which we can plan after this."

"This is ridiculous," Hudson murmured under his breath, before he got up and walked out.

I watched him go, knowing he had his own demons, and tried to understand what the hell was going on. "Why did he do this?" I asked, more to myself than anyone else.

"I never really knew the man, but apparently none of us did," Isabella said, staring off into the distance.

"Leave the paperwork and go," I ordered Winstone, and he didn't even mutter a peep. Instead, he practically ran out of the room. James and Flynn immediately went to the paperwork, and I knew they were scouring it. But from the way that their jaws tightened, I had a feeling that my father had found a way to make this legal. Because we would always have a choice to lose everything. That was the man.

"It's true," my mother put in. "You all share the same father. That was the deal when we got married, and when he decided to bring this other woman into our lives."

"I'm pretty sure you were the other woman," the other mom said.

I pinched the bridge of my nose.

"Stop. All of you." I stared at the group and realized that I was probably the eldest Cage here, other than the moms. I would deal with this. We didn't have a choice. "Whatever happens, we'll deal with it."

"You're in charge now?" Isabella asked, but Sophia shushed her.

I was grateful for that, because I had a feeling Isabella and I were going to butt heads more often than not.

I shrugged, trying to act as if my world hadn't been rocked. "I would say welcome to the Cages, because DNA evidence seems to point that way, however perhaps you were already one of us all along."

Kyler muttered something under his breath I couldn't hear before speaking up. "You have my eyes," he said.

I nodded. "Noticed that too."

The other man tilted his head. "So what, we do dinners and we make nice?"

I sighed. "We don't have to be adversaries."

"You say that as if you're the one in charge," Isabella said again.

"Because he is," Theo said, and they all stared at him.

I tried to tamp down the pride swelling at those words—along with the overwhelming pressure.

Theo continued. "He's the eldest. He's the one that takes care of us. And he's the CEO of Cage Enterprises. He's going to be the one that deals with the paperwork fallout."

"Because family is just paperwork?" Emily asked, her voice lost.

I shook my head. "No, family is insane, and apparently, it's been secret all along. And it looks like we have a few introductions to make, and a few tests to redo. But if it turns out it's true, we're Cages, and we don't back down."

"And what does that mean?" Isabella asked, her tone far too careful.

Theo was the one who finally answered. "It means we're going to have to figure shit out."

And for just an instant, the thought of that beautiful woman with that gorgeous smile came to mind, and I pushed those thoughts away. My family was breaking, or perhaps breaking open. And I didn't have time to worry about things like a woman who had made me smile.

The Cages needed me and after today's meeting there would be no going back to sanity.

Carrie Ann Ryan

Ever.

**In the mood to read another family saga?
Meet the Cage Family in The Forever Rule!**

From One Way Back to Me
Eli

When my morning begins with me standing ankle-deep in a basement full of water, I know I probably should have stayed in bed. Only, I was the boss, and I didn't get that choice.

"Hold on. I'm looking for it." East cursed underneath his breath as my younger brother bent down around the pipe, trying his best to turn off the valve. I sighed, waded through the muck in my work boots, and moved to help him. "I said I've got it," East snapped, but I ignored him.

I narrowed my eyes at the evil pipe. "It's old and rusted, and even though it passed an inspection over a year ago, we knew this was going to be a problem."

"And I'm the fucking handyman of this company. I've got this."

"And as a handyman, you need a hand."

"You're hilarious. Seriously. I don't know how I could ever manage without your wit and humor." The dryness in his tone made my lips twitch even as I did my best to ignore the smell of whatever water we stood in.

"Fuck you," I growled.

"No thanks. I'm a little too busy for that."

With a grunt, East shut off the water, and we both stood back, hands on our hips as we stared at the mess of this basement.

East let out a sigh. "I'm not going to have to turn the water off for the whole property, but I'm glad that we don't have tenants in this particular cabin."

I nodded tightly and held back a sigh. "This is probably why there aren't basements in Texas. Because everything seems to go wrong in these things."

"I'm pretty sure this is a storm shelter, or at least a tornado one. Not quite sure as it's one of the only basements in the area."

"It was probably the only one that they had the energy to make back in the day. Considering this whole place is built over clay and limestone."

East nodded, looked around. "I'll start the cleanup

with this water, and we'll look to see what we can do with the pipes."

I pinched the bridge of my nose. "I don't want to have to replace the plumbing for this whole place."

"At least it's not the villa itself, or the farmhouse, or the winery. Just a single cabin."

I glared at my younger brother, then reached out and knocked on a wooden pillar. "Shut your mouth. Don't say things like that to me. We are just now getting our feet under us."

East shrugged. "It's the truth, though. However much you weigh it, it could have been worse."

I pinched the bridge of my nose. "Jesus Christ. You were in the military for how long? A Wilder your entire life, and you say things like that? When the hell did you lose that superstition bone?"

"About the time that my Humvee was blown up, and when Evan's was, Everett's too. Hell, about the time that you almost fell out of the sky in your plane. Or when Elliot was nearly shot to death trying to help one of his men. So, yes, I pretty much lost all superstition when trying to toe the line ended up in near death and maiming."

I met my brother's gaze, that familiar pang thinking about all that we had lost and almost lost over the past few years.

East muttered under his breath, shaking his head. "And I sound more and more like Evan these days rather than myself."

I squeezed his shoulder and let out a breath, thinking of our brother who grunted more than spoke these days. "It's okay. We've been through a lot. But we're here."

Somehow, we were here. I wasn't quite sure if we had made the right decision about two years ago when we had formed this plan, or rather *I* had formed this plan, but there was no going back. We were in it, and we were going to have to find a way to make it work, flooded former tornado shelters and all.

East sighed. "I'll work on this now. Then I'll head on over to the main house. I have a few things to work on there."

"You know, we can hire you help. I know we had all the contractors and everything to work with us for some of the rebuilds and rehabs, but we can hire someone else for you on a day-to-day basis."

My brother shook his head. "We may be able to afford it, but I'd rather save that for a rainy day. Because when it rains, it pours here, and flash flooding is a major threat in this part of Texas." He winked as he said it, mixing his metaphors, and I just shook my head.

"You just let me know if you need it."

"You're the CEO, brother of mine, not the CFO. That's Everett."

"True, but we did talk about it so we can work on it." I paused, thinking about what other expenses might show up. "And what do you need to do with the villa?"

The villa was the main house where most things happened on the property. It contained the lobby, library, and atrium. My apartment was also on the top floor, so I could be there for emergencies. Our innkeeper lived on the other side of the house, but I was in the main loft because this was my project, my baby.

My other brothers, all five of them, lived in cabins on the property. We lived together, worked together, ate together, and fought together. We were the Wilder brothers. It was what we did.

I had left to join the Air Force at seventeen, having graduated early, leaving behind my kid brothers and sister. After nearly twenty years of doing what we needed to in order to survive, we hadn't spent as much time with one another as I would have liked. We hadn't been stationed together, so we hadn't seen one another for longer than holidays or in passing.

But now we were together. At least most of us. So I was going to make this work, even if it killed me.

East finally answered my question. "I just have to fix

a door that's a little too squeaky in one of the guestrooms. Not a big deal."

I raised a brow. "That's it?"

"It's one of the many things on my list. Thankfully, this place is big enough that I always have something to do. It's an unending list. And that the winery has its own team to work on all of that shit, because I'm not in the mood to learn to deal with any of the complicated machinery that comes with that world."

I snorted. "Honestly, same. I'm glad there are people that know what the fuck they're doing when it comes to wine making so that didn't have to be the two of us."

I left my brother to this job, knowing he liked time on his own, just like the rest of us did, and went to dry my boots. I was working by myself for most of the day, in interviews and other "boss business," as Elliot called it, so I had to focus and get clean.

I wasn't in the mood to deal with interviews, but it was part of my job. We had to fill positions that hadn't been working out over the past year, some more than others.

Wilder Retreat was a place that hadn't been even a spark in my mind my entire life. No, I had been too busy being a career military man—getting in my twenty, moving up the ranks, and ending up as a Lieutenant Colonel before I got out. I had been a commander of a squadron, and yet, it felt like I didn't know how to command where I was now.

When my sister Eliza had lost her husband when he was on deployment, it had been the last domino to fall in the Wilder brothers' military career. I had been ready to get out with twenty years in, knowing I needed a career outside of being a Lieutenant Colonel. I wasn't even forty yet, and the term retirement was a misnomer, but that's what happened when it came to my former job.

East had been getting out around that time for reasons of his own, and then Evan had been forced to. I rubbed my hand over my chest, that familiar pain, remembering the phone call from one of Evan's commanders when Evan had been hurt.

I thought I'd lost my baby brother then, and we nearly had. Everett had gotten hurt too, and Elijah and Elliot had needed out for their own reasons. Losing our baby sister's husband had just pushed us forward.

Finding out that Eliza's husband had been a cheating asshole had just cemented the fact that we needed to spend more time together as a family so we could be there for one another.

In retrospect, it would have been nice if Eliza would have been able to come down to Texas with us, to our suburb outside of San Antonio. Only, she had fallen in love again, with a man with a big family and a good heart up in Fort Collins, Colorado. She was still up there and traveled down enough that we actually got to get to know our sister again.

It was weird to think that, after so many years of always seeing each other in passing or through video calls, most of us were here, opening up a business. And all because I had been losing my mind.

Wilder Retreat and Winery was a villa and wedding venue outside of San Antonio. We were in hill country, at least what passed for hill country in South Texas, and the place had been owned by a former Air Force General who had wanted to retire and sell the place, since his kid didn't want it.

It was a large spread that used to be a ranch back in the day, nearly one hundred acres that the original owners had taken from a working ranch, and instead of making it a dude ranch or something similar, like others did around here, they'd added a winery using local help. We were close enough to Fredericksburg that it made sense in terms of the soil and weather. They had been able to add on additions, so it wasn't just the winery. Someone could come for the day for a winery tour or even a retreat tour, but most people came for the weekend or for a whole week. There were cabins and a farmhouse where we held weddings, dances, or other events. We had some chickens and ducks that gave us eggs, and goats that seemed to have a mind of their own and provided milk for cheese. Then there was the main annex, which housed all the equipment for the retreat villa.

The winery had its own section of buildings, and it was far bigger than anything I would have ever thought that we could handle. But, between the six of us, we did.

And the only reason we could even afford it, because one didn't afford something like this on a military salary, even with a decent retirement plan, was because of our uncles.

Our uncles, Edward and Edmond Wilder, had owned Wilder Wines down in Napa, California, for years. They had done well for themselves, and when we had been kids, we had gone out to visit. Evan had been the one that had clung to it and had been interested in wine making before he had changed his mind and gone into the military like the rest of us.

That was why Evan was in charge of the winery itself now. Because he knew what he was doing, even if he'd growled and said he didn't. Either way though, the place was huge, had multiple working parts at all times, and we had a staff that needed us. But when the uncles had died, they had left the money from the sale of the winery to us in equal parts. Eliza had taken hers to invest for her future children, and the rest of us had pooled our money together to buy this place and make it ours. A lot of the staff from the old owner had stayed, but some had left as well. Because they didn't want new owners who had no idea what they were doing, or they just retired. Either way, we were over a year in and doing okay.

Except for two positions that made me want to groan.

I had an interview with who would be our third wedding planner since we started this. The main component of the retreat was to have an actual wedding venue. To be able to host parties, and not just wine tours. Elliot was our major event planner that helped with our yearly and seasonal minute details, but he didn't want anything to do with the actual weddings. That was a whole other skill set, and so we wanted a wedding planner. We had gone through two wedding planners now, and we needed to hire a third. The first one had lied on her résumé, had given references that were her friends who had lied and had even created websites that were all fabrication, all so she could get into the business. Which, I understood, getting into the business is one thing. However, lying was another. Plus, we needed someone with actual experience because we didn't have any ourselves. We were going out on a limb here with this whole retreat business, and it was all because I had the harebrained idea of getting our family to work together, get along, and get to know one another. I wanted us to have a future, to be our own bosses.

And it was so far over my head that I knew that if I didn't get reliable help, we were going to fail.

Later, I had a meeting with that potential wedding planner. But first, I had to see what the fuck that smell was coming from the main kitchen in the villa.

The second wedding planner we hired was a guy with great and *true* references, one who was good at his job but hated everything to do with my brothers and me. He had hated the idea of the retreat and how rustic it was, even though we were in fucking South Texas. Yes, the buildings look slightly European because that was the theme that the original owners had gone for. Still, the guy had hated us, hadn't listened to us, and had called us white trash before he had walked away, jumped into his convertible, and sped off down the road, leaving us without help. He had been rude to our guests, and now Elliot was the one having to plan weddings for the past three weeks. My brother was going to strangle me soon if we didn't hire someone. And this person was going to be our last hope. As soon as she showed up, that was.

I looked down on my watch and tried to plan the rest of my day. I had thirty minutes to figure out what the hell was going on in the kitchen, and then I had to go to the meeting.

I nodded at a few guests who were sipping wine and eating a cheese plate and then at our innkeeper, Naomi. Naomi's honey-brown hair was cut in an angled bob that lit her face, and she grinned at me.

"Hello there, Boss Man," she whispered. "You might need to go to the kitchen."

"Do I want to know?" I asked with a grumble.

"I'm not sure. But I am going to go check in our next guest, and then Elliott needs to meet with the Henderson couple."

"He'll be there." I didn't say that Elliot would rather chew off his own arm rather than deal with this, considering we had a family event coming in, one that Elliot was on target with planning. The wedding for next year was an important one, so we needed to work on it.

Naomi was a fantastic innkeeper, far more organized than any of us—and that was saying something since my brothers and I knew our way around schedules, to-do lists, and spreadsheets. Naomi was personable, smiled, and kept us on our toes.

Without her, I knew we wouldn't be able to do this. Hell, without Amos, our vineyard manager, I knew that Evan and Elijah wouldn't be able to handle the winery as they did. Naomi and Amos had come with the place when we had bought it, and I would be forever grateful that they had decided to stay on.

I gave Naomi another nod, then headed back to the kitchen and nearly walked right back out.

Tony stood there, a scowl on his face and his hands on his hips. "I don't understand what the fuck is wrong with this oven."

"What's going on?" I asked as Everett stood by Tony. Everett was my quiet brother with usually a small smile on his face, only right then it looked like he was ready to scream.

I didn't know why Everett was even there since he was part responsible for the financials side of the company and usually worked with Elliot these days. Maybe he had come to the kitchen after the smell of burning as I had after Naomi's prodding.

Tony threw his hands in the air. "What's going on? This stove is a piece of shit. All of it is a piece of shit. I'm tired of this rustic place. I thought I would be coming to a Michelin star restaurant. To be my own chef. Instead, I have to make English breakfasts and pancakes with bananas. I might as well be at a bed and breakfast."

I pinched the bridge of my nose. "We're an inn, not a bed and breakfast."

"But I serve breakfast. That's all I do these days.

That and cheese platters. Nobody comes for dinner. Nobody comes for lunch."

That was a lie. Tony worked for the winery and the retreat itself and served all the meals. But Tony wanted to go crazy with the menu, to try new and fantastical items that just weren't going to work here.

And I had a feeling I was going to throw up if I wasn't careful.

"I quit," Tony snapped, and I knew right then, it was done for. I was done.

"You can't quit," I growled while Everett held back a sigh.

"Yes, I can. I'm done. I'm done with you and this ranch. You're not cowboys. You're not even Texans. You're just people moving in on our territory." And with that, Tony stomped away, throwing his chef's apron on the ground.

I was thankful that the kitchen was on the other side of the library and front area, where most of the guests were if they weren't out on one of the tours of the area and city that Elliott had arranged for them. That was the whole point of this retreat. They could come visit, and could relax, or we could set them up on a tour of downtown San Antonio, or Canyon Lake, or any of the other places that were nearby.

And yet, Tony had just thrown a wrench into all of

that. I didn't know what was worse, the smell of burning, Tony leaving, the water in the basement that wasn't truly a basement, or the fact that I was going to smell like charred food and wet jeans when I went to go meet this wedding planner.

"You're going to need to hire a new cook," Everett whispered.

I looked at my brother, at the man who did his best to make sure we didn't go bankrupt, and I wanted to just grumble. "I figured."

"I can help for now, but you know I'm only part-time. I can't stay away from my twins for too long," Sandy said as she came forward to take the pan off the stove. "I wish I could do full time, but this is all I can do for now."

Sandy had come back from maternity leave after we had already opened the retreat. She had been on with the former owners and was brilliant. But she had a right to be a mom and not want to work full time. I understood that, and I knew that Sandy didn't want to handle a whole kitchen by herself. She liked her position as a sous chef.

I was going to have to figure out what to do. Again.

"I'll get it done," I said while rubbing my temples.

"You know what we need to do," Everett whispered, and I shook my head.

"He'll kill us."

"Maybe, but it'll be worth it in the end. And speaking of, don't you have that interview soon? Or do you want me to take it?" His gaze tracked to my jeans.

I shook my head. "No, help Sandy."

Everett winced. "Just because I know how to slice an onion, it doesn't mean I'm good at cooking."

"I'm sorry, did you just say you could slice an onion? Get to it," Sandy put in with a smile, pointing at the sink. "Wash those hands."

"I cannot believe I just said that out loud. I just stepped right into it," Everett said with a sigh. "Go to the interview. You know what to ask."

"I do. And I hope we don't get screwed this time."

"You know, if we're lucky, we'll get someone as good as Roy's wedding planner, or at least that woman that we met. You know who she is." Everett grinned like a cat with the canary.

I narrowed my eyes. "Don't bring her up."

"Oh, I can't help it. A single dance, and you were drawn to her."

"What dance? You know what? No, I don't have time. We have to work on lunch and dinner. Tell me while you work," Sandy added with a wink.

Everett leaned toward her as he washed his hands.

"Well, you see, there was this dance, and he met the perfect woman, and then she got engaged."

Sandy's eyes widened. "Engaged? How did that happen? She was dating someone else?" she asked as she looked at me.

I pinched the bridge of my nose. "It was at Roy's place when we were looking at the venue to see if we wanted to buy the retreat here." I sighed, I knew if I just let it all out, she would move on from this conversation, and I would never have to deal with it again. "Somehow, I ended up at a wedding there, caught the garter. This woman caught the bouquet, and she happened to be the wedding planner. We danced, we laughed, and as she walked away, her boyfriend got down on one knee and proposed."

"No way!" She leaned forward with a fierce look on her face, her eyes bright. "What did she say?"

"I have no clue. I left." I ignored whatever feeling might want to show up at that thought. Everett gave me a glance, and I shook my head. "Enough of that. Yes, the wedding that she did was great, but I honestly have no idea who she is, and she has a job. She doesn't need to work here." And I didn't know what I would do if I saw her again or had to work with her. There had been such an intense connection that I knew it would be awkward as hell. But thankfully, she had her own business and wasn't going to come to the Wilder Retreat for a job.

I left Sandy and Everett on their own, knowing that they were capable, at least for now. And I knew who we would have to hire if she said yes, and if my other brother didn't kill me first.

I washed my hands in the sink on the way out, grateful that at least I looked somewhat decent, if not a little disheveled, and made my way out front, hoping that the wedding planner who came in through the doors would be the one that would stick. Because we needed some good luck. After the day we've had, we needed some good luck.

I turned the corner and nearly tripped over my feet.

Because, of course, fate was this way.

It was her.

Of all the wedding planners from all the wedding venues, it was her.

In the mood to read another family saga? Meet the Wilder Brothers in One Way Back to Me!

Acknowledgments

I've been at this writing gig of mine for nearly fifteen years and the team and circle that has helped make this happen has grown and ebbed over time.

No matter what, though, I know I could not have written this book without my team.

Thank you Brandi for not only digging into whatever was going on in Lex's head, but for keeping the series on target when I kept wondering what the Montgomerys were up to. Also...Its true, its true! And the other thing is, my sister had a baby...*cue weeping*

Ann - you are a powerhouse. I know that no matter how far fetched my ideas are, you'll be right there to make sure I find my path. Thank you for being the best team leader out there!

LB - You've now been with me long enough to read my mind. I am so sorry for that. But THANK YOU for all you do. I am literally in awe of your work and I'm so grateful for you!

Brianna, Classy, Ashley - Y'all are the dream team!

Thank you for taking on so much labor so I can do something called writing. After so many years, learning to give up control on a few things and actually finding people I can trust to keep the boat stead is phenomenal. I adore all of you and your talent!

Jenn, Emily, Tina - The Group Chat will always be my rock and I am so freaking happy to know you. Thank you for keeping me on target and not totally laughing at me as I try to write from my garden since apparently I've gone full Millennial Cottage Core with my gardening!

JoJo - I am so grateful for you, my friend. We're a community where, no matter the darkness, and I know that I am in safe hands here with you.

The Ryan Family - Y'all deal with so much with my life and career and I'm so happy I'm close by. Yes...you forced me to move to this state, but I know that I'm loved and cared for because you are here! Thank you for helping me stay on target with this book!

Sarah - Our spreadsheet knows no bounds. THANK YOU for making sure the audio for this book is AMAZING. I couldn't do this without you!

Lasheera - THANK YOU for getting this book into the hands of people who care for it! I am so grateful!

Lilly, Fedora, Brandi, and Britt - THANK YOU so much for you hard work on this project! I know my calendar is scary, but we're in this together. And please know I wrote this entire thing AFTER you edited... hence the typos and lack of punctuation.

And thank you THANK YOU to my dear readers. I met the Montgomerys over eleven years ago and I am forever grateful that you came along with me on this journey. We aren't leaving the Montgomery world any time soon and I am so happy you are here!

~

Carrie Ann

Also from Carrie Ann Ryan

The Montgomery Ink Legacy Series:
Book 1: Bittersweet Promises (Leif & Brooke)
Book 2: At First Meet (Nick & Lake)
Book 2.5: Happily Ever Never (May & Leo)
Book 3: Longtime Crush (Sebastian & Raven)
Book 4: Best Friend Temptation (Noah, Ford, and Greer)
Book 4.5: Happily Ever Maybe (Jennifer & Gus)
Book 5: Last First Kiss (Daisy & Hugh)
Book 6: His Second Chance (Kane & Phoebe)
Book 7: One Night with You (Kingston & Claire)
Book 8: Accidentally Forever (Crew & Aria)
Book 9: Last Chance Seduction (Lexington & Mercy)
Book 10: Kiss Me Forever (???? & ????)

Also from Carrie Ann Ryan

The Cage Family

Book 1: The Forever Rule (Aston & Blakely)
Book 2: An Unexpected Everything (Isabella & Weston)
Book 3: If You Were Mine (Dorian & Harper)
Book 4: One Quick Obsession (???? & ???)

Ashford Creek

Book 1: Legacy (Callum & Felicity)
Book 2: Crossroads (??? & ???)

Clover Lake

Book 1: Always a Fake Bridesmaid (Livvy & Ewan)
Book 2: Accidental Runaway Groom (??? & ???)

The Wilder Brothers Series:

Book 1: One Way Back to Me (Eli & Alexis)
Book 2: Always the One for Me (Evan & Kendall)
Book 3: The Path to You (Everett & Bethany)
Book 4: Coming Home for Us (Elijah & Maddie)
Book 5: Stay Here With Me (East & Lark)
Book 6: Finding the Road to Us (Elliot, Trace, and Sidney)
Book 7: Moments for You (Ridge & Aurora)
Book 7.5: A Wilder Wedding (Amos & Naomi)
Book 8: Forever For Us (Wyatt & Ava)

Book 9: Pieces of Me (Gabriel & Briar)
Book 10: Endlessly Yours (Brooks & Rory)

The First Time Series:
Book 1: Good Time Boyfriend (Heath & Devney)
Book 2: Last Minute Fiancé (Luca & Addison)
Book 3: Second Chance Husband (August & Paisley)

Montgomery Ink Denver:
Book 0.5: Ink Inspired (Shep & Shea)
Book 0.6: Ink Reunited (Sassy, Rare, and Ian)
Book 1: Delicate Ink (Austin & Sierra)
Book 1.5: Forever Ink (Callie & Morgan)
Book 2: Tempting Boundaries (Decker and Miranda)
Book 3: Harder than Words (Meghan & Luc)
Book 3.5: Finally Found You (Mason & Presley)
Book 4: Written in Ink (Griffin & Autumn)
Book 4.5: Hidden Ink (Hailey & Sloane)
Book 5: Ink Enduring (Maya, Jake, and Border)
Book 6: Ink Exposed (Alex & Tabby)
Book 6.5: Adoring Ink (Holly & Brody)
Book 6.6: Love, Honor, & Ink (Arianna & Harper)
Book 7: Inked Expressions (Storm & Everly)
Book 7.3: Dropout (Grayson & Kate)

Also from Carrie Ann Ryan

Book 7.5: Executive Ink (Jax & Ashlynn)
Book 8: Inked Memories (Wes & Jillian)
Book 8.5: Inked Nights (Derek & Olivia)
Book 8.7: Second Chance Ink (Brandon & Lauren)
Book 8.5: Montgomery Midnight Kisses (Alex & Tabby Bonus(
Bonus: Inked Kingdom (Stone & Sarina)

Montgomery Ink: Colorado Springs

Book 1: Fallen Ink (Adrienne & Mace)
Book 2: Restless Ink (Thea & Dimitri)
Book 2.5: Ashes to Ink (Abby & Ryan)
Book 3: Jagged Ink (Roxie & Carter)
Book 3.5: Ink by Numbers (Landon & Kaylee)

The Montgomery Ink: Boulder Series:

Book 1: Wrapped in Ink (Liam & Arden)
Book 2: Sated in Ink (Ethan, Lincoln, and Holland)
Book 3: Embraced in Ink (Bristol & Marcus)
Book 3: Moments in Ink (Zia & Meredith)
Book 4: Seduced in Ink (Aaron & Madison)
Book 4.5: Captured in Ink (Julia, Ronin, & Kincaid)
Book 4.7: Inked Fantasy (Secret ??)
Book 4.8: A Very Montgomery Christmas (The Entire Boulder Family)

Also from Carrie Ann Ryan

The Montgomery Ink: Fort Collins Series:

Book 1: Inked Persuasion (Jacob & Annabelle)
Book 2: Inked Obsession (Beckett & Eliza)
Book 3: Inked Devotion (Benjamin & Brenna)
Book 3.5: Nothing But Ink (Clay & Riggs)
Book 4: Inked Craving (Lee & Paige)
Book 5: Inked Temptation (Archer & Killian)

The Promise Me Series:

Book 1: Forever Only Once (Cross & Hazel)
Book 2: From That Moment (Prior & Paris)
Book 3: Far From Destined (Macon & Dakota)
Book 4: From Our First (Nate & Myra)

The Whiskey and Lies Series:

Book 1: Whiskey Secrets (Dare & Kenzie)
Book 2: Whiskey Reveals (Fox & Melody)
Book 3: Whiskey Undone (Loch & Ainsley)

The Gallagher Brothers Series:

Book 1: Love Restored (Graham & Blake)
Book 2: Passion Restored (Owen & Liz)
Book 3: Hope Restored (Murphy & Tessa)

The Less Than Series:

Book 1: Breathless With Her (Devin & Erin)

Also from Carrie Ann Ryan

Book 2: Reckless With You (Tucker & Amelia)
Book 3: Shameless With Him (Caleb & Zoey)

The Fractured Connections Series:
Book 1: Breaking Without You (Cameron & Violet)
Book 2: Shouldn't Have You (Brendon & Harmony)
Book 3: Falling With You (Aiden & Sienna)
Book 4: Taken With You (Beckham & Meadow)

The On My Own Series:
Book 0.5: My First Glance
Book 1: My One Night (Dillon & Elise)
Book 2: My Rebound (Pacey & Mackenzie)
Book 3: My Next Play (Miles & Nessa)
Book 4: My Bad Decisions (Tanner & Natalie)

The Ravenwood Coven Series:
Book 1: Dawn Unearthed
Book 2: Dusk Unveiled
Book 3: Evernight Unleashed

The Aspen Pack Series:
Book 1: Etched in Honor
Book 2: Hunted in Darkness
Book 3: Mated in Chaos
Book 4: Harbored in Silence

Also from Carrie Ann Ryan

Book 5: Marked in Flames

The Talon Pack:
Book 1: Tattered Loyalties
Book 2: An Alpha's Choice
Book 3: Mated in Mist
Book 4: Wolf Betrayed
Book 5: Fractured Silence
Book 6: Destiny Disgraced
Book 7: Eternal Mourning
Book 8: Strength Enduring
Book 9: Forever Broken
Book 10: Mated in Darkness
Book 11: Fated in Winter

Redwood Pack Series:
Book 0.5: An Alpha's Path
Book 1: A Taste for a Mate
Book 2: Trinity Bound
Book 2.5: A Night Away
Book 3: Enforcer's Redemption
Book 3.5: Blurred Expectations
Book 3.7: Forgiveness
Book 4: Shattered Emotions
Book 5: Hidden Destiny
Book 5.5: A Beta's Haven

Also from Carrie Ann Ryan

Book 6: Fighting Fate
Book 6.5: Loving the Omega
Book 6.7: The Hunted Heart
Book 7: Wicked Wolf

The Elements of Five Series:
Book 1: From Breath and Ruin
Book 2: From Flame and Ash
Book 3: From Spirit and Binding
Book 4: From Shadow and Silence

Dante's Circle Series:
Book 1: Dust of My Wings
Book 2: Her Warriors' Three Wishes
Book 3: An Unlucky Moon
Book 3.5: His Choice
Book 4: Tangled Innocence
Book 5: Fierce Enchantment
Book 6: An Immortal's Song
Book 7: Prowled Darkness
Book 8: Dante's Circle Reborn

Holiday, Montana Series:
Book 1: Charmed Spirits
Book 2: Santa's Executive
Book 3: Finding Abigail

Also from Carrie Ann Ryan

Book 4: <u>Her Lucky Love</u>
Book 5: Dreams of Ivory

The Branded Pack Series:
(Written with Alexandra Ivy)
Book 1: <u>Stolen and Forgiven</u>
Book 2: <u>Abandoned and Unseen</u>
Book 3: <u>Buried and Shadowed</u>

About the Author

Carrie Ann Ryan is the New York Times and USA Today bestselling author of contemporary, paranormal, and young adult romance. Her works include the Montgomery Ink, Redwood Pack, Fractured Connections, and Elements of Five series, which have sold over 3.0 million books worldwide. She started writing while in graduate school for her advanced degree in chemistry and hasn't stopped since. Carrie Ann has written over seventy-five novels and novellas with more in the works. When she's not losing herself in her emotional and action-packed worlds, she's reading as much as she can while wrangling her clowder of cats who have more followers than she does.

www.CarrieAnnRyan.com

www.ingramcontent.com/pod-product-compliance
Lightning Source LLC
Chambersburg PA
CBHW011210080925
32262CB00014B/78